I0451555

Dahlia's Bouquet

Tammara Aguado

Dahlia's Bouquet

Copyright 2010 Tammara Aguado

ISBN: 978-0-9840252-2-0

Tammaraaguado.com

ALL RIGHTS RESERVED

Acknowledgments

Thank you to all of my friends and family who gave me support when I needed it most. A special thanks to my husband, Larry Aguado, for giving me boundless opportunity to dream. Thank you Nola Summers for editing and cover design, and for listening to where I want to go, Platoon Chief Eric Cotter, Toronto Fire Services, and a big thank you to Margie Jacobs, my fairy godsister . . . you know why.

The difference between a
flower and a weed
is a judgment

~Author Unknown~

For Terra and Larissa

They'd come for Joseph.

He had whispered to Daisy to hide, if she managed to get away, to run toward the cliffs and remain there until he came for her. But there was only one way out of the tiny makeshift cabin Joseph built for the two of them, and that was in the midst of it all: the men, horses rearing back and forth, voices out of control.

BOOK 1

Daisy

Chickasaw Bluff
Memphis, Tennessee
1917

There was the finest multicolored forest, ever changing in autumn and in spring and summer more vibrant still. And at the back end of that abundant forest, flowed a stream that offered smallmouth bass and speckled trout. Low country land where white oak, hickory and cypress trees colonized the edges of steep bluffs overlooking the Mississippi River. An in-between time, after a man could no longer own another, after Auction, Exchange, Market, and Court Street were no longer centers for the business of bondage, before the Great Migration that pulled a race of people north swelled to a cosmic exodus—before Daisy could get her foothold into womanhood.

If she and Joseph had remained at the cabin that morning, they would have heard the horses maneuvering their way through the narrow path to the clearing. But on that stifling hot July morning, Daisy was restless from the humidity. She'd already tended to the small garden of corn, sweet potato and cabbage. She had already darned Joseph's socks and swept out the single clapboard floor of their one-room cabin. The quilt Birdie had given her for a wedding present had been pulled neatly over the corn shuck mattress. As far as Daisy was concerned, it was a full day's work.

"Why can't you skip the wood choppin for today?" Daisy swatted a mosquito lingering from the night before.

"I already told you why," Joseph said and readied another piece of wood for the next blow. Whack! "Ain't the time for easy livin if I'm gon make somethin of this land."

Whack!

Daisy put her hands over her ears. "Pleeeaase, Joseph. This air is so thick, I can hardly breathe."

Joseph put another log on the stump, mumbling, "That's what I get for hitchin myself to a house gal . . . don't know the meanin of real work."

Daisy smiled before she leaped off the porch and kissed his sleeveless arm, which was already raised high and ready to swing down again.

"Be careful, girl."

She put her hands on her hips. "You be careful."

Whack! Whack!

Joseph hacked two more times before the log split. It was only eleven o'clock, but the sun had already begun to change his forehead from chestnut to brown's darkest hue. Daisy watched him put another log into position. She had been listening to that whacking since dawn and was tired of it. It reminded her of her brother's stories, "If you don't go to sleep old Masta Neely gon come and chop yo head off."

Of course, they'd never had a master. Master Neely was just a name Daisy's brother conjured up to scare her. Nevertheless, his tale of a wrinkled old white man with half a face coming to chop off the heads of all the little girls who didn't do what they were told frightened her well into the latter part of twelve.

"Wanna watch me dance?" She swung her hips back and forth in front of Joseph.

"I wanna finish what I'm doin. Then I'll have the rest of the day to watch whatever you want me to."

She danced around him nonetheless, toying with her thick brown hair that should have been braided neatly at the back of her head, but instead swelled to sultry ripples down the sides of her shoulders. She raised her leg high and spun around similar to the ballerina in the music box back at the Collins' Mansion. Daisy peered over her shoulder to see if he was watching. He wasn't, which spurred a major modification in dance choice. She wiggled her hips back and forth pointing her toes with each step away from him. When she turned back around to see if she'd caught his attention, Joseph had stopped chopping to enjoy the performance. She shimmied her way closer and jumped on top of the wooden stump in front of him. He still held the axe in his hand when she blew into his face. Joseph closed his eyes and jerked his head back, when he opened them he stared at her.

"You got eyes the color of fall, girl," Joseph told her, softening a bit. "Gold, brown, green . . . they always changin up on me."

She shifted her hips to one side, "You talkin about my eyes, didn't you see my dance?"

Joseph dropped his axe and swung her around, letting her legs dangle in the air. "Don't you want me to build you a nice house?"

"It's hot and I want to go swimmin," Daisy pouted. She kissed him fast on the cheek. But Joseph set her down, moving her hair away from her face and kissed her as a husband does his wife. Daisy blushed, pressing her hand against his chest. "It's daylight, Joseph."

"Daylight, nighttime . . . don't matter." He pressed against her.

Daisy eased away. "Swimmin, Joseph. Then we can do what you want."

He bit the inside of his lip, hesitant. Then he shook his head. "I'm gon have to learn how to say no to you," his eyes still glued to hers. "Come on. But you'll be lookin for more than this broke down shack come winter."

They took the narrow path the Chickasaw Indians cut when the whole region was still theirs down to Daisy's favorite spot by the river. Dense masses of endless green surrounded them, and bald cypress stood watch doing the cooling. Joseph led the way, clearing the leafy branches that encroached the path, swatting swarms of whiteflies so that they'd break for Daisy. She hadn't fully adapted to life outside of the Collins' mansion in the city, but she was bending toward it. Despite his protests, Joseph liked to take this journey with her, each time seeing it fresh through the eyes of a girl once trapped in a house of chores, who now had the forest for a playground. They were quiet in their mission down to the river. The sounds of the steady forest balanced their silence until Daisy joined in. Joseph listened to her humming behind him. It was a happy tune—the sound of contentment. It made Joseph feel young, too.

The dappled forest sunlight had more power at the river's edge, shining openly on the river giving it a welcoming patina. Joseph had brought fishing poles with them, determined to make part of their adventure productive, but Daisy shed her clothes and jumped into the water before Joseph could set up his rod.

"You gon scare the fish!"

"I am a fish!" Daisy called back, darting in and out of the water like a gilded river nymph.

"Well, I already caught you!"

"I'm gettin away!" She swam out deeper.

Joseph grinned and snatched off his shirt. The cool water did feel good on his back. He watched for snakes as he entertained her, plunging deep under water, coming up and squirting it from his mouth, adapting to the playful ways of his young bride. Joseph, twenty-two years her senior, was determined to have a union of give and take with Daisy, who was just three days into nineteen. He watched her push the water through her arms, making angel wings along its surface. Her golden-brown skin glistened in the afternoon sunlight. Her hair had let go of its waves and clung to the back of her neck and down the small of her back. She would be the death of him: a good death.

She smiled.

He died: again.

After their sunny spot began to shade and Daisy grew tired, she wrapped her arms around Joseph's neck from behind, resting her cheek against him. He glided in circles around the water, holding her hands in place at his neck. She let him pull her through the water until he came to a standstill and her feet sank down against the back of his legs. She snuggled her face into his wide back. He felt it and smiled. They stood there, quietly fused, and Daisy wasn't hot anymore.

"This gon be our lives, Joseph?" Daisy's face still pressed against his back.

He squeezed the petite hands around his neck. "This gon be it."

It was near dark before the two of them returned to the cabin. They'd caught two bass, one small catfish not worth keeping, and Joseph's favorite—a speckled trout. Daisy removed her boots and set them down beside his at the side of the door. It was a two-mile hike back to the cabin, and the balls of her feet were tender to the touch. After they had settled in and Daisy started on cleaning the fish, Joseph pulled out his lucky deck of cards. He passed out two piles, playing against an imaginary partner, as he hadn't yet taught Daisy to play.

"Tell me again how you got all of this, Joseph. I'll bet that man about lost his mind when you flipped over them cards."

Joseph leaned back in his chair, stretching his arms out. "You want the fat version or the skinny one?"

"Whichever you feel like tellin." She hoped he'd tell the long version.

"Nawh, he wudn't happy that night." He started the tale as he had many times before, wherever Daisy placed the starting point. "I worked for Mista Forsythe since before I had fuzz on my chin—wudn't in no fields pickin cotton. I was the only colored man workin for him, but he used to say I was better than anybody in his shop. His pay sho didn't match his mouth. The master cabinet maker wudn't no master at all." He shifted in his chair, "Mista Forsythe knew I was the one with the skill, too."

"But he don't wanna put you in front of that other man." Daisy added.

Joseph shook his head. "Work for Mista Forsythe almost twenty years, watchin him get rich off me before I tell him I'm gon be movin on soon."

"He didn't like that."

"He was plenty mad, but he gave me a couple dollars more, expectin that was gon keep me from leavin. . . . Ain't right takin credit for another man's work."

"Sho' ain't." Daisy imitated, attempting to sound like her husband, but coming off as a distorted caricature of him.

Joseph grinned. He'd told her not to come down to him, but to bring him up to her, but he kept on with his tale. "Once he realized that didn't work, he start threatenin me with everything that come to mind. Said he was gon make it so I can't work for nobody else in Arkansas."

"But you weren't scared," Daisy stressed as if it were her part to tell.

"Nawh, Mista Forsythe wudn't that kind of white man . . . good down deep."

"Deep enough where he don't feel bad about givin that other man credit for your work."

Joseph's face tightened. Daisy wasn't sure if she'd overstepped her role in the tale. He hadn't solicited her opinion on the matter and from his expression, she was certain she'd violated some rule that existed between man and woman. So she advanced to the part of the story he liked most, "He loved to gamble though, huhh?"

"Yes indeed. Mista Forsythe had two loves, gamblin and money, and if they were women, money would be the mistress."

Daisy laughed, seeing that his relaxed mood had returned. "Taught you to play them cards."

"Almost every day after I finished my work. He used to say, 'Joseph, if you leave then who am I gon practice with?' Work for him for almost nothin, and entertain him for free. He didn't want to give that up. But I was determined. One day he just came into the shop and said, 'Get out of here then.' I picked up my tools right then and left."

They were at the part that gave Daisy a tickle. "Then you heard him knockin on the door."

"Yep, must have been two or three in the mornin, standin there with them cards in his hand. Lord, when I saw him wave that deed in front of me I almost pissed my pants from excitement."

"Then he made the bet," she said.

"If he wins I got to stay, and there'd be no more talk about leavin. But if I win, he'd give me the deed to this land in Tennessee. A chance to own land? I didn't care where it was. Then he dealt the hand."

"You weren't worried about him cheatin?"

"Told you Mista Forsythe treat them cards like they the Holy Bible. I saw him pin a man's knuckle to the table with a knife once for tryin to cheat him."

Daisy giggled, "He didn't know you were practicin with them cards."

Joseph cut an apple with his pocketknife and popped a piece into his mouth. "Had my own set of cards. Thought I'd make my way gamblin on the side to get money to open a shop of my own somewhere."

"And he didn't go back on his word like they do?" Daisy asked, as if she had firsthand knowledge of something she knew nothing about.

"Tell me when I win he don't have to sign nothin over to me—deal between colored and white don't mean nothin. But he did sign that land over to me. Say, 'If you lie you'll steal, if you steal, you'll kill.'"

Daisy put her hands out. "And all of this was yours."

"Yep, found out he'd won it from a man in a game two days before. Mista Forsythe don't care nothin about no yellow fever land in Memphis, least that's what he told me it was. I don't know if he was tryin to scare me or what. When I looked at that deed and it said a hundred sixty acres. . . ."

The two of them sat a few moments more, sharing the apple Joseph cut into equal parts.

Daisy's feet still hurt, but it was time to cook the fish. Joseph opened the small wood clad box that sat by the fire and set his cards inside. He pulled out his plans for the new house and spread them out on the table, eating the rest of his share of the apple while he pondered over the worn papers in front of him. "I'll start with our bedroom. It's gon face east so we know it's time to get up in the mornin."

"I already know when it's time to get up in the mornin," Daisy said. "When you start gropin at me."

Joseph cut his eyes at her, playful like before he went on. "This room is gon be for entertainin."

Daisy's mood darkened. "My family gawn up north. All I know is Birdie and the Collins. They sho won't be comin'."

Joseph was quiet for only a second. "You got my family. You haven't met them yet, but you'll sit right with 'em. You'll like my momma. I told you she work up at the Medford house in Memphis. 'Round Christmas, they let her come for a day and visit. And don't forget about my sister Leotha, just married too. You and her about the same age. She real smart. Her and her man work the fields now, but they savin up for a place down on Beale Street. Colored folk got shops and restaurants and everything over there. They probably bring us some goods when they come. So we gon have lots of company."

Daisy lit up as if it were already Christmas. "I want a rocking chair and a big dinner table where all of my babies can sit." Joseph grinned. "Lots of space for us to sit together and sing and be proper—like the white folks, a stove to cook on instead of this fire, a cabinet, a bigger space out front where I can do my plantin and . . ." She couldn't recall everything she wanted. It was a long list of items that changed from day to day.

"First we start with more chairs to match that one," Joseph said.

He continued with his dreams for the second level, describing three more rooms that would house the children she had not yet borne. Daisy's mind wandered back to the chair.

The Green Striped Chair

Daisy had no last name she could benefit from, nor a past worth mentioning—her future just as bleak. Her history was a compilation of many like her, one seldom detailed in books, but rather by oral accounts salvaged by those who listened. Daisy's mother had said, "If you work real hard, we can send you to school and then maybe you can go on to the teacher's college down in Tuskegee when you older."

That was eight years ago. Laundress was her goal now. Then she could come in, do her work, and promptly leave at the day's end. However, as part of the live-in staff at the Collins' mansion, work, and more work, was all she knew. Daisy was housed and fed in exchange for twelve to fourteen hour days of fulfilling innumerable tasks for the Missus; the money earned, two dollars and twenty cents a week, was sent home to the family by Mrs. Collins.

Daisy never even saw it.

Over fifty years had passed since the Civil War, but Daisy, just as her mother, had a life of servitude.

The Collins were considered a good family to work for, as much as good was worth. Daisy thought herself lucky. Most colored girls were sent out at ten years old to work. Daisy's mother had held on to her until she was twelve.

"Daisy, it seems your family has gawn up north to Philadelphia," Mrs. Collins had said. "Do you know where that is?"

"No, ma'am," Daisy answered, but was still processing Mrs. Collins first comment.

"How old are you now?"

"Fifteen, ma'am."

Mrs. Collins went silent. "Well, that's hardly an age for you to go chasin up after them. It's about time you handle your own affairs anyway. Birdie knows her money—she can help you with yours." Then she raised her scant eyebrows, "You been touched?"

"No, ma'am!" Daisy felt her cheeks flush.

"Mr. Collins?"

"No, ma'am! He ain't never come after me!"

Mrs. Collins paused again, seeming surprised by her outburst. Daisy hoped she believed her. It was the truth. After Mrs. Collins' stern face relaxed its jaw, she said, "There are many dangers for a white woman alone down here in Memphis—doubly so for colored."

Daisy knew she was right. On the river, a woman had two choices: belong to one man, or fall prey to many. It was a new beginning for Memphis, a phoenix blossoming from the ashes of yellow fever, re-inhabited by a combination of rural settlers, gambling gunslingers and robber barons all living amongst one another. She was relatively safe inside the walls of the Collins' mansion.

Marriage to an older man could have sentenced Daisy to a life of oppression: backbreaking chores and acquiescent, one-sided conditions at night's fall, essentially trading one life of servitude for another. But she would have accepted a life with a man half as good-natured as Joseph to get out from under the Collins' residence and out of the rough-and-tumble town of Memphis.

Daisy's morning had started out like any other. She was in the kitchen helping Birdie, the cook, peeling potatoes when the colored man arrived with the piece of furniture. She'd watched him from the kitchen window walk around to the back entrance with the chair in his arms. It was covered in broadcloth, but Daisy could see four legs peeking out from the bottom. Birdie told the man that he could set it down on the floor, that he could have a drink of water, settle himself while he waited for Mrs. Collins.

"No thank you," he said to all three proposals. "I been carryin it in my arms all this way, might as well hold it a little while longer."

"Suit yourself." Birdie went back to peeling potatoes. Daisy eyed the cloaked chair, wondering why he guarded it so. It was an amusement her mind could play with while her hands busied with her work.

If Mrs. Collins had talked with the man in the kitchen or the breakfast room, Daisy would have peeled the rest of the potatoes and minded her business, but Mrs. Collins had escorted the man to the dining room! Neither Daisy nor her kind was welcome in there except for serving and cleaning. She ignored Birdie's unyielding warnings and peeped into the dining room just as the man began to unveil the piece. He uncovered it gently—taking his time, as if he were performing a magic trick. She understood why as her eyes feasted on the unveiled chair.

It was the most beautiful thing Daisy had ever seen. The legs were carved to perfection, with a sheen that caressed the length down to its clawed feet. The seat and back curved like a woman's hourglass form, and it was covered with exquisite green striped upholstery.

"Daisy!" Mrs. Collins called from the dining room.

Daisy jumped back against the wall and waited a moment before she entered, so that it would seem as if she were in the kitchen helping Birdie where she belonged. Mrs. Collins had scolded her just yesterday about poking around white folk's business and not minding her chores.

"Yes, ma'am?"

"Take this," Mrs. Collins pointed to the broadcloth. "And bring me a cup of tea."

"Yes, ma'am." Daisy hurried back with the tea as fast she could so that she could marvel at the chair again.

The new Mrs. Collins, replacing the more temperate first, made an unconvincing attempt at appearing unimpressed by the magnificent craftsmanship. But her eyes danced about it. She ran her fingers along its ornately rolled arms, caressed the fabric, and finally parked her backside in it as if she were the Queen of England. The mansions of Memphis were spacious and comfortable, rather than grand and stylish. Many streets still needed pavement and lights. Mr. Collins, a wealthy cotton merchant, had returned seven months ago from a trip to South Carolina with candy and fine dresses for his three girls, a pistol for his young son, and a new wife for himself to replace the one dead.

The second Mrs. Collins' tastes were refined and opulent, and she went about the metamorphosis of the mansion's simple décor with vigor.

"You made this chair yourself?"

"Yes, ma'am. Carpentry been my life since I was a baby. My Daddy say he gave me a piece of wood to cut my teeth on."

Mrs. Collins ignored the man and went to her writing desk. Daisy watched her unlock the top drawer and pull out a handful of money.

"Do you know how to count?"

"Yes, ma'am." He said proud, but then relaxed his shoulders a bit to remain respectful.

"Sixty was what we agreed upon. Here is sixty for the one and another hundred for the wood to get started. . . You'll get the rest when you finish the other five," she said, and counted out the money very slow as if she hadn't heard him say that he could count. "I expect the others to be just as precisely made as this one."

"Yes, ma'am."

Mrs. Collins caressed the back of the chair. "This is along the lines of the kind of furnishins I was brought up with in Charleston," she said. "Of course I couldn't bring everything with me."

"Of course, ma'am," the man nodded as if it mattered that he agreed.

Daisy had never seen a colored man paid that much money in her life. Her mouth was wide open in awe of the whole matter, which stirred Mrs. Collins, "I don't want you puttin your grimy hands on it. Go back to the kitchen!"

"Yes, ma'am, I mean . . . no, ma'am," Daisy answered quickly. But it was too late. She'd already fallen in love with the chair and made a point of traveling past the dining room to marvel at it daily. She fancied having the chair as her own, just so she could admire it. No one would ever, ever be allowed to sit on something so splendid, not even her. She hadn't given the maker of that fine chair a thought until the third was completed.

Joseph admired Daisy from the first.

By the time the fourth chair was completed, Daisy was convinced she could make a life with him. When he finished the sixth chair, he took her with him. And on their wedding night, in the cabin built for only one full round of seasons, was a beautiful bed carved from chestnut. And there in the corner, was her wedding gift—the seventh chair, as exquisitely crafted as the first. It was the last of Joseph's green striped fabric.

Goodbye Joseph

Daisy directed her attention back to Joseph, who was still going on about the house he planned to build, only now describing the type of wood he was going to use and which trees he would cut. She nodded her head and said a couple of "*hmmms*" to convince him that she was still paying attention before she'd drift again, this time to Joseph's boots sitting next to hers. The difference between the two sizes tickled her.

She was just getting to know him. Just beginning to learn how to sleep with his arms wound so tightly around her that she could barely breathe a cricket's breath. Just understanding that his voice naturally carried a thunderous tone that didn't necessarily mean he was upset with her. She liked the way he carried her as if she weighed nothing at all. How he was determined to keep her from ever working for something that wasn't hers, and that as long as he was alive, neither one of them would sharecrop. How he was patient and gentle with her at night. She'd decided that tonight she'd reward him by wrapping her legs around him tightly to help him put a baby in her belly.

Just as Daisy gutted and cleaned the last fish, they heard the horses rearing outside. One of the men called out to Joseph, "Hey boy! Get yo black ass out here!"

It wasn't the first time men had tried to run them off their land, but Daisy had married a vigilant man, protective of what belonged to him. Joseph loaded his rifle before they called a second time, and was out on the porch just as quick. She heard his rifle go off only a few seconds later. Joseph was fast with a gun and even quicker with his hands. But the skill of one man against a group armed and prepared was futile—a hero's tale spun for children gathered around a campfire. She heard Joseph's body fall hard against the porch. The gunshots ceased then, but the chaos continued. One of the men yelled, "Hold him tight!" She heard them dragging her husband off the porch, and she attempted to count the voices against her husband: four, maybe five. Joseph was a big, robust man. It would take that many to bring him down.

Daisy didn't know what to do. It was happening so fast that her body couldn't keep up with what her mind already knew. Instinct told her to crouch behind the bed. She clasped her hands against her ears to block out Joseph's cries, praying that they wouldn't kill him, but merely give a lesson; Tennessee was known for teaching colored land owners a thing or two about limitations. She clasped her hands tighter over her ears, rocking her body back and forth, crying. After what felt like eternity, the commotion outside the cabin quieted. Daisy released her hands slowly, listening deeply now for any sounds of life from Joseph.

Nothing.

No moans, no pleading from Joseph, only the muffled sounds of laughter from the men outside. Daisy remained crouched behind the bed, waiting for the men to leave so that she could go out to him. Then the cabin door burst open. She squatted smaller and put her hand over her mouth. She heard footsteps cross the dirt floor, stopping very close to the bed…

Outside the cabin, two of the men stumbled and giggled like school girls, still passing back and forth the bottle of gin they'd brought to stoke the bravado they found only in numbers. One of them kicked at Joseph's lifeless body, disappointed that he had died so quickly.

Another man leaned against an oak tree and let the bark dig into his back as he smoked a cigarette. He looked up at the tree's sturdy brown branches and wondered why Joseph built the house so close to it. "It's done. Let's go," he ordered to the other two.

"Come on, Dean, let's stay for a while," said one of them and picked up a stick to poke at Joseph's castrated manhood. He grinned and said, "We got time for a wiener roast."

His brother picked up a stick to join in, but stumbled over a log and fell to the ground, spilling the bottle of gin in his other hand. "Shit," he hissed but then the two of them burst into drunken laughter, poking and wrestling one another beside Joseph's bloody body, as if Joseph were a dead bird, not worth giving a second thought.

Dean loathed these two. They were stupid little men barely out of boyhood and easily manipulated. The two jumped at the chance to do something favorable in Dean's eyes. Very few men had been to college. Dean had gone for two years. He didn't graduate, but it didn't matter. He had been to Nashville and that was farther than many would ever go.

Killing Joseph was personal for Dean. He left for college with all the dreams a white man has of making his mark in the world. Dean was smarter than most, armed with quickness in thought, and a favorable manner that convinced him and most in town that he was destined for something big. But in Nashville they were smarter—cleverer. His small town wit didn't fare well with the professors or his classmates, and in a year and a half Dean learned that he wouldn't make it big, but would take the train ride back to Memphis.

While he was away, the town seemed to have matured behind his back. There was a new grocery store called the Piggly Wiggly, and a new church where there were socials once a month. Even the girls he knew (of which he could have had his pick before he left), were married off now, or spoken for by a more promising suitor. His father, during a heated argument vocalized his son's shortcomings, chiding that there was even a tall black man named Joseph from Arkansas who had more of a future than he.

The remark was a harder blow than intended.

Dean's first encounter with Joseph only fueled his animosity as he witnessed him walk right past a white couple without making the customary move off of the sidewalk and onto the street. He had rode past Joseph's land and saw the chimney smoke while his own family froze from the Tennessee winter air. Reconstruction had brought too many changes too quickly for Dean to digest, and this firsthand account of colored progress frightened him. He let that fear and discontent fester toward Joseph until his face was the root of why he couldn't find a good job, why he couldn't get the respect he had when he left for college, why he wasn't the golden boy anymore.

He started rumors about Joseph bringing other coloreds to stir up the ones who knew their place, how Joseph was going to build other homes on Rodney's land and let other coloreds buy from him, how that was going to make him richer than most whites in Memphis.

"Dean I don't know about that," said Egan Banks looking at the other men gathered in the shed in the back of the grain and food store. "He don't bother nobody, and from what I hear he just wants to grow a few crops and raise a family."

"That's what he says but we all know of coloreds in Louisiana that got more than we'll ever have. And when I was in Nashville there were schools teaching them to move right on past us." The other men nodded in agreement. "Now I'm telling you we got to get a handle on this before we're all working for him."

They had all agreed, but when it came down to it, only Rodney, the two brothers and Dean were on board.

Dean gave one last backward glance to the brothers wrestling beside Joseph's lifeless body and turned toward the gaping cabin door.

Inside the cabin, Rodney was having a rough time. His stomach convulsed, ill equipped to handle the bloody scene just moments ago. He wanted to run, but the vomit kept him hostage and he bent over with his hands on his knees for support. He wanted Joseph dead as much as Dean, but not for the same reasons. The land Joseph called his was owned by Rodney's uncle, an avid gambler. There was a feud between his uncle and his father that Rodney still didn't understand completely. All Rodney knew was that two years after that fight, a colored man named Joseph had legal papers on the land. Land Rodney always thought would be his.

Daisy heard one of the men yell to the one inside the cabin. "Are you gon be alright!"

Rodney yelled back that he was, but the depth of death still boiled in his stomach and twisted his gut. "I'm just seeing if he got anything to drink in here!"

Daisy heard the man come inside the cabin with the other.

"Whew wee, he was a fightin bull wasn't he? Better be glad Angus and Arlen can't see you in here all hunched over like this. You'd never hear the end of it."

Rodney cleared his throat and stood upright. "Did you pull them two idiots up off the ground so we can get out of here?"

"Figured I'd let them roll around a bit longer while you checked out your place—Auwwh shit! Look what that boy did to my boots."

Rodney laughed and said, "That's your own blood, fool."

"Betcha twenty acres it ain't. . . . Shit." He inspected his boots.

Daisy concentrated on squatting very still behind the bed, even though her thighs burned. She prayed to God again to make them leave, to make her Joseph be alive, to be invisible just this once. She listened to the men shovel through their belongings. One of them said, "Damn, look at this. . . . Now where the hell you think that boy got the money to buy this fancy chair?"

"No telling, probably stole it like he did my land."

"Let me have it, Rodney. You got the land and all."

"Take it . . . and the bed, too."

"Whew wee! I'm givin 'em to my momma. Watch my daddy shit his pants."

Daisy heard them walk toward the door. "I can't believe he ain't got no hooch," said Rodney.

"Maybe not, but I think he got somethin much better."

The bed was flipped over before Daisy knew it, exposing her to the two men looming over her. Two more men entered, young men with identical faces. Daisy coiled against the cabin wall. A man with a bloodied lip dangled her boots from his hand and said, "Looky what we got here, a pretty little mouse. You behave now, or I'll squash you."

BOOK 2

Lilly

Mistaken Identity

Lilly had let go of her mother's hand and wandered off, for the drug and goods store was her favorite place. At five, the people in the store only smiled at her as she poked at the big sack of beans stacked alongside the jelly. On a dusty shelf, not far from her mother, sugar and gingersnaps caught her attention, but the lineup of candy displayed on the back counter was where she was headed. After eyeing several choices, she settled on the swirling lollipop, imagining the different flavors combining in her mouth.

"Little princess where is your mother?" A finely dressed old woman standing next to the candy shelf asked. Lilly pointed to the front counter, where two women stood.

"Well I don't think your mother would mind me buying such a sweet, pretty little girl something even sweeter," she said and handed Lilly the lollipop.

"Thank you, ma'am," said Lilly with a charming wee voice.

"You are most welcome, darlin." Her thick Irish accent sounded like a song to Lilly's ears. The brooch over her breast twinkled, and Lilly thought she might be a queen hiding away from a far off place. She could trust this one— her smiling eyes proved it, and Lilly was sure she wasn't a queen, but a fairy hiding within an old woman's body.

"What's your name little angel?" asked the old woman.

"Lilly."

"Well, tell me, Lilly, can I steal those pretty green eyes of yours just for a little while?"

"Nooo," Lilly giggled.

"I just want to borrow them for the weekend. I promise I'll give them back on Monday."

Lilly giggled again, but eyed the clerk putting the bolt of material back on the shelf after he'd cut her mother's fabric. Soon she would have to leave the nice old woman giving her so much attention and go with her mother. For an instant, Lilly imagined going home with the gentle lady. All that it would have taken was an extended hand, a nod, a kiss to tell her that she belonged to her. Then she could have all the candy and gingersnaps she would ever want. She thought about a fancy house with dolls to play with and beds with comfortable pillows. She whispered under her breath, "Take me with you."

The woman from the front counter headed toward Lilly and the older woman.

"Your little girl is a pleasure. She reminds me of my grandniece in Louisiana," said the old woman and stroked Lilly's hair. "I hope you don't mind me buying her a little treat."

"She is precious, but she isn't mine," said the younger woman.

"Not yours?"

"No."

"Who are you here with child?" pressed the old woman, now with some concern. Lilly pointed again at the counter just as Daisy finished and headed toward them.

"I hope she wasn't botherin you none," Daisy said. She looked down at Lilly with the candy and glared.

"What is that in your mouth? You know I can't pay for that." She went to take the candy out of Lilly's hand, but the old woman pushed her hand back.

"I bought it for her."

"Can't I have it, Momma?" Lilly begged.

"Momma?" The younger woman put her hand over her mouth and sucked her breath. "Lawd, she's as white as us."

Lilly saw the old woman's eyes narrow. "Is this your child?" Folding her arms and stepping back.

"Yes, ma'am—she's mine." Daisy confessed as if she'd committed the most reprehensible crime. She quickly scooped Lilly's hands in hers and headed for the door. Sometimes these incidents were small—sometimes there was a big production.

"Wait a minute!" scolded the old woman. Lilly felt her mother's hand grip hers tightly. The old woman walked slowly up to the two of them. Lilly remembered the kind face of the old woman just moments before. Her face seemed to collapse now, reminding her not of a fairy but of a witch in a story. She started to cry.

"Give me that lollipop," snapped the old woman. She tried to take the candy from Lilly's hand, but Lilly ran behind her mother.

Mr. Frank, the owner stepped in. "Ladies, Daisy didn't mean you no harm. Her little gal can't help the way she looks. . . . Ain't cause for all this excitement. Now Daisy, you get on home."

"Not until she gives me that lollipop." The old woman reached for Lilly, but Daisy put her arm in front of her daughter to protect her. She would be the one to pry the candy from Lilly's hand.

"Here," said Daisy, looking at the woman straight on. The old woman hesitated, and then she grabbed the candy from Daisy and crushed it under her shoe. "You had better get a sign for her so that good people will know she's nigra."

"Mrs. Tillman, you gon have to pay for that." Mr. Frank pointed out.

Down the dirt road home, Daisy lectured, "You ought to know better than to wander off like that . . . vicious old hag,"

Daisy rambled. "I got enough to worry 'bout sides you. . . . You be thankful for Mista Frank, he a good man."

"Yes, Momma," said Lilly. Mr. Frank was nice to her and her mother. His checkerboard smile warmed Lilly even on the coldest days. And when no one was around, he'd let her look through the pages of children's books in his store. It comforted Lilly to pretend that he were her father, even though she knew he wasn't. Daisy's anger had slipped into an inaudible whisper that almost sounded like a prayer to Lilly. It was an odd prayer that wasn't meant for God or anything beneath him. It was her mother's way of calming herself. She mumbled and whispered the rest of the way home, which left Lilly perfectly content to linger in her own thoughts. She felt her mother's grip on her hand soften and caress her intertwined fingers. She could feel her love seep through. Tonight, Lilly would tell God she was sorry for wanting to go with the old woman, and she would try harder to be a good girl. She held her mother's hand as tightly as her little fingers could muster and whispered under her breath, "I never want to leave you."

Varying degrees of color, that in rare instances went all the way to its lightest tone was accepted, or conveniently tolerated in the colored community. Lilly was acknowledged as colored in a distant, formal sort of way. She'd grown accustomed to the odd stares that let her know she wasn't really one of them, and the more blatant instances where the younger ones would touch her hair, or rub at her skin to see if there was color underneath.

Franks General Store wasn't far from the little shack the two of them called home, but to Lilly, it was the other side of the world. Those last few moments with the old woman were like a nightmare, but before, precious moments before, Lilly belonged somewhere different in the world.

Depression

"Daisy, you could sew two rags together and make heaven," beamed Roberta Clemons.

"Thank you, Miss Roberta."

"You just got the gift," Roberta complimented again, admiring herself in the mirror.

Lilly wasn't sure if Miss Clemons was talking about her mother or herself. It was 1926 and Roberta and other high-spirited women came to Daisy, the best seamstress in town, for the new, modern look. Roberta flicked her long cigarette right on the floor and did a provocative shimmy.

"If Steve thought he carried a torch for me before, just wait till he sees me in this." Roberta spun around admiring herself this time from behind. "Bee's knees, honey, bees knees."

Lilly sat in the corner of the two room shack and admired the woman in the dress her mother had called flapper. On her lap lay scraps of material in tones of blue, red, a small strip of silver, and Kelly green. Leftovers from the many dresses Daisy made for everyone but herself. Lilly collected the discarded pieces to make doll clothes. Daisy would say, "Practice sewing straight pretty lines baby, like you makin a dress for a real woman. Then you ain't got to work on yo hands and knees."

Roberta turned her attention to Lilly, "Soon you're gonna be wearin somethin pretty too. Find you a nice colored boy and have lots of cute little picaninnies."

Daisy stood behind Roberta and rolled her eyes. "You gon pay me today, Miss Roberta?"

"Of course I'm gonna pay you, Daisy." She pinched Lilly on the cheek and then handed Daisy the money.

At seven years old, Lilly knew her mother didn't like Miss Clemons. By eight, she began to understand why. Roberta was notorious for picking up a dress, and paying her mother two or three weeks later. She'd arrive in a tizzy with the money complaining about some minor defect that her mother knew was Roberta's own doing, and always after the dress had been worn several times. Lilly didn't like the way she felt around her. Daisy would say she gave compliments with a "teaspoon of vinegar." However, she brought her mother four other white clients who paid on the regular. The steady money combined with the extra from private sales of Daisy's prohibition hooch she made in the back woods, enabled Lilly to go to school and when she returned home, there was not just collards, but meat in the pot for supper.

Four years of reading and writing for Lilly, four years of "living decent" as her mother would say. But the Depression hit hard, and Daisy's small dress making business couldn't survive the blow.

Even the most menial jobs were saved for whites that needed the work. With the assistance of Roberta, who had settled down and become Dr. Steven Banks' wife, Daisy was able to find work among the rich as a domestic. Since they had no man to come home to, most of the families let her and Lilly stay on at their homes. Lilly saw the change in her mother when she went back to working on her knees. She knew of the story of her mother's life at the Collins' residence, of the time before Joseph, the man who was supposed to be her father. One night, in the very late evening, when all the work was done, Daisy had said to her, "Colored folk ain't made no progress at all."

The two of them survived like this—nomads shuffling from one home to the next, cooking and cleaning for the better families of Tennessee. All the while, Lilly grew up observing the mannerisms of the upper-class whites she and her mother worked for.

She watched the way they ate their food, and what was eaten, how white women sat in a chair and how they got up. She watched the young girls become women and how they maneuvered around the boys becoming men.

Lilly was a beautiful child, and had developed into nothing short of dazzling as a young woman. Her skin held on to its delicately pale hue, only taking on a more reddish, sunburned appearance in the summer, rather than a tanned tint that would trace her back to Daisy. In winter, her fair, almost translucent complexion confused as many as in her childhood. Her figure had blossomed earlier than most, giving old and hand-me-down clothes a whole new life when she put them on. Daisy, observing the budding of her handsome daughter, taught Lilly early on how to blend into the woodwork and seams of the homes they worked in, and to never be caught alone with the men of the house.

"Work ably, without being seen or heard," her mother said often.

There was only one compromising incident in all the homes they worked; it was at the Crowley's residence, where she and her mother worked for nine months. Benjamin Crowley was the same age as Lilly, but he had the build and nature of someone much older. He was the youngest of three—clearly Mrs. Crowley's favorite. Lilly knew that Benjamin had his eye on her from the very beginning. Daisy noticed it too. "Keep yo distance from that one," she had said.

He'd put toads or anything else that had at least four legs in his sister's drawers. He'd wait in dark corridors to scare them *and* the help. Nonetheless, he brought field flowers to his mother for no reason at all. He'd make a constant clucking sound with his mouth that drove everyone insane. But he'd stop clucking when Lilly was around. He was a sly nuisance that could easily change direction and become a danger if Daisy didn't keep a watchful eye.

A Crowley's Christmas

The Christmas season had Mrs. Crowley hopping about more than usual because of unexpected guests coming in from New York. Daisy's and Lilly's chores doubled, disrupting their routine of working together. Daisy was instructed to wash the banisters and scrub all the bathroom floors before getting started on the holiday meals—a task that would certainly keep her up well into the night. Lilly was to wipe down all the woodwork, change all the linens, and help Daisy with the rest of the chores. While Mrs. Crowley was upstairs getting ready to receive her guests, Lilly was at the back of the house changing the sheets in the guest quarters.

"Hi, Lilly," Benjamin said and closed the bedroom door behind him.

"Benjamin," said Lilly without pause from her work.

"You know you supposed to call me Mister Benjamin." He had a stern, hard gaze. Then he grinned, "I'm just kiddin, Lilly. We're friends aren't we?"

"We can't be friends."

"Well, why the hell not? I been trying to be your friend since you got here."

"White boys and colored girls don't make good friends," Lilly said matter-of-fact. She hadn't meant to sound sassy nor so candid. He was just making her nervous. She ran her hands along the top sheet to smooth out the wrinkles, feeling his eyes follow her hands and every other move she made. She hoped that he just wanted to watch her—a habit she could do nothing about.

He moved toward the bed. "Here I'll help ya." Benjamin grinned again and fluffed the pillow on the other side of the bed, never taking his eyes off her.

Lilly stopped working. "No need for your help, I can do it just fine by myself."

"Don't be like that." He slinked around the edge of the bed to the side she was working on. Lilly searched out the quickest way around him. She watched him rub his hands together in a nervous, anxious sort of way, as if he were getting ready to catch a rabbit for the first time. She could feel the goose bumps flare against her skin.

"How 'bout you and me take a walk in the woods later?" He moved within arm's-length of her.

"I can't. I have to help Momma with—"

Benjamin rushed toward her before she could finish and grabbed her roughly around the waist. "I'm gonna be nice to you!" He whispered in her ear just as coarse. He pushed her against the wall and pressed his face hard against her neck. He smelled of perspiration and dirt, as if he'd been running through the woods and climbing trees just moments before. He groped at her quickly—harshly, then softly—easing up on his grip, and then harshly again as if he wasn't sure of how he was going to go about it. Lilly attempted to free herself, but he grabbed her hair tightly and snarled, "Don't you ever push me away!"

The word *ever* stung her senses. Lilly knew that ultimately she would be to blame in Mrs. Crowley's eyes if she complained afterward. He was just a kid who had celebrated his fifteenth birthday only three months before. But his hands were all over her body, grabbing at her breasts, under her dress—back at her wrists.

He unzipped his pants.

Lilly decided then that she wouldn't be his toy all season while he tried to figure out what to do with a girl. No one was going to just take it from her. Lilly grabbed for his crotch and squeezed as hard as she could.

"Whoa now, Lilly!" The boy winced. She clutched harder

and backed him up to the door. "Come on now girl, be sensible. All I got to do is tell my momma you wanted it. You and your momma'll lose your job!"

"You're gonna lose something too if you don't open that door!"

"H-h-how can I open the door w-w-with you holding on to me like this!" He struggled hard to get a hold on his words.

"Ain't my job to figure that out for you!" Lilly said and tightened her grip, despite the boy's efforts to grope for the doorknob. She didn't let go until the door was open. She ran down the hall. He limped the other way out of sight.

Three days later, Daisy and Lilly left to work for another family, for it would only be a matter of time before Benjamin would be back with a better plan.

Cloak-and-Daggers

Lilly spied her mother pull the covers tightly around her neck. They had moved on from the Crowley's estate in Tennessee, to Paducah, Kentucky, again with the recommendation from Roberta. The Bradley residence was now home for the two of them. Lilly hated the place from the start. They arrived in the middle of an ice storm and truly never thawed out. The drafty estate was tolerable on the main floors, but the attic, where Lilly and her mother roomed, bore a constant chill that nipped at their fingers and toes in winter. In the summer, the attic was just as brutal. Hot and sticky all of the time, and if there was a breeze at night, Lilly swore it was a dragon's breath.

The Bradleys were frugal people, hiring only the two of them instead of the four or five needed for the massive estate. Despite their thriftiness, Mrs. Bradley's rituals for the upkeep of the mansion bordered on fanatical. Typical workdays consisted of twelve to fourteen hour days with one break at lunchtime. They were to clean the floors, wash the windows, mend any clothing that needed repair, cook, and clean up afterward, and make sure the young ones were clean and properly dressed. The list went on and on. Mrs. Sara Bradley checked everything. She'd rub her fingers across the dining room table to make sure it was dusted and polished, inspect her plate before she ate a single morsel as if she were in a fine restaurant, even checked behind the toilets for dirt. Lilly hated the way Miss Sara stared at her, as if she were an oddity she hadn't quite figured out. Lilly would stare back at her, to whom Daisy would warn, "You better stop eyeing that woman, she can look at you any way she wants to."

Miss Sara's glances annoyed Lilly, but her constant undermining irritated her to no end. "Lilly, do you call this clean?" She would say just about everything. It was an incessant and specific hounding, which had nothing to do with Daisy but all to do with Lilly—as if Miss Sara wanted to make crystal clear to Lilly that white skin had no relevance to Lilly's station—she was colored. The two performed this dance daily. Lilly figured she would have something to say no matter how well she cleaned, so why should she break her back trying to please her.

One evening they were quite surprised to see Miss Sara standing in the middle of their attic room. Daisy and Lilly's days ran together in a continuous string of labor, but being Friday, Miss Sara was dressed for her weekly night out with Mr. Bradley.

"Miss Sara, did you need anything else tonight?" Daisy asked.

Mrs. Bradley gazed around the room with a frown on her face as if it had an odor that didn't suit her. "Lilly, I figured since you can't clean worth a damn, I might as well give you this old typewriter I was going to get rid of. You probably can't learn how to type either, but at least. . . looking the way you do, you can learn to peck your name."

Lilly stared at the machine sitting on the two-drawer dresser where she and her mother stored their uniforms.

"Thank you, Miss Sara," Daisy spoke up for Lilly.

"I nearly worked myself up a heart attack bringing this old thing up here."

"Did you want to sit down, Miss Sara? Rest up a bit?" Daisy motioned for her to sit on the bed.

"Oh, no, I'll be fine, Daisy." Then she said under her breath, "Soon as I get myself back downstairs."

Lilly fixed her eyes on Mrs. Bradley. It was obvious she was ill at ease alone with the two of them. This was her home—all of it, yet Lilly imagined the climb up to the attic must have felt like another world to Miss Sara, a world unsafe and dark.

"Thank you, Miss Sara," Lilly said. Miss Sara's response was a curt half-witted smile and another disdainful glance around the room. Her red pumps clunked all the way back down the stairs.

"I told you she ain't all bad, now didn't I?" Daisy beamed. She wanted Lilly off her hands and knees, and learning to type was the quickest way to stand. She went to sleep to the sound of Lilly pecking her way through the alphabet, and in a while, the pecking lullaby progressed to a continuous motion along its keys.

After that night, Lilly and Miss Sara still watched one another, but with a different gaze.

Lilly waited until her mother was in the deep, dog-tired sleep she sank into nightly before applying the lipstick Miss Sara had discarded the day before. She'd thrown it in the master bedroom wastebasket while Lilly made the bed. "I just bought this lipstick. It's called Chinese Red. It must look better on a geisha—oh, that's Japanese. Regardless, it's all wrong for me. It might suit you better though, with your more, you know . . . odd coloring."

"There's nothing odd about my coloring. It's the same as yours!" Lilly wanted to say, but knew better. She'd just emptied that wastebasket and figured that was another one of Miss Sara's back-ended ways of giving her something.

Lilly twisted her hair up in the back, similar to Miss Sara's style. Miss Sara's demeanor had undergone a major modification. Lilly hadn't heard a peep from her about her domestic abilities in weeks. Fashion was her new obsession. Mr. Bradley inherited a life-altering sum of money, which transformed the frugal couple seemingly overnight. Lilly had to admit that she admired Miss Sara's new look and deportment. She'd collected plenty of Miss Sara's discarded make-up and kept it in a box at the back of her drawer.

Lilly pranced across the attic floor and scolded, "Daisy, you're just going to have to stay up all night and finish this washing." Lilly was carefully quiet, so that her mother wouldn't wake. "Now I know I expect a lot from you, Daisy, but if you and Lilly want to stay on here, you're going to have to work much harder." Lilly dropped a shirt on top of a pile of clothing assembled in the middle of the floor and said, "Mr. Bradley and I are going out for dinner, but I expect all of this to be done when I return." She checked herself in the mirror, meaning to mock Miss Sara's regal manner and then head for the closet door to complete her scenario. But the reflection of Daisy now sitting up in bed, stern faced stopped her cold.

How long had her mother been awake? What did she hear? What did she see? Excuses flooded Lilly's mind, but none of them would make sense outside of her head. Could she find a way to explain to her mother that she hadn't meant to belittle her, but that at night, when no one was looking, she could be who she was and not who she was told she was? This had been Lilly's secret for three years. The world had played a vicious trick on her, and with night's fall, she could play it right back. The hours of darkness were her only friends, holding secrets to a life her mirror reflected. It was the only time she could practice being refined and splendid—white.

Lilly fell to her knees in front of Daisy. "I'm sorry, Momma!" Forgiveness would be her plea once she calmed down, once she could come up with some sort of justification for what she'd done. She wiped her wet face on Daisy's bare thighs, holding onto them until she felt her mother's hands on her head.

"Look at me!" Daisy put her hands out. "My hands are still raw from washing those clothes."

"I wasn't making fun of you, Momma. I promise I wasn't. I'm just trying to . . . I don't know!" Lilly couldn't stop crying. She attempted to wrap her arms around her mother's waist, but Daisy pulled away from her and firmly held Lilly's hands.

"How long you been doin this?"

"A while," Lilly answered, avoiding Daisy's glare.

Daisy turned Lilly's face back to her. "We both'll be out on the street if you caught acting like that, you hear? She done put up with a lot from you, but ain't no white woman gone stand for you mockin her."

"Yes, ma'am," Lilly nodded quickly, hoping she was near the end of a reprimand that in the end was useless. Lilly remained on her knees even as Daisy got up from the bed and slowly paced from one corner of the attic to the other. It was the middle of July and sweat beaded Daisy's forehead.

"Watching you act like that. The way you spoke. Lawd, if I didn't know you was my own child. . . ." She handed Lilly a rag to wipe her nose. "Stop cryin! You eighteen years old, not a baby no more." Daisy sat down on the bed again. "You've opened my eyes to more than I wanted to see." She rubbed the back of her neck, which Lilly knew meant she was thinking something through. "Ain't no young man comin around here to claim you—not no colored man," Daisy finally said. "Nothing but hobos for miles anyway. . . . Stand up!" Lilly jumped to her feet. Daisy inspected her from head to toe. "What you gon do when I'm gone? No white woman is gon let you work up in they house looking like you do around they men folk. I don't have money to send you nowhere to school or to Europe or somewhere. And stop that snifflin before you answer."

Lilly wiped her nose and sniffed one last time. "I-I can type."

"Who is gon give you a job around here?"

Lilly didn't know what her mother wanted her to say. She hadn't considered life without her, and it frightened her to think about it now.

"I could go back to Tennessee and work for Mr. Frank."

Daisy gave her daughter a long hard look. "Mr. Frank don't hire colored, 'cept for old man Willie who sweeps out the place."

Lilly looked down at the floor. She hadn't thought about working for anyone. Mr. Frank was the only person that came to mind. "I won't do it again, Momma."

Daisy grimaced, pressing her eyes shut, "I love you, Lilly. You got to know that, but you got to know by now that I'm sick, child. You gon have to make your own way."

It came to Lilly just then, that she did want a small part of the colored world—her mother. "Momma, I can work. I can sew. . . . I can take care of you."

"Nobody lookin for dresses right now, baby. You see how hard it is for me—for you cause you're with me." Daisy's eyes filled. "You're my daughter, but only by blood." She shook her head, "There ain't no place for you in my world." Daisy grabbed hold of Lilly tightly then and even as she clutched her in her arms said, "You gon have to go away from here."

"No, Momma! Where am I going to go?" She was scared to death. "I don't want to go!"

Daisy smiled and stroked her daughter's hair. "Quiet baby, I'm not sending you out unprepared for this world." Daisy sat back down on the bed and rubbed her thighs, still thinking all of it through. "We gon practice, just like you been doin, until you can't hardly remember I'm your mother. Thank God I saw to it that you learn to read and write. Got to know how to do that if you gon make it. . . . Practice your typin—forget about sewin. We're on to somethin bigger now. Mr. Frank can't hire you cause he knows you're mine, but out there, nobody has to know. Only you gon know when the time is right to leave. We ain't gon talk about it. If you see an openin to make your way into that life, then you take it. . . . Don't worry 'bout me."

An odd feeling of calmness swept over Lilly. She didn't have to hide anymore. Her mother was sick. That was something she couldn't change. However, what she could change was her own future.

"I love you, Momma."

"I know, baby." Daisy caressed the top of Lilly's head, rocking back and forth. "I guess God got somethin else in store for you, making you the way you are." She kissed Lilly's forehead. "No reason to cry, baby. You and me in this together now."

From then on, Daisy hesitated before correcting those who assumed Lilly was white. It depended on the circumstance—whether it benefited them to disclose the details of Lilly's true pedigree or not. Lilly started using proper English—no more country talk. Typing became a necessity rather than a hobby. While Miss Sara hosted luncheons and dinner parties, Lilly stayed in the kitchen to help prepare; Miss Sara didn't want her out serving and confusing the guests. Lilly was fine with the arrangement, it gave her time to listen in and make mental notes. The two of them experimented on both the colored and white culture whenever possible. It not only benefited Lilly to have real life experiences, but also Daisy. She seemed to relish watching white men open doors for Lilly, even while letting them slam on herself. It didn't appear to bother her to relinquish parental authority over Lilly, and instead, abide respectfully in public to Lilly's wishes. Lilly figured it was her mother's way of getting back at a world that showed her so much ill will.

Once, while up in Metropolis, Daisy insisted she recognized one of the men that raped her the night her Joseph was killed. Lilly was inside a pharmacy while Daisy waited outside. The man was dressed in gentlemen's attire, nothing like the shabby clothing he wore that night. His hair was grizzled salt and pepper now, and cut short and neat around the ears. Yet he still had the face of her nightmares. Daisy ran behind the side of the pharmacy as if almost twenty years hadn't passed since she was Joseph's young bride in Memphis. She peeped out slowly, afraid for herself and Lilly, who was just leaving the store.

"Pardon me, miss," The man said to Lilly and tipped his hat respectfully.

Daisy didn't mince her words later. "He was the foulest of the four," she said to Lilly after they were a safe distance away from him. She was painstakingly thorough about her depiction of the several rounds he'd gone with her that night. Lilly could have done without the gruesome details of how she came to be, but was under the opinion that Daisy needed to tell her—to tell someone who would listen. ". . . Now, this same man tilting his hat to you, who could be of his own flesh and blood," Daisy took a deep cleansing breath. It was a minute dose of satisfaction. It was all a colored woman could wish for in 1936.

Cornbread

Lilly's choice of the mustard colored dress with the felt ribbon fastened neatly around her waist gave her the confidence she needed today. It was the first dress she'd made without Daisy's guidance. She looked good in it, despite the few flaws only a highly skilled seamstress would notice. She combed her hair carefully, brushing the permanent waves so that her fine, shoulder length hair softly framed her face. She put on the fedora hat that reminded her of one of Greta Garbo's in the *Marie Claire Magazine* she peeped through when Miss Sara was out. It was the same mustard hue as her dress. She tilted it to one side and gazed around the room one last time: the twin beds that sagged in the middle, the window that let the wind whistle through it in the winter, the old typewriter, the note she placed inside her mother's scarf on the bedside table. Lilly stored it all in her mind, but then thought better of it. Her mother was the only good thing about this place—nothing else.

She eased downstairs to the kitchen. Cornbread was still sitting on the stove. Lilly took a small piece and stuffed it in her mouth, savoring every crumb of her mother's bread. When she finished she wiped the edges of her mouth with her middle finger, very dainty-like, and wrapped another piece to put in her purse. Daisy was already outside helping Miss Sara in the garden.

She slipped out the side door.

The end of the block came quicker than she expected, too quick for her heart to handle. Each step away from Daisy brought a fresh wound, heavy and injurious. She couldn't breathe. *Just put one foot in front of the other.* She kept telling herself. A chance at a real life was out there in another town, another state, waiting for her to make it her own. She kept walking, legs transporting her to somewhere else.

It was the *else* that caused her panic.

She hadn't realized how fast she was moving now, the quick pace of a woman anxious and afraid. Her mind was spinning from endless possibilities of a foreign world. She started to run, until she was down a street all too familiar.

It was a ridiculous idea. She'd run upstairs and put on her uniform before Miss Sara got wind of it. When she reached the backyard, she took a minute to catch her breath, peering through the large bushes to make sure it was clear to sneak back in from the side door. Then she saw Daisy there on her knees, digging hard against the ground to make holes as Miss Sara stood over her, directing the placement of each bulb, as she was particular about her prized garden. She'd seen her mother this way many times, but never as a stranger would see her—as if Lilly was just passing through and needed directions. She and her mother were the same. Lilly could have easily been the one on her knees, broken and tired, aged ahead of time. She watched Daisy rub the sweat from her forehead, coughing from the sickness she still hadn't revealed to Miss Sara. They were the same, but not. Standing behind the bushes in her mustard suit, they were not the same, but profoundly different. Daisy was trapped in a barring skin that would always be rough, cut, bleeding, afraid, raped, laughed at, ignored. Her mother didn't have a choice, but as sure as she was standing up straight now, she did. That servant's uniform meant death. And Lilly planned on living.

"It's so hot out here today, I'm about to die if I don't get some lemonade," said Miss Sara. Daisy started to go in and get it. "No, you stay put. I'll get it myself. It'll give me a chance to get out of this heat."

Lilly waited until Miss Sara went inside. She hadn't offered to get Daisy a drink or even the water hose. Three years of working for the Bradleys and the only thing that had changed for Daisy and Lilly were their ages.

Without thinking, Lilly stepped slightly out of the bushes.

Daisy smiled at her, but a wash of sadness swiftly followed when she spotted the large bag dangling from Lilly's hand. They stared at one another from across the yard for a long time. Lilly remembered how it felt to hold her mother's hand when she was a child. How she could make her feel love instead of saying it aloud. She wanted to pull Daisy up from her knees and together leave Miss Sara and her flowers behind. But then Daisy said, "No need for long goodbyes. Those are for loved ones you'll see again."

Lilly started to cry. Daisy smiled, nodding encouragement. Miss Sara returned with her single glass of lemonade and Lilly crept back out of sight.

They both knew there could be no connection between the two of them once Lilly crossed the threshold for good. She would have to live for the both of them.

Later that night, Daisy picked up the scarf with the note Lilly had left her. It was a picture of a heart colored in with chalk. She sat down on her bed and gently caressed Lilly's goodbye letter.

Daisy never learned to read.

Rebirth

"How old are you?"

"Twenty-four," Lilly's first lie.

"The pay is twelve dollars a week, and Saturdays and Sundays off," said Mr. Norton, head of accounting, and in charge of hiring the small typing pool at Goodman's Automotive Supplies in Detroit. "I'd expect you to be here on time and pull your weight along with the other clerical staff. One of our girls is getting married so we need a replacement." He looked up from her application. "A good looking woman like yourself probably will be getting married and staying home to raise a family, too."

"No, sir. I'm new in town. I won't be getting married any time soon."

Lilly guessed by his tone that he was making a statement rather than asking a question.

She was right.

"A married woman needs to be at home," Mr. Norton said. He looked at her again and she suspected that he was waiting for her to agree.

She couldn't.

He walked quickly down the row of women behind their typewriters, making Lilly practically trot to keep up. The sound of so many fingers tapping against the keys excited Lilly. In an odd way, the typing pool appeared glamorous to her and she was eager to be a part of it. Mr. Norton showed her the tiny desk in the back corner of the office. "This is where all the new girls start." Lilly frowned. "Is this a problem for you, Miss Carter?"

Lilly quickly caught herself and put on a wide, eager smile, "It's perfect."

"I don't want to waste my time or yours if this isn't what you had in mind."

"I'd love to work here, Mr. Norton," Lilly assured him. This was her first attempt at working alongside whites. The desk at the back of the room reminded her of coloreds in the back—a knee jerk reaction that was clearly misunderstood by Mr. Norton. She'd have to be more careful, she scolded herself. If she was going to make a go of this new life, then she had better not just live as if she were white, but think it too!

Mr. Norton was on the move again, back to his office, a small stuffy room with a glass window that looked out upon the typing pool. He plopped down in his chair and motioned for her to sit down. "I'd be taking a chance with you. You type fast, but you're not as accurate as the others," he said, reviewing her typing test.

"Mr. Norton, I know I don't have experience . . . or proper training, but I'm good with numbers and it would take me no time to settle in."

He spit mucus into his handkerchief and stuffed it back in his shirt. "I've got four other girls to interview before I can make any decisions. I'll let you know by the end of the week," He placed her application in the pile with the others. "Good day, Miss Carter." Mr. Norton extended his hand toward the door without moving from his chair and began to clear his rumbling throat until he spit again into his hanky.

Lilly's heart fell to her stomach. She looked at the half-eaten sandwich on his desk. It was more than she'd eaten all day. She swallowed deeply, and before she lost her nerve, picked up a paper from the typing bin stacked high on the corner of his desk.

"I'll type this free of charge. If there are any mistakes I'll leave without saying another word." She raced out of his office to the back desk before he could reply and typed as quickly and as accurately as she could. She hadn't noticed that the other women stopped typing to gawk and whisper until she finished. Lilly snatched up the letter and charged back to his office.

"That was fast," Mr. Norton said. He popped the last of the sandwich into his mouth and then leaned back in his chair to scan the letter. Lilly swallowed again, imagining a turkey sandwich with lettuce and tomato—lots of mayonnaise. She was afraid to move in the chair across from him, afraid to breathe. She had exactly four dollars and twenty cents left of the twenty-five dollars she'd saved to last until she found a job.

"Where did you say you're from?"

"Georgia. Well, that's where the convent was." Lilly clutched her hands together in her lap.

"It would be nice to have someone right away . . . " Mr. Norton rubbed his forehead. "Are you sure you want a job here? I don't need any peacocks sitting with a bunch of chickens."

For the first time, Lilly surveyed the pool of women in the office—she was a bit overdressed. But she guessed he wasn't talking about her attire. A beautiful woman working with a room full of *Plain Janes* could slow down productivity—cause problems with the others. Lilly snatched the faux mink collar off of her jacket right in front of him.

"I assure you Mr. Norton, I won't cluck any louder than the rest."

Mr. Norton toyed with the pen between his teeth. "Well, you'd certainly improve the view around here."

It was a man's world. Lilly understood that, so she sat up straight and crossed her legs to force him off the fence. After he'd eyed her legs he said, "I'm going to give you a crack at it. Welcome to Detroit."

"Thank you, Mr. Norton!" Lilly jumped from her seat and extended her hand.

"Don't disappoint me."

"Yes, sir. I mean no, sir."

A Letter for Daisy

Dear Mother,

How can I begin to tell you what life is like for me? I feel giddy every time I think about how far I've come. I love Detroit, Momma. Everything we planned is falling into place for me. I work as a typist. The pay is terrible, but it's enough to get by. I've got my own desk. At first I thought my boss was going to be trouble, but he turned out to be harmless. In fact, he started out with giving me letters that weren't very important, but after a couple of months, he's begun to give me more significant documents to type. He's even moved me from the back of the room to a middle desk.

"What can I get you, honey?" That's what the waitress said to me at the lunch counter the first day I set foot in Detroit. No one yelled at me or pulled me off the stool. No spitting. No police. I was shaking all over, and the waitress even asked me if I were alright, if she could get me a glass of water! I finally settled down and ate the best burger I ever had. I found a place to stay too. It's nothing special, but it's far from 'Paradise Valley', where all the coloreds live.

I spend a lot of time at the library. There's so much to learn. I'm even teaching myself French. I met a very nice lady at an art exhibit on women and their role in art history. Her name is Doris and I think she comes from money, but you would like her, I just know it.

I wish you could read, Momma. I wish there was a way to do this without leaving you behind. I pray that the world will catch up to a place where we can re-unite. I pray that you know I love and miss you, and that my heart aches.

Your loving daughter always, Lilly

Lilly reviewed the letter she'd written. It didn't matter that Daisy couldn't read as the letter would never be sent. Any evidence of Lilly's life back in the South could be used against her. It was Friday night and the boarding house was empty except for Moira who was busy with sweeping the hall. Her aunt Arleen owned the place, and had sent for the shy and hopelessly skinny girl all the way from Ireland. Even so, Lilly lit a match and burned the letter down to its ashes. It felt good to write it down. In a small way, she felt this connected her to her mother. It would become her method of keeping Daisy close.

Grosse Pointe

"Are you sure it's alright if I come?"

"You're my best friend, Lilly," Doris Remming laughed. "Besides, it's my party and I'll kill anybody who tries to ruin it—eight o'clock?"

"Eight o'clock," Lilly confirmed.

She ate nothing but cereal and cans of soup for a week to save for the material to make her dress for Doris' birthday party. Lilly and Doris were fast friends for a year now, yet, Lilly had never visited the Remming's home. Going out together was one thing, but coming to the Remming's home and mingling with them socially was another.

Stanley Remming, Doris' father, was senior partner at Remming, Felton and Huntley law firm, the biggest firm in Detroit, who counseled most of the auto barons in Grosse Pointe. Lilly often combed the society pages to see if Doris or her family appeared. Usually it was her older sister Elizabeth: she was the beautiful one.

Although Lilly was cautious around Doris in the beginning, she eventually let down her guard. Doris was a genuine friend who went out of her way to make her feel comfortable. She knew that Lilly wasn't a socialite, but then Doris didn't consider herself part of that set either—despite her last name. She'd studied abroad and returned with a fresh outlook on the world, which didn't include class distinction. Lilly was delighted to call her a best friend and she couldn't wait to celebrate Doris' birthday with her. She had to admit that mingling with the cultured set had her beguiled.

The night of the party, Lilly asked Marcello, a friend from the mailroom at Goodman's, to drive her there. He was the only person she knew with a car that she could be proud to get out of.

Jefferson, which bowed into Lakeshore Drive, the dividing line between Detroit and the stunning village of Grosse Pointe, seemed like a fairy tale to Lilly. Stately English Tudors and Colonials sat adjacent to massive French Renaissance and sprawling Italian villas. She stretched her neck like a child as they passed the wondrous homes nestled behind regal evergreen trees, and immaculate, velvety lawns, each home more spectacular than the last. It was seven forty-five and Lake St. Clair sparkled like diamonds on the other side of the street. The community was breathtaking, and Lilly couldn't decide where her eyes should rest. She tried to quiet the heart that pounded mercilessly against her chest. It was more than what she had imagined—a storybook come to life.

"I can't believe you're invited to a place like this, Lilly," Marcello said as they pulled up to the drive of the Remming's mansion.

"Why not?" Lilly asked, instantly irritated with him.

"Don't go so fast, Lilly." He grabbed her hand. "You know I didn't mean it like that."

"I have to go in, Marcello."

"I know I sometimes don't say the right things," his Italian accent heavy. "I try to think of the words, but they don't come out the way they should."

Lilly wanted to jump out of the car. She knew what was coming next.

"You know I care for you, Lilly."

"I know," she smiled at him. "You're sweet, Marcello."

"I don't have all of this but one day—"

"Ten-thirty, right?" She cut him off and gently eased her hand away.

"Right," he sighed.

She smiled again to cheer him up. Twice Marcello had asked to marry her. Lilly wished she could say yes. But she knew they were only compatible by circumstance—both from a far off place, both lonely. It was only a matter of time before Marcello knew it too.

"I can let myself out, Marcello," Lilly opened the car door before he could object. Walking her to the door would only lead to more awkward conditions, and she was already nervous. Counting the stairs up to the massive entry calmed her butterflies.

"Good evening, ma'am," said the butler, a tall, elegant coal-black man. Two and a half years of passing for white, and Lilly still hadn't become accustomed to colored folk speaking to her with obligated respect.

Inside, the foyer was no smaller than many of the homes she'd lived in as a child. Masters Matisse and Gauguin she recognized from books at the library, the others she couldn't recall. The room's entry was dark and mysterious, but a luminous shimmer gleamed over the entire space, which Lilly thought gave it romance. She would have been happy to have stayed there and marvel at the room's magnificence all night, but the butler took her coat and led her to the ballroom.

It was much brighter inside of this room. The decorations were flamboyantly colorful—as if she were under the big top at the circus. There was a live band playing and the women swung around the room in flowing dresses Lilly couldn't afford. They reminded her of a Hollywood movie with Myrna Loy, Betty Davis, and Joan Crawford all at the same party. She stood at the entrance for a moment, taking it all in. A slim, stylish man whistled when he caught sight of her.

"Down boy!" Doris hissed and hit him on the arm. "Hi, Doll." She kissed Lilly on the cheek and handed her a crystal glass filled with punch. "You look beautiful as always."

"So do you, Doris."

"Liar, but this dress is straight from Paris. This is as good as it's going to get." She gave Lilly another quick look. "With your face, I wouldn't need Paris.

"Modesty is not your best quality," Lilly teased.

"No." Doris set her own glass on a table and moved her hands down her shapely hips. "It certainly isn't."

"You're terrible." It was one of the reasons Lilly liked her so much.

"It's my birthday. I'm entitled." Doris and Lawrence Colby locked eyes.

"Ahhh, I see what you're up to."

Lilly was relieved Doris had found her right away. It took the edge off of not knowing anyone else. She took a sip from the sparkling glass and gagged.

Doris winked. "Good, isn't it?" She lifted her glass back up toward Lilly's. "To good friends."

It only took a half glass of the punch laced with what tasted like Daisy's old hooch before Lilly began to loosen up.

"Come on, let's make a round." She took Lilly's arm and guided her around the room. "That's Brian . . . railroad family. Over there is Dennis . . . insurance, which you'll need with him dancing on your toes all night. Oh, and that's Martin." She leaned in close to Lilly's ear, "Descendant of one of the old French families. You two might hit it off, how's your French?"

"I'm just here for you, Doris." Lilly whispered back. "It's your birthday, and I want to celebrate it with *you*."

Doris put on a wise grin, "Sweet, but don't be foolish. You're the prettiest girl here—nab one."

Elizabeth, Doris' sister was already on her fifth taste of gin from Stewart's flask. She'd settled onto his lap in the corner of the ballroom far away from judging eyes, but close enough to be seen. Stewart Fillmore had been her date to these kinds of social events for the last seven months. He had the charm and good looks Elizabeth required—a Harvard man, but more importantly, his family was worth a fortune. He was what her mother called a "front of the line" candidate for a husband.

Elizabeth whispered in Stewart's ear, "Give it to me."

"Don't you think you've had enough?" Stewart scolded.

She rolled her eyes, but then gave him a flirtatious look and leaned in close to his ear again. "You used to like me this way."

"The operative words are *used to*." He pulled back. "It's your sister's party."

"What's wrong with you?"

"Nothing. I just don't want you to upstage Doris tonight."

"I'm not going to ruin her little party."

"Little? There must be at least two hundred people here."

"Hundred and twenty, if everyone showed." Elizabeth took one more sip and shoved the flask back to Stewart before anyone noticed. She pushed herself off of his lap and straightened her dress. Despite her lack of judgment with liquor, Elizabeth was dazzling. She wore confidence as well as couture and most women in Grosse Pointe conceded that they didn't have a chance when she was in the room. "There she is again," Elizabeth said after catching sight of Lilly "I told Daddy that Doris had practically invited the help."

"Why does that girl bother you so much? A little healthy competition never bothered you before."

"I welcome competition. Even thrive on it—when I *see* it."

Stewart glanced at Lilly one more time, "Maybe you should start wearing your glasses."

"Ha Ha." She pressed her lips. "I suppose she's pleasant looking enough, if you're into the economical type. No one's told my sister that it's alright to coddle a stray cat, as long as you don't bring it home."

"Now I need a drink."

"Stew, it's just that every time I turn around she's hanging onto Doris. She's out of her league. . . . We're the Paris of the Midwest, and I want to keep it that way." Elizabeth shrugged her shoulders, then added in case he needed clarity, "She just isn't one of God's chosen."

Stewart looked at her, narrowing his eyes. "I'm going to see if I can find some of *'God's chosen'* and have a drink outside."

He had already started to walk away before she could talk her way back onto his good side. She looked around the room to see if anyone had noticed his quick departure and gathered her wits before heading toward Doris and Lilly.

The liquor guided.

"So Lilly, you decided to join us." She said, loud for such a small audience.

"Hello, Elizabeth."

"Don't you look . . . quaint."

"Your dress is stunning. I've been admiring it all night." Lilly complimented, ignoring the poke.

Elizabeth smiled. "Since you're practically part of the family, what is your last name?"

"Carter," Lilly said, trying to sound convincing. It was Mumford before she left Daisy. The name belonged to Joseph. He wasn't her real father, so she didn't feel bad about changing it. Still, a panicky surge of tension shot through her with claiming the new one.

"Carter, of the Carter Trading Company out of New York?"

"No." Lilly could feel the panic rising.

"Carter . . . Carter . . . let me think. I pride myself on knowing all the leading families along the East Coast."

"You wouldn't know my family, Elizabeth." Lilly face beamed red.

"You'd be surprised at who I know. But enlighten me.

Enlighten us. Who are you, Lilly?" Elizabeth raised her eyebrows, still with that plastic smile. Before Lilly could answer, she added, "Oh, I know. Doris, didn't we have a gardener named Carter?" The group near them snickered. Lilly just stood there, helpless.

"No. Carter was the name of the English fella you let feel you up at the club last year," said Doris with the wit she was famous for.

The group laughed out loud. Elizabeth caught sight of Stewart grinning, too. He raised his hands in the air to surrender. "Hey, you jumped in the mud, now you're going to have to clean yourself up," he said.

The group laughed harder. "You fickle . . ." She didn't finish, but stormed out of the room. Drama was her specialty.

Stewart didn't run after her. He liked Elizabeth—she felt good in his arms, and she was smart although she tried to hide it, even fun when she wasn't assigning everyone to a category. However, he was more compliant than in love. A man with his breeding and responsibility to family lineage didn't have the privilege of such an emotion.

"Aren't you going to go after her?" his friend Brian asked.

"She was looking for attention, and she got it," Stewart answered. He tilted his drink toward Doris offering a silent "touché" and took a long gulp of the punch.

"You're going to pay for it later," his friend warned.

"Maybe." Stewart poured the last few drops of gin from his flask into his glass of punch. "Brian . . . our fore-fathers used up all the adventure a man could boast about in his old age. This pointless shindig is just another constant reminder."

"Cheer up. They've done all the hard work for us, my good man." Brian slapped Stewart on the back and then looked over at Cindy Beasley. "It's time to reap the benefits."

The band began to play a Benny Goodman melody and the group coupled off. Lawrence Colby asked Doris to dance.

"Are you alright, Lilly? Don't let my sister upset you. She's a cow."

"I'm fine. It's your birthday. Go dance." Lilly assured her and nudged her toward Lawrence. Yet she wasn't fine. She was drowning in humiliation. Elizabeth had pointed out to the entire room that she didn't belong. She looked around at the men left without a dance partner. They avoided her gaze and nestled together in idle conversation. One of the men in the huddle looked her way, which led Lilly to believe they were talking about her. Lilly couldn't hear them, nonetheless, she imagined their words, *"Great to look at, but not to touch—at least not in public."* She wondered how many women knew her dress wasn't couture. Skin color wasn't the issue, but class. She took a deep breath and turned her attention toward the dancing couples. She wasn't going to let them get the best of her. If she could manage to appear unaffected by her encounter with Elizabeth until the song ended, Doris would come back. She could stay a while longer to save face, then she'd tell Doris thank you for inviting her, but she had to go.

Lilly closed her eyes to block out Elizabeth, the men making jokes about her, even how she was going to pass the time since it was only nine-thirty—Marcello wouldn't be back for her for another hour. She let it all go and imaged just for a moment she belonged there.

"Do you dance?"

Lilly jumped, spilling her drink on her hand.

"I've been known for a lot of things, but scaring pretty ladies isn't one of them," Stewart said. He took his handkerchief out of his pocket and wiped her hand.

"Thank you," She pulled her hand away.

Stewart grinned and gave her a quick glance from head to toe. "You didn't answer my question."

"Dance? Not really." she said.

"Well, we have to change that." He removed the punch from her hand, and pulled her to the dance floor in one quick swoop. She was still suspicious of Stewart and anyone else at the party besides Doris, but they were already in the middle of the floor before she had time to refuse. She looked at the others swinging around her.

"Don't look at them. Watch me. Rock, step, triple step, triple step, rock, step."

Lilly mimicked his steps, mouthing his directions. He was a good lead and guided her with just enough force to cover her missteps.

"Hey, you two are looking pretty good!" Doris said swinging past with Lawrence.

"She's a quick study!" said Stewart.

Lilly couldn't tell if he was making her woozy, or if the punch had made its way to her head. Whatever it was she liked it. Then the music slowed.

"Thank you," Lilly murmured out of breath.

Stewart eyed her again. "I think I'm supposed to say that."

Her stomach swirled—part fright, part delight. She wasn't sure if she should walk away, wait for him to escort her off the floor, say something—do something other than stand in the middle of the floor while everyone else danced around them. He hadn't moved away, in fact, he gave the impression that the motion surrounding them didn't affect him at all. Her bare shoulders quivered as if the temperature in the room had fallen and she rubbed her arms.

"Let's try something slower," he said and slid his arm around her waist.

"I should get back."

"Get back to. . . ."

"Doris is waiting for me."

He smiled, then he turned oddly serious, "Doris is dancing."

"Oh." Oh, Lilly repeated in her head. She thought she sounded completely ridiculous. She guessed he must have thought so too, because he let go of her.

"I'm Stewart Fillmore," he stuck his hand out for Lilly to shake. "You are Doris' friend, Lilly—we've officially met. Now, will you dance with me?"

Two glasses of punch still warmed her body. Were her eyes still closed and this simply imagery she'd conjured up in her head? If this was real, she was sure he'd come to his senses at any moment, excuse himself and run. But he must have felt something, because he didn't run and he didn't wait for Lilly to say yes. He embraced her again. Lilly fumbled her fingers between his.

"This way." He placed her hand properly in his.

Neither one of them said a word throughout most of *Moonlight Serenade*, her new favorite tune. She held her breath through most of it, inhaling just enough to keep a pulse. She was so scared that she barely touched him as they moved around the dance floor. Stewart held her hand tight enough for the both of them. She tried to relax, telling herself to calm down.

But he was beautiful.

Not like a movie star, but like an ordinary man with unordinary appeal. His sharp, chiseled features were almost too severe, but his eyes were a soothing bluish grey. Comforting, peaceful eyes that should have put her at ease but didn't. She couldn't help but look up at him, which she gathered the courage to do only once in his arms.

"Is this your first time?"

"I'm not very good."

He pulled her closer, his mouth at her right ear. "Don't worry, I am."

Blood rushed to Lilly's face. This *was* the first time she'd danced with a man, the first time she'd been held without fear. He snuggled her closer.

Lilly imagined he'd meant to dance with her as a sympathetic gesture Doris must have put him up to. She'd always remember his kindness. But the way he held her didn't feel like kindness. It felt new and warm, and remarkably tangible. Many white men had looked at her, even before she passed—a look she'd learned as a child to avoid. But that world and this one were poles apart. She felt different in his arms: safe.

"Should you be dancing with Elizabeth?"

Stewart looked at her, seemingly surprised by her decision to suppress the obvious by bringing up Elizabeth. "If you'd asked me an hour ago I would have said yes and I would have handed you off to Doris . . . but now I'm not so sure." Then he stroked the side of her face—unintentionally it appeared by the way he drew back his hand. Unsettling waves of nerves began to get the best of Lilly. He was looking at her too intensely, too deeply.

Why?

Why did she dance with him? Let him hold her like this. Her whole body went rigid at just the thought of the risk she was taking in his arms. But he smiled and said, "It's alright, Lilly." She felt his hand on her back press her closer and they danced to two more songs.

She could have lived off of the scent of him, lived off of this one night. It would have to be enough, for she was no match for Elizabeth.

Lilly told herself not to aim so high.

Obligation

"You and Elizabeth will make a fine match," Stewart's father told him.

"Do you mean me and Elizabeth or our two families?"

"Both," his father said. He was firm about his convictions. The pictures on the walls in his study read like a postcard of his life: fishing trips in Panama, safaris in Africa, a picture of Stewart's mother at eighteen, Stewart and his brother Sam sitting on his lap when they were children. He poured a glass of Scotch and handed it to Stewart. "Everyone has a place in this world—stay the course." Then he poured himself a glass and added, "We all have desires, son."

"Dad—"

"I heard about the party. Some woman with all the right curves and all the wrong background got you thinking." Stewart fidgeted. "We've got this new factory to open and you're going to run it." He swallowed the rest of his drink and looked at his son. "Elizabeth's the one. Some poor lucky bastard will marry the other. He'll take her to the movies while you take Elizabeth on holiday. He'll get into fist fights over her at the bowling alley, and afterward, they'll have a grand old time between the sheets. He'll go on to fight another day—happy and in love. And you will have a good life with Elizabeth—sons and daughters to build an empire for."

On an evening far less glamorous than the night of the party, Lilly and Doris met for dinner.

"I only let him kiss me twice that night," Doris said. Lilly's eyes narrowed. "Well, three or four times, tops."

"Three or four long and extended kisses I'll bet," Lilly joked.

Doris sighed and took out a cigarette. The restaurant was crowded but Doris, using her father's name, was able to get a nice table in the back of the room. "I can't help it, Lilly. I can talk to him about everything. . . I'm not beautiful."

"Don't say that."

"Why? I'm not." She took a long drag off her cigarette. "My mother and Elizabeth used up that gene. They left me the brains. So I'm lucky. Lawrence likes *me* . . . Doris. And not because I'm standing on top of Daddy's fortune."

Lilly squeezed her hand and said, "He's the lucky one."

"Anyway, you looked pretty comfy with Stewart at my party. You know he's here at the bar with Brian don't you?"

Lilly resisted the urge to turn around. It had been two weeks since the party, and he was all she could think about since.

"I've always liked Stewart. He's one of the few things I admire about my sister." They had a good laugh, then Doris whispered, "Heads up, he's coming this way."

Stewart nodded to the both of them, but didn't sit down.

"Hi, Stew," said Doris.

"Hello, ladies." His "hello" clearly directed toward Lilly.

"Excuse me for a moment. A girl can never have on too much powder," Doris said immediately and most obvious. She darted toward the powder room leaving an awkward pause between Stewart and Lilly. Stewart remained standing even after Doris left.

"Did you have a good time at the party?"

"Yes," Lilly said.

"So did I."

Quiet.

"You looked . . . nice that night. . . . You look nice tonight."

"Thank you."

"You're welcome."

Quiet.

Lilly's knees were shaking under the table. She tried to think of something provocative to say but all she could think about was his arms around her. "Do you have dinner here often?" Lilly finally found her words.

"No, just drinks."

Quiet.

"Are you always this quiet?"

"No, not at all," Lilly said with more strength than was needed.

It embarrassed the both of them, but then Stewart said, "Good."

Every time she looked at Stewart she blushed. She knew he liked her, too. She just didn't know to what extent. She was sure of her side of it, though. Lilly was just getting comfortable with this new life. She hadn't dared to dream of a relationship. It was one of the reasons she hadn't thought of Marcello the way he thought of her. But she'd fallen in deep two weeks ago on the dance floor.

"Well, what did I miss?" Doris slid into her chair.

Stewart smiled. "Awful timing Doris."

"It's cold in there!"

Lilly put to memory his tailored suit, his face, his eyes, his lips.

He stood over them, staring at Lilly.

"Why don't you sit down and join us?" Doris tried to help him.

"I better not. You two have a good evening . . . Lilly."

Arleen's Advice

"Lilly!" Arleen, the boarding house mother yelled from outside Lilly's room. Lilly opened the door before she could knock.

"There's some fancy gentleman downstairs asking for you. It's almost ten o'clock. That is far too late for any man to come callin." She scolded. Lilly ran to the window and looked outside. It was Stewart! He was leaning on the porch post holding his hat. A few of the other boarders had gathered in the hallway.

"Nice car, Lilly," One of the women said. "If I were you, I'd do something I shouldn't to make him mine before this night was over."

"Cara, please," Arleen called from the top of the stairs. "Try to fake like you're a lady."

Spending so much time with Doris made Lilly forget where she lived. Times like these made her remember.

"He seems to think it awfully important to talk to you tonight. I'm not in the habit of lettin women run wild at my place. I'm runnin a good clean house here . . . but he seems like a nice man." Arleen looked out the window one more time. ". . . and that is an awfully nice car."

Lilly hadn't heard half of what Arleen had said. She was too busy racing through her closet to find something appropriate to put on before she went downstairs. She was about to change into another dress, when Arleen stopped her.

"Darlin, I'm just an old woman, but men haven't changed. If he came all the way over here to see you, then let him see you." She smoothed the collar on the dress Lilly was already wearing. "He's seen plenty of those fancy dresses on the other side of town. He's obviously here for something else."

Lilly took a deep breath and nodded her head in agreement. She kissed Arleen on the cheek and raced down the stairs.

"Slow down. He'll wait," Arleen said.

Lilly looked back at Arleen and then walked slowly down the stairs. When she opened the door, Arleen yelled to Stewart. "You've got ten minutes. I'll be lookin out my window checkin up on you. This is a place for clean, nice women!"

"Yes, ma'am!" Stewart yelled back. Grinning, "Hello, Lilly."

"Hi, Stewart."

"It took me a while to find this place. Uh, Doris gave me your address."

"You have to know where you're going. You're probably not used to coming this way."

"No, but if I find my way once, I . . . I don't forget."

Doris had given her sister's boyfriend the address of another woman. Lilly would never fully understand her, but Stewart Fillmore was standing on her front porch and she was going to burst. Stewart started to say something but then hesitated. The awkward silence that plagued them continued to haunt. Lilly looked down at her shoes, embarrassed. He stared at her the way he had that night at the party, and then suddenly backed away. "I'm sorry for bothering you so late, Lilly," he said and started down the stairs.

What just happened! Lilly was in a panic and blurted out before she could think it through, "I think you're wonderful!"

Stewart stopped in his tracks and turned back to her. "Look—" he ran back up the stairs just as fast as he ran down. "Let me tell you all the reasons why you and I won't work." Lilly's heart sank. "You didn't grow up the same way I did, so we have nothing in common. You have no family. You're quiet, I'm not."

"I'm not quiet," Lilly pleaded.

Stewart took a breath. "I have family obligations—a company I'm going to run soon."

Lilly listened, nodding her head in agreement for some reason she couldn't quite understand. She watched him close his eyes and take another deep breath.

"Now let me tell you all the reasons why we will. You didn't grow up the same way I did—thank God," he moved as close to her as he could without touching her. Arleen knocked on the window to let them know she was watching. "I'll be your family," he kissed her hands. Arleen knocked on the window harder. "I have obligations, but my first will always be to you." Then he kissed her lips.

Arleen went nuts.

"Take me with you," Lilly whispered for the second time in her life.

A Visit with Martha

"More tea, Dear?"

"No thank you," Lilly said. She set the fine porcelain teacup on the saucer. In the eleven months of Lilly and Stewart's courtship, she'd won over everyone in his family. She'd weaved a tale of her parents being killed in an accident, and of herself growing up in a monastery for girls to heart wrenching perfection. Stewart's father took one look at her and understood why Elizabeth was no longer viable. And when women of Mrs. Fillmore's inner circle politely inquired about her son's choice in a wife, she rallied to Lilly's defense. Fortunes were being made all over the country, and some of the new money families were settling in Grosse Pointe. The community was careful not to insult one of its leading old money families, at least not in public.

Stewart's grandmother, Martha Fillmore had been traveling in Asia for the year and had not yet met Lilly.

"Asia was fabulous, but I am entirely too dark. I figure at my age, who cares?" She put her glasses on and gave Lilly a zealous stare. "Now who is this villain who is taking my favorite grandchild away from me?"

"I know how important family is to Stewart—especially you," said Lilly. "It would be silly for a scoundrel like me to even consider competing with such a beautiful woman."

Martha smiled, then got to the point, "You are a smart dresser, Lilly. I can tell you have great style. Give me a suggestion to make this parlor more glamorous."

Lilly sat quietly for a moment to collect her thoughts and observe the room. She knew a simple "everything looks beautiful", wouldn't do. The sumptuous parlor was exotic in décor with many artifacts from her travels. However, the answer to Martha's question had nothing to do with admiration. "Well, the room is magnificent. There are only a few minor changes I would make."

"Ohhh?" The old woman raised her left eyebrow.

"I would switch the Seurat painting to the west facing wall so that the sun would show its true beauty in detail while you have your morning tea. That chair I would put next to it instead of over by the window—the tones seem to go well together. I'd place the sculpture beside you at the entrance on that table over there, so that it's the first thing you'd see when you walk in."

Martha nodded. "I think all that's left is the wallpaper, or would you have me change that also?"

"No, ma'am," Lilly blushed. "I hope that I wasn't too outspoken."

"Better outspoken than in," Martha said. "I can't sit more than five minutes with the delicate types." Martha and Stewart grinned at one another, as if there were a secret just between the two of them, and then she put her feet on the footstool under the table to get more comfortable.

Lilly chose her words carefully during the next two hours with Martha. She knew Stewart's grandmother meant the world to him, and she needed her endorsement if not her affection. She tried to remember everything she'd read and everything she'd observed working for the upper class South. She took small bites from the crustless tea sandwiches and other savories, she broke her scone apart one piece at a time, rather than slathering the whole scone with jam and cream; she remembered to sip her tea without making a sound, to hold her cup properly—no pinky since it had a handle. She resisted the urge to eat more than one cookie and one tiny cake for dessert, all the while, making sure she carried her weight in the conversation.

By early evening, Martha had witnessed only a few breaches of etiquette—minor infractions that could be corrected with proper guidance. "You're about to become a member of Grosse Pointe royalty, Lilly." Stewart rolled his eyes. "If you won't tell her I will. We were here before the Peninsular Electric Light Company put streetlights and drinking water into the community," she said, straightening her back. "There's high regard for us Fillmores, but I came across the ocean from England in low tier quarters, so I know a thing or two about re-invention." She relaxed her shoulders. "You have a very interesting nature, Lilly," Martha finally said and leaned forward to be more intimate. "I suspect that you've survived more than I can imagine. It's in your eyes . . . a sadness I hope my grandson's love can diminish."

By the end of the visit, Martha accepted Lilly, pinching Stewart's cheek before they got up from the table.

"Your French is weak, but I can help you with that," she said.

"I'd be very grateful," Lilly responded.

"We'll see," Martha teased.

Martha and Elizabeth's grandmother were good friends, but her favorite grandson's happiness meant more to her than friendship. Lilly was an apt pupil and absorbed everything Martha put to her. She was stern in her teaching, speaking only French to Lilly, perfecting her conversation and manners. And neither Martha nor Lilly ever spoke of the sculpture which had been repositioned at the entrance of the parlor as Lilly had suggested.

The morning of her wedding Lilly wrote another letter to her mother.

Dear Mother,

I feel as if I am saying goodbye to you all over again. I've met a man, lovely in every way. I know that you'd want the very best for me, and Momma, he is. I'm completely in love and am marrying him on this day. With this new life, I must put behind the old. I know that you would understand. I will pray for you, Momma. But I will not put pen to paper again.

Lilly

She lit a match and the last remnants of a life before Stewart, smoked and blackened in the ashes. The wedding was the talk of the Grosse Pointe circle. Lilly wore a drop shoulder slender fit satin dress, a hat with a netted face veil and full-length gloves. She was nothing short of stunning. A famous Swedish baker made the cake. Doris was Lilly's maid of honor and enjoyed every minute of watching her best friend wed one of Michigan's most eligible bachelors. Her sister Elizabeth married a Count and moved to France, intentionally timed three weeks before.

The Couple

"The ship is beautiful, Stewart," Lilly said.

"We're having dinner with the Captain tomorrow." Stewart leaned in to nestle her closer. "Tonight we have other plans."

The cruise liner to Italy would begin their three-month tour of Europe and its quarters were as extravagant as Stewart's gifts to her. During their engagement, Lilly gave Stewart what was proper—her hand, kisses with long embraces that might have at times included caressing the back of his neck. With no money and influence to fall back on, her virtue was all she had. But her wedding night was different. Lilly guessed Stewart expected a timid wife, covered in her gown and tucked securely under the coverlet, but Lilly lay on the bed fully naked, with one knee slightly bent and opened.

When he saw her, he took off his robe and slowly pushed his pants to the floor. Never taking his eyes off her, he took her hands and pulled her up to her knees. He played with her lips, barely touching them at first—skimming them. Lilly followed his lead, teasing his mouth back until he was pressing hard against her. Their breath quickened in and out, both unable to catch enough air to continue the slow burn rising. He slid his hand down her spine, kissing her mouth hard now, cupping the under part of her buttocks so that she felt the wet, rigid tip of him between her thighs. She squeezed. His drone-like moan hummed at her ear and he gently pushed her down on the bed. Lilly looked at him, half crazed with excitement and anticipation. She felt the weight of his body press down onto her—a solid, chiseled mass of a man she'd wanted to feel against her from the day they'd met. She braced herself, waiting for the quick, sharp pain she'd only heard about. But he pulled back and kissed her mouth, then he kissed her neck, her shoulders, her stomach, he took her left leg in his right arm and kissed her inner thighs. Shaking now, Lilly tried to pull him back up to her. He slowed her, flipping her over onto her stomach, discovering all of her, until Lilly couldn't wait any longer. She turned back around to face him with a wild unhinged look. He spread her legs . . .

There was spun-out passion. The jolting kind that scares a woman into believing she's made a mistake afterward. But Stewart had loved her back with the same intensity and they laughed later with the security of knowing they were equally matched. Stewart was a surprise gift her new life presented and she vowed to be the very best wife.

To Stewart's delight, Lilly could hold an engaging conversation with the best of them. Their discussions about art and history, and at times business, lasted for hours.

One of New York's finest architects built their mansion on Grosse Pointe Shores. They named it Daisy Manor, which Stewart believed to be Lilly's favorite flower, and he brought her a bouquet weekly.

Lilly settled into her role as a socialite straight away. She hosted the grandest parties and brought her new grandmother a dozen fresh roses every Tuesday to low tea. She was known to be both outspoken and affable with her friends, and Stewart's family thought they were lucky to have her among them.

Then the rain came.

Tula

It was the constant storms of 1942 that took Martha's health, and the humidity's thickness choked the life from her. She didn't fight its strangle. At eighty-seven, the world had changed all around her and she'd had enough of it.

Martha left Stewart her most cherished antiques, money he didn't need, and a colored maid named Tula she'd had in her employment for twenty years. Naturally, Tula could have moved on to another family or gone back south to help her sister with an emerging cake business. But that was in Alabama—the last place she'd go back to. Stewart offered her two dollars more a week than with his grandmother, plus he was willing to hire her son, Martin as grounds keeper as well. Tula always liked Stewart. While the other grandchildren (none of whom were older than ten years of age when she first came to work for Martha), treated Tula as if they ran the place, Stewart had a more gentle nature toward her.

She had a matter-of-fact view of the world, with no room for contemplation. According to Tula, the world was simply what it was and put no effort into questioning it. She'd shrugged off Alabama like a bad cold, but brought its views with her to Michigan. And when Martin had doubts about the Lord's decision to make them carry the burden of color, he was firmly and unequivocally told, "It's right here in the Bible."

All in His Head

"Stand up straight and none of that 'Yes suh, nawh suh here.
. . . Mr. Fillmore don't like that kind a talk," Tula said,
smoothing down the collar on Baby Count's freshly pressed
white shirt.

"I ain't stupid, Aunt Tula. Daddy already told me what's
expected."

"Look at him when you talk, but not directly," Tula
ignored him and kept on. "Let him know you're gonna do a
good job here and be sure and tell him you worked for the
Wesley's in Charleston."

"I *will*, Aunt Tula."

"I already told him all about your momma and me workin
for the same family back in Alabama."

"You tell him I ain't really your nephew?"

"Boy, Mr. Fillmore don't care nothin about that, he just
wants to know that you gon do a good job." Tula helped him
put on his father's suit jacket and murmured under her
breath, "White folks think we all related anyway."

"Thanks for sending me the money to come," said Baby
Count.

"Uhmm. Go on now. Mr. Fillmore don't like to be kept
waitin." She nudged him out of the kitchen.

"Good morning, Mr. Fillmore." Baby Count said as soon as
Stewart entered the knotty pine walled library.

"Mr. Count Vansant." Stewart put his hand out to shake.

"Baby Count, sir. That's what people call me."

"Baby Count," Stewart repeated with a strange look on his face. "Tula has already informed me about your experience as a driver in Alabama, and that now you're looking to fill the position here at Daisy Manor."

"Yes, sir. I'm a good driver, and I don't stay up all night drinking and things so I won't have no trouble getting up bright and early," Baby Count said hurried and nervous. Stewart grinned just a little. "I brought you a couple of recommendations." Stewart was in the process of looking over them just as Lilly entered with a burst of activity.

"It's so dark in here!" She stepped behind Stewart's desk to kiss him on the cheek. "You are going to go blind." She pulled back the curtains, standing there for a moment directly in the late afternoon light. "Sorry I'm late."

Stewart looked at his watch and let out a long breath. "This is Mrs. Fillmore. Lilly, this is Co—Baby Count Vansant.

She was just as tickled by his name and laughed openly about it. "Baby Count, it's nice to meet you." She put out her hand. He hesitated for a second, trying to decide if it was proper in the North to shake hands with a white woman. She nodded, signaling that it was fine.

"Likewise, ma'am."

"I was just looking over his recommendations." Stewart handed them to Lilly, but she set them down without giving them a glance.

"Tula's told me all about you."

Baby Count looked down at his shoes.

"Don't be shy. You and I are going to be spending a lot of time together."

"Yes, ma'am."

"Where did you get such a name, Baby Count?"

Baby Count looked up at Lilly strangely and then turned his attention to Stewart. "Well, my Daddy's name is Count—he's the first, so my Momma, God rest her soul, thought it fitting to call me Baby Count. I guess I'll be stuck with the name till my Daddy pass."

"I guess so," Stewart said. "However, my wife inquired about your name, not me. I suggest you address Mrs. Fillmore if she asks you a question. She's the one you'll be driving."

"Yes, sir,"

Stewart snipped the end of a cigar before lighting it. "What do you think, Lilly?"

The scent of the cigar began to fill the room and Baby Count again looked quickly at Lilly then down at his shoes. Lilly asked, "Do you smoke, Baby Count?"

"No, ma'am. I sure don't."

"You've got the job then. I don't want to smell smoke every time I get into my car." Giving Stewart the eye for smoking while she was in the room, "Tula will give you my schedule and your uniform. You can start immediately."

"Thank you, ma'am." He looked at Stewart. "Thank you, sir."

Stewart watched his wife leave the room, admiring her form until she disappeared. "I'm entrusting you with my wife's safety when she's out," Stewart said, now looking down at his cigar. "She's the reason I get up in the morning, you understand?" And then he gave Baby Count the most menacing stare. "Don't mistake my generosity for weakness."

"No sir, Mr. Fillmore."

The driver quickly acquainted himself to Lilly's comings and goings and was dependable with his directions and time. Tula was glad Baby Count had made such a speedy transition, and fed him gravy and biscuits every morning before the Fillmores came down for breakfast.

"Aunt Tula, Mrs. Fillmore from here?" He cleaned his plate with the last half of biscuit and stuffed it in his mouth.

"Mrs. Fillmore ain't from nowhere. Poor woman grew up in an orphanage down south," Tula said.

"What parts?"

"I don't know, Georgia I think."

"Georgia?"

"I believe." She took out the pork for tonight's dinner.

"Where 'bouts?"

"Why you so interested in Mrs. Fillmore, boy!" Tula suddenly snapped. "I'll put your head in this stove myself if I catch you sniffing up around her."

"No, Aunt Tula! Ain't nothing like that. I just wonder about her that's all."

"Well you better put your head to wondering about something else quick, fast and in a hurry, 'cause they hang our men here just like they do back home."

"Yes'm—I mean Yes, ma'am."

Baby Count sat quietly for a moment, fiddling with his uniform hat. He watched Tula rub her own mixture of herb seasoning on each of the pork chops.

"It's just that about five or six years back Daddy took us to see Mamma's side of the family in Kentucky. My cousin Blinky and me was—"

"Blinky—Lawd have mercy, you all don't have no sense about what to call yourselves. How's someone gon take you seriously with names like Baby Count and Blinky?"

Baby Count laughed. "He got some kind of eye tremblin so we call him Blinky. Anyway, sometimes we'd go swimmin in the creek and sit by the bank afterward. Blinky say if we wait a bit we gon see the prettiest black girl in Paducah. So, we wait hidin there by the creek until this black woman and a white girl come round the bank with this basket full of laundry. I'm thinkin all this time we waiting for this black beauty to come and all I see is a white girl. Beautiful yeah, but

I wasn't gon take no chance of gettin strung up by lookin at her real good. . . . Blinky say that's who he talkin about. I get a better look at her 'cause she still don't see me and Blinky. She looked white alright. Blinky say she work with her mamma for a family in town, and they pick up laundry on his side of town every Tuesday and Sunday. Me and Blinky watch her and her mamma pass by like that all summer long. Then he paused, almost afraid to say, "Mrs. Fillmore look just like her."

Tula was busy stuffing the pork chops with an apple and berry mixture, barely paying Baby Count any attention.

"It ain't her."

"Just look like her that's all I'm sayin."

"That woman's white as they come," Tula said. She covered the stuffed pork and set it in the refrigerator. "You don't have time for no fairy tales, Baby Count. You got the car filled up? Miss Lilly's going downtown today." She removed Baby Count's breakfast plate from the table. "You got a good thing here. You owe it to your mamma to—" They heard footsteps nearing the breakfast room.

"I'm not gon mess this up, Auntie," Baby Count whispered and slipped out the back door.

Tula had heard stories of light-skinned Negroes passing in the South. She even knew of a family with two sons, Brandon and Randolph who had supposedly passed and brought home their earnings once a month. They were just stories to her—nothing proven. Nothing she needed to worry about, anyway. She had the rest of dinner to prepare.

Unraveling
1943

The world began to unravel the night Stewart's factory was set on fire. It was the second day of clashes between blacks and whites in Detroit, rumored to have started on the island park of Belle Isle. Looting and spurts of vandalism from the riot claimed several businesses. Stewart's factory was one of them. Fear was all around Detroit's inner city and had filtered out to Grosse Pointe. Before dinner, Lilly explained to the staff that this was a difficult night for Stewart. "Tensions are high all around," she said.

There was no need for Lilly to explain further. The colored staff was well aware of what was going on outside of glossy Grosse Pointe.

Stewart had already yelled at Baby Count for not cleaning the car. He didn't come in and look for Lilly, which was customary, but went straight to his study. At dinner, Lilly and Stewart sat in silence. Lilly knew that he was beyond upset, but she couldn't take the silence any longer.

"Will our insurance cover the damages?"

"I haven't spoken with Dennis yet," It was obvious he wasn't ready to talk about it.

Lilly pressed anyway. "Is the fire out?"

"Yes."

"Do the police have any idea who started it?"

"Blacks!" Stewart snapped.

She paused before she said delicately, "I just want to know what's happened, Stewart."

"What's happened is they've burned half the building down."

He shook his head, closed his eyes and took a deep breath all at once. Then he said more calmly, "I just want to eat dinner right now. We can talk about it later."

They'd had disagreements before—heated differences that sometimes lasted for hours. Lilly felt comfortable voicing her opinion on his business, his friends, his tie—anything.

She was no doormat.

But Lilly had never seen Stewart like this. She couldn't find her footing. Partly because he'd never talked to her as if she were ignorant, but also because this was a matter that involved the part of her that she'd kept hidden from him. She couldn't defend the activities of the rioters, even though she knew the deep-rooted anger from being treated as less than human. She couldn't go along with the condemnation of the rioters either. She was caught in the middle, so she just kept quiet.

Stewart played with his food for a moment before he looked up at her, sick to his stomach. "The factory looks like it was bombed, Lilly. . . . They have a few suspects, but no real leads."

Lilly reached her hand across the table to Stewart. "We'll get through this."

"I know we will. It's going to take some time to get things up and running again, but I'll do it." He gulped down a full glass of wine. "If I could get my hands on one of them…." Just then, Tula walked in to fill their glasses.

Tula heard what he said. When white folks were in a bad mood (this being a very bad mood), she knew to tread lightly around them. "Would you like some more wine, Mista Stewart?" Stewart nodded his head yes. She was a bundle of nerves this evening, which was the cause of her leaning the bottle of wine on top of his now full glass, which spilled all over his plate and into his lap. He jumped up wiping himself with his napkin.

"I'm sorry, Mista Stewart! I'll get something to clean that right up!" Tula fled to the kitchen.

"Stupid niggers."

"Stewart!" Lilly was sure Tula had heard him, too.

Tula returned quickly with a dishtowel and dabbed at the mess on the table. Stewart was still standing. He snatched the bottle of wine off the table and poured himself another glass.

Lilly just sat there. Her plate was fine. If she didn't look anywhere else but at the dish in front of her—her napkin still in her lap, she could pretend that nothing had happened. But pretending would be difficult with Tula dabbing at the stained tablecloth Stewart's grandmother had given them, his roasted chicken and fresh snap peas pooled in one of his best bottles of red, and Stewart standing there with the front of his pants soaked, oddly still drinking his glass of wine as if he hadn't just said what all three of them were trying to ignore. She'd seen this strange occurrence between colored and white many times before. Just never in her home.

Her husband was a fair man, one of the first to hire black men at the factory. A pragmatist too, often arguing that the Negroes worked just as hard as the Italians, Polish, and the Irish. His open-minded nature was one of the things Lilly loved about him. She thought back to a discussion she and Stewart had about the time his father overheard him call a boy working in the yard, nigger.

"Stewart!" His father had called from his study. Stewart remembered that he knew by his father's tone that he had done something wrong.

"Yes, sir?"

"We are all God's creatures," his father had said without looking up from his writing. "The coloreds are already at the bottom. There's no need to remind them." His father had looked up at him then. "Leave them with a little dignity, and they will give more to you than their own children. Call them that and you'll worry about your meals, your sleep, and your woman."

Stewart had told Lilly that he was a young boy at the time and didn't quite understand all that was intended in that conversation. But he felt it was the first time his father had talked to him like a man. The first time he'd been called into his father's study to talk about life and how to conduct himself. "I heard my friend say it to their grounds keeper. . . . I'd heard his father say it under his breath." Stewart had told her. "I only wanted the boy to get my ball before it went into the bushes."

In three years of marriage, this was the only other time Lilly had heard Stewart say it.

"I'll speak to Tula," Stewart said after he'd finished his glass of wine.

Lilly nodded her head. That was all she could do. She was too off-put: woozy. "I'm not feeling well. I need to lie down," she said and stood up from the table.

"This is nothing for you to worry about, darling. This whole night has been a disaster," He rubbed Lilly's arms and pulled her close to him. She wanted to forget tonight, she wanted to wrap her arms around him and help him forget too. But at the moment his arms felt strangely foreign to her. She looked at his still damp pants and wondered if the stain would come out.

"Why don't you take a hot bath before you lay down? It'll make you feel better." Stewart said, putting his arms around her waist as he escorted her up the spiral staircase.

Later that night Lilly stood in her lavish bedroom suite and looked at herself. It had been five years since she'd stepped off the train from Kentucky, a lifetime since she'd written a letter for Daisy. She didn't know if her mother was alive or dead. She'd forgotten about that life. She didn't consider herself a pretender anymore.

She was white.

But what was she to do now with the part of Stewart she cherished most growing inside her? There was too much power in the word nigger. She'd seen and heard its power too many times before moving North. She sat on the edge of her bed and rubbed her stomach.

One month before, when Lilly had just suspected she was pregnant, Stewart had taken her with him to California on business. Lilly went shopping alone, looking to bring a little Hollywood glamour back east. She passed quite a few storefronts before she stopped at the quaint shop on the corner with the beautiful black dress in the window. There was only one other woman inside, strikingly fine looking. The woman noticed Lilly's gaze and nodded as women of means did when they admired one of their own. But the woman's smile disappeared as she caught Lilly's eye. It didn't bother Lilly at first. She'd become accustomed to this dance among beautiful women—smiling faces, that at times seethed underneath. However, it wasn't jealousy and competition in this woman's gaze. It was something else that scared Lilly to death. Instinct told her to leave—quickly! *Calm down Lilly*, she told herself instead. *She can't prove anything.*

"I'll wrap these things for you, Mrs. Murdock," the shopkeeper said to the woman and went to the back room. As soon as the shopkeeper was out of sight, the woman made a beeline toward Lilly.

"How long have you been passing?" she whispered.

Lilly froze. Images of when she was a child and the old woman taking her candy flooded her mind. Her legs wouldn't move and the air in her lungs disappeared. Her heart felt like it was going to explode.

It can't end this way.

She needed to get to the door and speak nothing of it to Stewart. *Stay calm*, she told herself again. *She can't prove anything!* Lilly walked away from the woman, petrified, but determined to maintain her composure. She ran her fingers through the rack of dresses at the front of the store. The woman followed her though, looking around anxiously.

"We don't have much time—she'll be back in a minute," said the woman. She hesitated. Her mouth moved but nothing came out. Then the woman leaned in close to Lilly. "It's been so long since I've talked to anyone like me—the last time was in New York—that was three years ago. It's hard keeping this inside all the time. . . . I have to let it out."

Lilly stopped pushing the dresses back and forth. She scrutinized the stunning woman standing before her. There was no hint of color in her translucent complexion. Her light, sandy brown hair was fine, nose slim and pointed, lips thinner than many women in Stewart's family. Yet it was there, right in front of her. Color found only if you were looking for it.

"Sometimes I feel like I'm trying to get caught." The woman smiled nervously, fondling the hats on display. The longing in this woman's eyes was overwhelming. Lilly knew that longing. This kind of secret was so alienating that she felt she too would go insane at times. But this woman was living dangerously—coming up to complete strangers. It was absolutely out of the question. Many times Lilly had looked at women on the street and wondered, but she would never be foolish enough to take a chance like this.

"Do you have any children?" Lilly asked, admitting nothing.

"Yes, two. A boy and a—"

"Are they white?" Lilly interrupted, forgetting to keep her guard.

"Blessed yes, as white as right," smiled the woman and grabbed Lilly's hand. Lilly tensed, but didn't pull away. It was the only time in her life that she would feel such a connection.

The shopkeeper headed toward them with her hands full of neatly wrapped bags and hatboxes. The woman quickly let go of Lilly.

"Will that be all, ma'am?" The shopkeeper asked.

"No." The fine woman quickly collected herself, holding a beautiful green dress toward the shopkeeper. "I'd like to know if this dress comes in any other colors."

The shopkeeper set the items down and took the dress. "It only comes in green, ma'am."

Lilly moved away from them, following the fair woman's lead. As she headed toward the door, the woman said, "It was nice meeting you." Lilly turned back to her and smiled. "Did you wrap them separately? I won't have my things wrinkled when I get back to my hotel."

Lilly opened the door, but paid attention to the shopkeeper's response, "Yes, ma'am. . . . I took special care."

Motherhood

"Give me one more big push, Lilly!" The doctor commanded. Lilly, with her hair plastered against her forehead, gave one final excruciating push before her baby entered the world. The doctor stared at the baby and then called for Stewart.

"NO! It can't be true!" Stewart cried.

The doctor glared at Lilly with disgust.

That was the dream Lilly woke up to the last five days of her pregnancy—Stewart falling to his knees about the tawny baby she'd just liberated from her womb.

But in reality, there were no shrieks from Stewart and no falling out in shame. Stewart had a son, blond from his first day and skin just as pale. They named him Stewart Nathaniel, after his father, and grandfather. The Fillmore clan couldn't have been happier. Lilly relaxed after the birth of her second son Matthew, who had sandy brown hair and beautiful brown eyes, almost too pretty for a boy.

Lilly was the overseer of all the boys' activities. She wanted them cultured. Art, language and music were taught, but she was also the kind of mother who got right down on her hands and knees and played marbles with them. She adored those boys and they returned it as little boys do. They caught frogs and worms as gifts for her, and curled around her tightly while she read their favorite bedtime stories. Throughout the years that followed, their hair had grown slightly curly, but Stewart's mother only boasted that they'd inherited her side of the family's "Nordic locks."

The incident the night of the factory fire was a distant memory. Stewart apologized to Tula, and the following morning had even given her and the rest of the staff the day off with pay. He'd done exactly what he'd said he would and had the factory up and running again in four months time. All was forgotten. And Stewart's embrace was again familiar, anticipated. Lilly was perfectly content. Her two boys, Nathan and Matthew (three if she counted Stewart), were the extraordinary delight of her life, surpassing her meager ambition to pass.

It was her picture perfect world.

However, Stewart's picture wasn't finished without one more—wishing for a girl as pretty as his wife—a princess for Lilly to dress up, buy dolls for and take to tea. After the third child, he would commission a painter to do their family portrait.

Lilly no longer struggled with the decision she'd made years ago. But the pressure to have one more made her think about what her life could have been if she'd made another choice. Among coloreds, she would have been a considerable prize. Moving along the right circles could have put her in position to marry a colored doctor or businessman in no time. But why settle when she could reign supreme? She was where she should be—nestled into the incredible lightness of being white.

W orld War II had come and Lilly kept herself busy by helping with community support centers and USO activities. When that war ended and the war between the races escalated, Lilly hadn't found herself stuck in the middle as before, she quietly dismissed herself from it and stood on the sidelines—away from the hostility, the dogs—the violence. Through it all, Stewart hadn't forgotten about his desire for another child and many nights were spent attempting to fulfill his desire. Until one morning, the busiest of mornings, Lilly sat behind her poached egg and felt the familiar nausea from years past.

Just One More

"What time is it Tula?" Lilly asked sitting up in bed.

"Nine-thirty, Miss Lilly," Tula set Lilly's breakfast tray down over her lap.

"I was so tired."

"This one sure got you beat down, Miss Lilly. You get as much rest as you need, you hear?"

"I've got a luncheon at the Club today, so I don't want to overeat this morning."

"You got to eat something now, so that baby of yours'll be healthy."

Lilly took a couple of bites of toast. "The boys kicked and turned all night long. This one lets me sleep."

"Your appetite's down with this one, too. It's gonna be a girl," said Tula.

Lilly leaned back and rubbed her stomach. "Stewart's been beside himself about this one. Just between you and me, I think it makes him feel like a teen again."

"Awhh he may not be no spring chicken, but he ain't all the way sprung yet, Miss Lilly." They laughed. "Now come on and eat something."

Stewart had said that Lilly would jinx it if she picked out a boy name so she only concentrated on names for girls. They decided to name her Beatrice if it were a girl, her mother-in-law's name. But Daisy had crept into her mind often during the last few months. She couldn't stop thinking about her. She still wondered if Daisy were dead, or worse, alive and penniless. She wished she could let Daisy know she was better than alright—that she had a wonderful family, a husband she adored, a dream life that was finer than the lives of the people they had worked for. Except it was a life without Daisy. A life she couldn't risk undoing by contacting her, not even once. A mother's love can cause confusion. She knew because she was a mother now. She couldn't have Daisy showing up at her doorstep one day.

Her Little Bundle

Lilly wasn't sure if it was the clashes of rolling thunder or the pain that woke her. The early onset of labor was as unexpected as the storm, and Lilly was caught between the two. Stewart was out of town and the boys were visiting their grandparents, leaving Tula alone to act as midwife. So, three weeks earlier than expected, she clutched her pillow with one hand and held on to Tula's with the other.

"Come on now, Miss Lilly, it's time for you to push!" A flash of brilliant light lit the room and then a deafening boom roared across the sky. The lamp flickered off and then back on again. "It was just a stutter, Miss Lilly—Push!"

The medieval torture from the contractions left Lilly barely able to speak. "Did you—try—calling the doctor again?"

"Phone's dead and the road's flooded. Ain't no doctor coming before this baby, Miss Lilly—Now push!"

"Tula, I c-can't!" Lilly thought she would pass out from the pain as it moved relentlessly from shallow valleys to blinding peaks that left her gasping for air—no start, no end.

"I know it hurts, Miss Lilly, but you got to help it out."

Tula had experience delivering her son's daughter so she knew what she was doing. "Your baby is right there, Miss Lilly. I can see it!"

Lilly belted out a pitchy scream that started low but ended high.

"Push it on out, Miss Lilly!

Lilly grunted one more time, pushing as hard as she could. "It's a girl, Miss Lilly!" The baby let out a healthy cry.

Lilly's weary nod accompanied an exhausted, muttered sound. "Let me see her," she said.

"Just one minute, Miss Lilly. Let me cut the cord and wipe her off for you. She got you all over her right now." Tula started to wipe the baby's face with the water and damp cloth on the side of the bed.

"Just give her to me, Tula," Lilly repeated softly, but this time more firm. "I want to see my little girl."

Tula didn't answer.

"Tula? What's the matter? Is she alright?"

"What'd you do, Miss Lilly?" Her tone was suddenly flat and loathsome.

Lilly tried to get a better view, but Tula's back was turned to her.

"This can't be Mista Stewart's baby?" Tula said and turned toward Lilly so that she could see the child in full view.

"It—" Lilly couldn't find her words. What she'd feared the most lay in Tula's arms, truth uncovered and bare with tiny arms and legs. The child that lay in Tula's arms wasn't black, but there was no denying that the skin, the soul and even the blood that pulsed through this child was absolutely and undisputedly something other.

"Lawd, Jesus!" Tula said. "You done the worst thing possible to Mista Stewart—the worst thing. It's not Baby Count's, or—or my Martin's baby is it?"

"It's Stewart's child!" Lilly cried. "—No one else's. No one else's I swear!"

"Mista Stewart a good man, Miss Lilly. You gon kill him."

"I swear this is our baby—me and Stewart's." Lilly whimpered. "I swear it."

"This baby come from a union of two people, and one of them ain't Mista Stewart, so either you been messing with someone or you—" Tula didn't finish. She glared at Lilly as if a light had switched on in her head. "Baby Count guessed it. I didn't believe him when he told me. You're the girl he saw!"

Lilly had no idea what she was talking about. She started to cry. "My mother is—"

"Colored!" Tula riled before Lilly could say. Her face scrunched in like a shriveled pumpkin.

Lilly didn't deny it. She couldn't anymore. Confirmation was right there in Tula's arms. Her tears seemed to fuel Tula's anger. "You think cause you got white skin you better? Hmmph," she shook her head, disgusted. "Can't stand your kind . . . . High yella marrying high yella. Paper bag tests to keep my dark face out your clubs. You worst than them! Get the best jobs, best menfolk. Leaving the rest of us with the pickins. Well you ain't better than the rest of us. We all colored! Don't matter what shade you get." The baby started to cry. Tula glared at Lilly with hard eyes, "Here. Take what's yours."

The anger in Tula's voice frightened Lilly. Just this morning Tula was an employee, beneath Lilly by no fault of hers, but by a country that had set both of their fates.

"I didn't set out to fall in love with Stewart. But I did. I love him! I love my sons!" Lilly cried and at the same time tried to soothe the baby.

"What about this little colored thing, huh? You love her too—gon let her sit down at the dining room table with her family? Show her off to all your fine friends?"

"I don't know."

Lilly didn't know. All she could do was look down at the child in her arms.

"Yeah you cry. Cry hard and good girl. We'll see what kind of life you gon' have now." She pulled the baby from Lilly's arms. "Wait till these white folks find out about how this Negro with green eyes tricked 'um."

"Please, Tula!" Lilly screamed. "I can give you money. Anything!" She was desperate. "Think of the boys, Tula—you love them too. Think about what would happen to them if anyone found out." The baby quieted with the scent of Lilly, or quite possibly her voice. Like other newborns, she looked up at her mother, beginning to make the connection that lasts a lifetime. Lilly was too busy trying to save herself to notice. She wasn't thinking rationally. All she wanted was her life back to the way it was only hours before. "We could get rid of her. You would know what to do with her, Tula."

"You're talkin crazy now," was what she said in rebuttal. But Tula did love those boys, and they too would have to pay for their mother's recklessness. She stared at Lilly for a moment. "If I do anything, and I didn't say I would, it's for them boys and Mista Stewart—not you." Then she took the baby from Lilly.

"We can't tell anyone. You've got to do it quick," Lilly kept on.

"It'll be quick alright. Ought to be easy to smother a baby."

The words stung Lilly like one hundred bees. There would be no dolls for this baby, no dresses or tea parties. Clear thought returned with the cruel company of pain and agony. But it was too late to take back her words. How do you explain to your baby girl why she has to die?

Lilly started to cry hysterically. "Let me hold her again, Tula."

"Why? You don't want her. Don't make no sense to hold something you ain't gon keep."

"Let me hold her. Please!" Lilly wept.

Tula didn't want to give an ounce of mercy to Lilly, but she was a mother too, so she handed the swaddled baby back to Lilly.

"Say your goodbyes quick. I got to get over to my—our side of town before I do anything with her."

Lilly caressed the smooth sandy-brown hair that lay flat against her baby's head and took a long look at her for the first time. Her faintly olive skin would become darker with time, Lilly was certain. She smiled at her daughter. She truly was a beautiful baby—deliciously beautiful. She simply had the wrong set of parents. Lilly pressed her lips to the baby's forehead for an unbound moment, trying to give her the love of a mother's lifetime within minutes. She closed her eyes, engraving the scent of her child in her mind. She wanted to nurse her, to nourish her with her milk as she had the boys. It would be a small part of her love that she could give—it took all of her strength to resist. "I wish I knew another way." Lilly whispered. "I can't do this to my boys—to Stewart. You'll tear us apart." Her face dripping, she kissed her baby several more times—quick tender little kisses.

"She don't know what you're sayin," Tula told her, her tone back to grim and stringent. She'd finished cleaning up the mess of bloodied rags.

"You get to go to God!" Lilly cried as Tula pulled the baby from Lilly's arms again. She set the baby down in a chair and took the fine-looking onyx necklace out of Lilly's jewel case, and stashed it in her bloodstained apron. Tula would put away her Bible and look at the world differently now. She picked up the baby and left the room, leaving Lilly lying there, bloody and childless.

Stewart was told the baby had been born dead. He mourned with the sorrow of a father knowing almost instantly he would never hold another newborn in his arms and call it his.

Lilly mourned differently.

The After Death

The night Lilly and Stewart attended the symphony was surprisingly beautiful. It was early August and the air had been stifling hot for the last three days. However, tonight there was a spirited, cool breeze that felt good on Lilly's skin. She would have preferred to skip the symphony and just take a walk along the shore with Stewart. After the symphony, she wanted nothing more than to avoid the many familiar faces in the procession out to the atrium. Stewart had convinced her that it would be good to mingle with their friends again. He meant well. But all Lilly could think about was going home.

"Stewart," Dr. Wallingford called to them. He and his wife were one of the first to greet Stewart and Lilly in the atrium.

"Mr. and Mrs. Kris Kringle," Lilly whispered to Stewart before they were in earshot.

"We'll say hello and leave," Stewart said quickly before they were in hearing range. "Dr. Wallingford, Mrs. Wallingford, how are you?"

"Wonderful after such a performance, just wonderful. Wasn't it absolutely riveting?" he asked Lilly.

"Absolutely!" Lilly said, mocking the jolly man. Stewart pinched her waist.

Mrs. Wallingford pulled Lilly to the side then. "How are you dear, really?"

"I'm fine."

"Are you? The best thing to do in these cases is to get right back on the horse." She lowered her eyebrows. "If you know what I mean."

"I do," Lilly said, and then she looked at Stewart for help. The last thing she wanted to talk about with Mrs. Wallingford was having another child.

Several other couples surrounded them and soon the two were separated. Lilly was on one side with the women, and Stewart was on the other with the men. Lilly's group chattered on about absolutely nothing. She wished Doris were home from her trip to Africa. She had been away for eight months, and Lilly missed their lively debates. The conversation around her varied from Sunday bridge club to who was the better actress, Bette Davis or Joan Crawford, with the jovial Mrs. Wallingford leading the conversation. Ten minutes was spent on the up and coming Elizabeth Taylor. Just when Lilly felt as if she would suffocate from the mindless noise, Stewart came up behind her and said, "We're going to head home now. It's been great seeing all of you."

He was good that way. Lilly could count on him knowing when enough was enough. In the car, she was grateful for the quiet that the drive home afforded, away from the clink of the champagne glasses and noise of the crowd. After several blocks of silence Stewart asked, "Are you happy, Lilly?"

"As happy as I *can* be." A simple yes was what she wanted to say—what she had wanted him to hear. She kissed his hand and smiled wearily. "You've always been the love of my life."

"Show me tonight," he said.

Lilly wanted to assure him. Make him feel as if they were still the passionate couple her friends envied. She scooted over the wide seat of their Cadillac and slid her arm under his. She dropped her head to his shoulder and he kissed the top of it. If she could explain her distant behavior, her lack of desire, she would. She did love Stewart, more than any woman should love a man. But there was no way to explain what she had done to stay with him and the boys. Tula was right. It would kill him if he knew. Instead, she would love him tonight and make him believe nothing had changed.

He felt the same—kissed her the same. She felt his tongue run along her neck and back to her lips. He held her head tight to look at her. There was question in his eyes though her body tried to console him. She felt his thrusts become more direct and cherished the familiar intensity in his breath.

But it had been a long time since it was just she and Stewart in the room.

Lilly lay awake long after Stewart had fallen asleep, his arm coiled around her waist. She gently caressed it, making sure not to disturb him, and thought about the second time she saw her daughter.

Tula left her employment four months after the night Lilly had given birth—the weight of the secret between them too heavy for a working relationship. Lilly was giving the new maid instructions about her bedroom when she glanced over at her dressing table and saw the toddler sitting on top of it.

Her heart stopped!

Then it started again, beating hard against her chest. Heat soared from her toes to the top of her head like a rocket. She thought that she would actually levitate off the floor.

"Mrs. Fillmore, Mrs. Fillmore! Are you alright? Let me get you some water before you faint, ma'am."

"I don't need any water. I need you to leave me!" She practically pushed the maid out the door.

"Mrs. Fillmore?" Lilly could hear the maid ask from the other side. She hadn't meant to shut the door in her face, but this was no time for manners. Lilly turned quickly back to the infant. She was still there.

"Thank you, God. Thank you," she prayed softly. Lilly sat down on the bed to look at her from a distance—she didn't want to frighten her. In toddler form, no older than two or three, sitting on top of the dressing table playing with the pearl necklace Lilly had set there earlier, was the child she never spoke of. Only six months had passed since that horrendous night, but Lilly knew in an instant that the child was unmistakably hers. Overwhelming love resonated around the room, bouncing off the walls and the furniture, pulsating deeply throughout Lilly's body, through her hair follicles, and her knees. It brushed across her lips and tickled up her spine, until it settled down deep into her pounding heart. Lilly was crying but smiling too. A long missed joy consumed her.

This child sparkled. Her wild, loose curls flowed like her brothers' at that age—chiseled nose like Stewart, her skin dazzled gold, like an ancient relic too beautiful for existence in the here and now. She was the prettiest little girl she had ever seen. Her daughter finally looked up. Her eyes were brilliantly navy black. She giggled sweetly and held her hands out to her mother.

Lilly's legs couldn't carry her fast enough. Then, just as Lilly approached the dresser the child disappeared.

"Nooo!" she screamed out loud. In her head she pleaded, *Come back. . . come back.* Her limbs buckled under her and she collapsed on the floor.

"Is everything alright, Mrs. Fillmore?" She heard the maid on the other side of the door.

"Go away!"

Lilly cried until her eyes swelled. But with her grief came a discerning expectation that her baby would return. Misery arrived in a combination of sorrow and regret. In the kitchen, sitting in a sink full of water too high for safety—at the top of the staircase, about to attempt the winding set of steps dangerously on her own—in the garden, close to the forests' edge, looking back at Lilly just as she stepped into its darkness. All places that Lilly's daughter appeared. Scenes played out only to Lilly, only for Lilly. Always the same, just as Lilly ran to her aid, the child would disappear. It had been four gloriously agonizing months of this.

This much she knew. She was losing her mind, and there was nothing she could do about it. What she didn't know was how fast it would happen.

Lilly, still wrapped in Stewart's arms, looked down at the end of the bed to watch her daughter wiggle toward the edge. It was where she always sat, waiting for Lilly to waken before she scooted to the edge of the bed, fell off, and vanished. Lilly closed her eyes and held Stewart closer.

Tula's Rewards

"This money's gonna set me up fine in New York, Miss Lilly," Tula said. "I don't know why I still call you that." Tula came around occasionally when Stewart was busy at the factory, and when she wanted something.

"I can't give you any more," Lilly told her, emotionless and barely standing up straight.

"You on something?"

"What do you care?"

"What about that green brooch you never wear."

Lilly took it out of her jewelry chest and handed it to Tula.

"You got plenty. You won't even miss it." Tula raised the brooch up to the light and then stuffed it into her bag. She had barely noticed Lilly drag her feet over to the bed and lay down. "You need to pull it together, Miss Lilly. You're lookin a little ragged." Lilly responded by turning away from her. "You ain't gotta listen to me, but for your own sake. . . ." Tula pressed her lips and started to leave, but then she paused at the door. She fixed her eyes on Lilly. "It's not as bad as you're makin it. You still got your family, your life." She pressed the bag of loot to her chest and leaned against the door. "I'm the one that don't have nothin. I was a good woman, Miss Lilly. Now I can't even gather up enough courage to go to church to ask for forgiveness."

Confession

Stewart couldn't hide Lilly's condition anymore. She'd begun to talk to herself, not only with him and the boys, but in public. He told Nathan and Matthew that their mother was having a difficult time recovering from the death of the baby. However, a year had passed and Lilly's hallucinations and listlessness were becoming more and more frequent. Friends and family assured Stewart that eventually Lilly would get better, that she would be back to her old self with a little rest. She didn't get better though, and eventually friends, then family stopped coming. The invitations to parties were replaced with caring notes on Lilly's behalf. The boys got used to their mother holding them for hours at a time, letting go only after they promised to never leave her.

Stewart took her away to Canada for a while. She had hot baths and cold ones, sunlight and dark rooms. The prescriptions kept coming, but Lilly stayed the same. Eventually Stewart had no choice but to commit Lilly to a hospital where she'd have constant care.

"She needs me, Stewart. She's all alone." Lilly would whine and pull at him. Her babbling of a black baby coming to haunt her, and how she needed to go to her soon, was seen as merely part of her mental illness—nothing more. She'd even mentioned Daisy's name in one of her rants.

Stewart tried to comfort her—to understand, but she didn't make any sense. He was a successful businessman from an established family. There was no reason to imagine that his beloved wife was the daughter of a colored woman named Daisy. It was all so muddled. Stewart and the doctors just couldn't put the pieces together.

Then on an unusually warm Easter Sunday, while a nurse was fixing her bed, Lilly told her the entire story: How she passed for white, how she met her husband through a white socialite named Doris, how she gave birth to two white sons, and how she had to kill her black baby girl. Just like that she said it—clear and precise as if God had given her clarity just for the holiday. Afterward, Lilly never spoke another sane word.

Unlike her nightmares, Stewart didn't scream and holler when he was told. He just sat there in the hospital room, watching her sleep. Lilly looked more peaceful than he had seen her in months. There was no sign of tension in her slumber as he'd witnessed so many nights before. Her breathing was deep and restorative, as if she were cleansing her body from years of deceit.

He stayed until the morning.

"Mr. Fillmore. . . . Mr. Fillmore."

Stewart had fallen asleep in the chair beside Lilly's bed. He opened his eyes to a man dressed in a cheap suit and matching tie. He glanced at Lilly who was awake and at the window. She was talking to a bird that sat outside on the ledge.

The ill-suited man cleared his throat and swallowed as if he needed to muster up the courage to speak. "Mr. Fillmore, we have a delicate situation here. As part of the administrative staff, I've been informed of your wife's . . . condition." He struggled to find the right words. "I know this is a troubling time for you and your family, but our strict separate but equal policy must be maintained. I can make no exceptions." He looked down at the floor, relieved to have gotten through it.

Stewart took in a deep breath and exhaled just as deeply. "Where are you sending her?"

"Oh, we take great care of our Negroes on the fourth floor," The man said particularly proud. "We have one of the leading Negro psychologists on staff, Dr. Singletary. And the nursing staff. . . ." he paused, "Well, as I said, it's a difficult situation all around, sir. Of course, this is if you're still willing to pay for her expenses."

Suddenly Lilly broke into a hearty laugh, which startled both of the men. She tapped at the bird, the source of her entertainment, until it flew away from the window.

"I will," was all that Stewart said. The fourth floor was where Lilly was moved. And that was where Stewart planned to leave her.

Telling the boys their mother was very sick and that they couldn't visit her was the hardest. Stewart hadn't lied to them—Lilly was sick. But he couldn't say what was really wrong. That even if she got better, she couldn't come home.

"When is she coming back?" Nathan, the eldest boy asked. He was only eight, but he knew his father wasn't telling it all.

"I don't know." Stewart grabbed the Scotch from the shelf and poured a full glass. He was shaking, letting the large gulps of alcohol tear at the back of his throat until the glass was empty. He poured another one quickly, but broke down before he could bring it to his lips.

"Don't cry, Dad," Matthew said, mimicking his mother when he'd fallen down or was sad about something. Matthew was six years old and had never seen his father cry. He rubbed Stewart's leg to comfort him.

"I'm alright, Matthew," easing away from the boy. "I just need some time alone. Nathan take your brother to the kitchen. . . . Get some cookies."

"What's happened to her, Dad?" Nathan pressed.

"Your mother—" Stewart's voice cracked.

Nathan eyes swelled, fearing the worst. "What happened to Mom?"

"She'll be alright. I mean. . . . she's ill . . . very ill. The truth is I don't know if she will ever be well enough to come back."

"I want to see her." Nathan demanded.

"You can't."

"Why not?"

"Because you can't!" Matthew began to cry loudly now and grabbed his father's leg. "Stop it, Matthew. . . . You two have to be big boys now." It was all he could think of to say to the two of them—he'd already begun to shut them out. Nathan grabbed his waist tightly. "Nathan," Stewart begged. He tried to pry Nathan's hands from around his waist but the boy held onto him even tighter, as if he knew something so horrific had transpired that if his father succeeded in separating them, it would be forever. Matthew, following his brother, latched even tighter onto his father's leg. Stewart stood there sandwiched between them—limp. He didn't hold them. He couldn't. He shut his eyes tight. These were Lilly's children.

They were black.

"YOU'RE NOT MINE!" He shook Nathan by the shoulders. "You're not mine," he said again softly. This set Matthew into complete hysteria, crying at the top of his lungs but still clutching Stewart's pants.

"DAD!" Nathan started to cry, too.

Stewart fell to his knees. The weight of the whole mess had finally hit him. Everything he'd believed, had known was blown out from under him. Mayhem had taken its course and they were in the middle of a hurricane trapped together. He wished for separation.

He wished he could pack their bags and rid himself of them—every man for himself.

He couldn't breathe. His lungs and chest tightened.

Suffocation would be a way out.

He wished that insufficient air could stifle his thoughts of what would happen to them if he left—what it would do to them. He wanted to be someone else. The kind of someone else who'd push and shove—kick if need be to break free of them. *Lilly ruined EVERYTHING! Everything.*

But how does a man leave his children?

As soon as he let his mind ask the question, he had let the possibility of another way seep in. These were his children, his boys and the love he had for them was irrevocable. Stewart clutched them tightly in his arms, and the air and he united.

He broke free of them, but only to stand. "Nathan, calm down." He kissed his forehead. "Matthew." Stewart wiped his face and picked him up, even though he was six and long. "No matter what, you're my children . . . Fillmores." He would make a way for them. If nothing else, he owed that to Lilly.

White Hope

Stewart's move to France was a somewhat hasty decision, but there he and the boys could have a fresh start. Nathan and Matthew could easily pass for white, and in France they could avoid the possible gossip about their mother. Stewart's family didn't try to convince him otherwise. His wife's background was a devastating blow to the family. It was easier on all sides if they left.

"It'll be an adventure," was what Stewart sprung on the boys. He bought a beautiful country estate in Southern France, where Nathan and Matthew had acres to roam and play, and he could forget about Lilly. His plans were to divorce her and quickly re-marry a woman with unquestionable pedigree to help raise the boys. Stewart was still a good-looking man with a sizable purse to boot, and there were quite a few women interested. But he couldn't find a woman who would accept the small part of his heart that Lilly didn't fill. The fine dining and walks in the park were surreal and uneventful. Stewart's lackluster approach to the women he courted teetered between hopelessness and utter nonsense. His memory of Lilly was steadfast, an irreversible condition that after a full year abroad, brought about the sale of his estate and their return to Grosse Pointe.

Home

"Hello, Lilly," Stewart knelt down next to Lilly's chair out in the hospital garden. "How are you?" He leaned in closer. "Lilly. . . Lilly, it's Stewart."

Lilly gazed at him but said nothing. Stewart had been warned of her current condition. She was prone to fits, and at times needed sedation. She had dark circles under her eyes, and her skin had darkened to a dusky tan as if she'd been left to sit and weather in the sun. Her hair had grown out and was combed straight back. A year alone in the hospital had put ten years on her face.

Stewart's eyes wet. "I'm going to take care of you, Lilly. I'm going to make you well." She looked at him again for only a second, and then she looked past him out toward the garden. "The boys are doing fine. I'll see to it that they're raised properly." He put her hand in his.

"No!" She yelped and pulled her hand away. "No," she said again more quietly.

"Alright, Lilly," Stewart said. "I won't hurt you. . . . We've got time."

There were many visits, but Lilly couldn't distinguish Stewart from the doctors and nurses that cared for her. Some visits Lilly sat vacantly still while Stewart talked to her about the boys and her old friend, Doris and the world that was growing up without her. Sometimes Lilly cried hysterically about the baby.

"The hard part is that I can't help her," Stewart said to Dr. Singletary after one of Lilly's fits. "She doesn't even know I'm there."

"I know this is very difficult for you," Dr. Singletary said. He placed his hand on Stewart's back to console him. "Keep trying."

"What if this is all that's left of her? I can't do it anymore. I can't."

A colored nurse walked by and looked at Stewart. Dr. Singletary gave her the eye as if to say, *Mind your business.* Once she turned the corner, the doctor said, "You're all she's got."

Stewart *was* all Lilly had, at least in the sane world. Stewart nodded his head and tried to pull himself together.

"Look," Dr. Singletary went on, "You've had a hard time with her today. She's sedated now. It's cold outside but it might do you some good to get a little fresh air."

Stewart took Dr. Singletary's advice and went for a walk. The street's barren sidewalk reflected January's vigor, and the still cold air bit at Stewart's nose. He turned his face toward a small shop to protect himself from the gust of billowing wind. The window, blurred with ice and snow hid the store's contents. From a small transparent spot, Stewart could see a sewing machine that looked as if it were at least ten years old propped on top of a console, a piece of costume jewelry that was a poor imitation for rubies, and in the corner display, a doll in a cradle.

Her Smile

"I hope she'll bring you back to me, Lilly," said Stewart.

He gently laid the caramel-colored doll he'd bought from the shop onto Lilly's lap. Its head peeped out of the receiving blanket the nurses had swaddled it in. For a long moment she looked at Stewart as if she recognized a small part of him.

"Lilly," Stewart beamed at the sanguine ray of light in her eyes. And then he realized the light was for the thing she cupped in her arms. Lilly caressed its head gently, then its angelic rubber face.

"My baby," Lilly cried, rocking the doll back and forth. "You've come back to me. I'm going to bathe you, and feed you, and teach you to ride a horse, and teach you French and . . . do all the things a good mother should."

Stewart might as well have left the room then. Lilly was complete. Her world didn't include him and probably never would again. But she looked so exquisitely happy with the doll that he sat at the end of the bed and watched her be a mother once more.

Lilly nestled the doll next to her and pulled the covers over the both of them. "You came back to me. . . . Nothing's going to keep us apart." Stewart sat silently at the end of the bed for almost an hour. He watched his wife fuss with the doll: counting its toes, caressing its fingers, singing lullabies to it until she fell asleep. Then he pulled the covers over Lilly's shoulders, kissed her forehead, and left for the night.

Perhaps he could make that kiss his last. She didn't need him anymore. Lilly had someone now—her baby. He would discuss it with Dr. Singletary in the morning.

Stewart slept better than he had in weeks. He met with Dr. Singletary outside on the freshly shoveled path that the patients walked in the spring and summer. The air was frigid but bearable.

"I know you were against giving her the doll, but Lilly needed it," said Stewart.

"You're not helping her get well. There are methods we haven't tried yet."

"No more," Stewart said firm. "I don't want her poked and prodded anymore." He was quiet for a moment, and then he said, "I've had ten wonderful years with Lilly. She gave me two sons, Matthew and Nathan. I've had more than most."

Dr. Singletary nodded his head. "You must have."

"I was so busy trying to make her well that I forgot about myself. I needed healing too. She lied about the world she came from, not about her love for me and the boys. It took me a while to finally realize that."

"I have to tell you, I didn't think you would stick around. I'm a doctor, but not in the eyes of some."

Stewart smiled, understanding what the doctor meant. Dr. Singletary looked at him solemnly. "She probably won't ever be the woman you remember."

Stewart stopped walking. "On the way here I planned to tell you that this was my last visit." It had started to snow and Stewart looked up at the sky. "Did you know that you can see Lilly's window from the parking lot?"

"No, I just want to get home to my family after my shift—" Regret immediately washed over the doctor's face.

"It's alright," Stewart assured him. "I remember those days. How many children?"

"Three—and my wife is five months pregnant."

Stewart whistled.

They both laughed.

"I look up at Lilly's window every time I visit. . . . I don't know why. Maybe I half expect that she'll be there waving to me one day, completely recovered." Stewart fell silent for a moment. Dr. Singletary didn't rush him. He gave Stewart all the time he needed. "There's a bird's nest up there. Lilly's bird—sometimes she talks to it. The last couple of visits I noticed that the bird wasn't there. I think it's gone for good. It came to me today that I can't leave Lilly. I know she can't come back to me. But I can come to her."

It took some time, but eventually Stewart was able to caress Lilly's hair, and on rare occasions, when she was especially calm, he was able to hold her hand. She even began to smile when he entered the room. Dr. Singletary was still convinced that Lilly didn't recognize her husband, and he guardedly warned Stewart who believed otherwise. The day Lilly allowed him to hold her was Stewart's sign of their reunion. He held her from behind while she cooed at her baby until she fell asleep in his arms. Over time, his hugs turned into kisses on the cheek, each kiss closer and closer to her lips.

Stewart didn't tell Nathan and Matthew the truth about their mother until the youngest was old enough to understand. In the time of children being *seen and not heard*, the colored floor for the mentally ill was hardly the place for children. But when it was time to disclose their mother's background, her condition—her appearance, Stewart did it with such grace and respect that their hearts stayed true to Lilly. She didn't shy away from the boys as Stewart feared. She touched their faces and stroked their hair, staring at them as if she were searching her memory for clues of a past she should know. The boys were advised that they shouldn't expect much, so her touch brought Matthew to tears. Nathan, now twelve could control his. It was a fleeting moment of love and affection that could have passed as sanity. But once again her attention returned to her baby resting in the crib that Stewart bought. It had been four years since they'd seen their mother.

Her caress was enough.

Outside of the family, Stewart never reported to the world his boy's true identity. Though he did confide in Doris, who looked at it as something no dirtier than the laundry of many of the families they'd grown up with—secrets respectfully overlooked. "If you look deep enough in any of our blue-blooded lines, you're bound to stir up some trouble." She'd said to comfort him. Money and stature shielded the boys. Stewart and his family joined forces to use both. Nathan and Matthew were sent to the best boarding schools abroad, and on visits home, were taken to see their mother. They grew up telling Lilly all about their football games, the girls they liked, both of their acceptances to Harvard, and what their weddings were like. Lilly still never spoke a word back, but every once in awhile they imagined a smile from her.

Doris visited in the beginning, until it became abundantly clear that she didn't have the strength to see Lilly locked away—a weakness she despised in herself the rest of her days.

New nurses questioned the old about the white woman in room 408, and the man that came every Tuesday and Friday with a box of candy and flowers to sit and talk with her.

Unexpectedly, Stewart and Dr. Singletary's relationship developed into a deep-rooted friendship. Marches and boycotts fortified their resolve to bring the races together. And later, when they stood together among the many thousands in the crowd as Dr. King spoke of a dream, Stewart thought of the adventure he'd envied of his forefathers long ago.

He never remarried.

＋ BOOK 3 ＋

Violet

Train to Chicago

People say that time heals all wounds. People need to stop lying. Bad things don't just happen. There has to be a reason, a purpose—somebody's wrong doing, thought Violet. To right those wrongs takes some effort. It was only a matter of time before blame found its victim, but Violet was sixty-three not twenty-three, so she could take it.

"How long are you gonna stay?" Rueben asked.

"I already told you—about three weeks." Violet answered, but didn't stop folding her clothing neatly on the bed. Rueben sat at the end and watched Violet pack her underwear into her suitcase. Violet grinned. *Old as that man is, he still gets excited looking at my panties.*

Rueben grabbed his wife's bag of rollers and setting lotion out of the bathroom drawer. Thirty-seven years of marriage provided him with enough experience to know what kind of supplies she needed to take on a trip.

"Sure you don't want me to go with you?"

"Honey, you know your back can't take that train ride."

"If you'd take a plane like normal people do we could be there in about two hours."

Violet sat down on the bed and looked at him. She knew he made that comment mainly because he just liked to hear her talk. It didn't matter what Violet was talking about, as long as they were communicating. Sometimes he would do or say things just to get a response from her. They didn't need to creep around one another and say nice things all the time. They had the rapport of old love. So, for his benefit—she let him have it.

"You expect me to get on a plane with no room to stretch out my swollen legs, and trust somebody I've never even seen to take me so high up in the air that I can't see where I'm going, and then give me some nasty food that I know don't have enough seasoning, and by the time I get everything open, cause you know my arthritis is gonna flare up, have one of them air waitresses take it from me cause we're about to land, and then bang me to the ground—" Violet took a deep breath and then raised her eyebrows. "And I'm supposed to pay for all that to boot?—Humph." She reached down and slipped on one of her Naturalizer shoes. "Train will be just fine thank you."

"They don't *give* you food on the plane anymore—you pay for it, Violet."

"Well if you would take me somewhere sometime I would know that."

Rueben looked at her for a moment. "You ought to be ashamed for even letting that fall out of your mouth."

Violet instantly felt bad. Rueben did take her places. Only four months earlier, they had driven to Miami. Throughout their marriage they'd traveled all through the U.S. Reuben had said: "Before you leave the country you should see your own." And they did see the country, and a few others. Then his back began to bother him, and the surgery, and then the colon cancer. She was just happy he was alive and strong enough to pull through.

"I guess we've gone a few places." Violet conciliated. "But I'm still not getting on a plane. It's too much trouble these days."

Rueben shrugged and then bent down to help Violet put on her other shoe. "Alright then, sit on the train for nineteen hours." He headed toward the kitchen and mumbled, "When the Lord made woman, he said, 'What for?'"

Violet poked her head into the hallway and yelled back. "And when he made man he just said—'What?'"

The train ride from Georgia to Illinois had Violet bored out of her mind at Tennessee. The young man one seat in front of her coughed continuously, a little girl couldn't sit still and played up and down the aisle. The woman across from her wore a wig that needed to be shifted slightly to the left, which bothered Violet all the way to Kentucky. She thought that the best thing to do was to close her eyes and go to sleep. She'd slept through Kentucky and part of Southern Illinois before she heard, "Excuse me, ma,am? Ma,am?" Violet opened her eyes and looked over at the woman with the lopsided wig. "Can you tell me what time you have?"

"Two-thirty," Violet said, trying her best to look unfriendly.

"Where are ya headed?"

"Chicago."

"Oh, I love Chicago, is this your first visit?" asked the woman.

"No."

"I'm going to my sister's wedding. The woman put her hand up to the side of her mouth as if she were telling a secret, "She's marrying some man she met online two months ago."

Violet watched the woman's mouth move, catching only echoes of her words as she dragged on with her story. She nodded when appropriate, and raised her eyebrows up and down since the woman was obviously immune to inhospitable posturing.

"How long are you going to be in Chicago?" The woman asked.

"I'm not sure."

"Visiting family?"

"My granddaughter."

"Got any pictures?" The woman perked up.

"No," Violet said and turned her head toward the window to signal the finality of their conversation. She wasn't intentionally rude, she simply had a lot on her mind. She closed her eyes again and thought about Taylor's phone call. Violet barely heard from her son-in-law, except for the customary Christmas and Easter greetings, and even those calls were strained on both ends of the line. She was convinced that it was better that way. A nineteen-hour train ride was what kept her memories at bay for nine years. Violet rested her back into the seat and tried to think about what she was going to say when she saw Dahlia again.

The Arrival

"Momma Violet," Taylor said as if it had been only a few weeks since they'd seen one another. He wasn't fooling anyone. Violet could tell from his hug that he was uneasy.

"Good to see you, Taylor."

"It's been a while."

"That it has."

They stood in the foyer staring at one another.

"How's your mother doing?"

Taylor stuck his hands in his pocket. "Uh, she died a couple a years ago, Violet."

"Oh, I'm sorry to hear that. . . . Your sisters are doing fine?"

"Yeah, Jackie's in Vegas. I haven't had a chance to get out there and see her yet."

"How long has she been out there?"

"About eight years," he said, obviously uncomfortable with admitting how long it had been.

"And the other one?"

"Katrina."

Violet nodded her head.

"She's fine."

Violet figured from his tone that he didn't know if she was fine, either. He was getting fidgety, annoyed with her questions. She decided to give him a little slack about the youngest sister, Katrina. Violet remembered she was loud and embarrassing at the wedding. She wore an apple green satin dress that must have been a size fourteen, when she needed a sixteen. It hadn't restrained her on the dance floor. Her butt looked as if it were spread across two continents, bumping and grinding all evening with a drink in her hand. *Poor Taylor*, Violet thought. *Can't pick your family.*

"I wish I had time to catch up, but I have to make this flight."

"That's alright. Where is she?"

"Upstairs." He grabbed the suitcase propped against one of the six-foot urns at the side of the front door. "She isn't allowed to go anywhere unless it's with you, and I took her phone. She can't have it for two days."

Who the hell did he think was going to enforce that? Violet watched him run around the foyer looking for his car keys. He caught the corner of the wall with his elbow.

"Damn it!"

Violet stood still a moment and tried to stay out of his way. Two things crossed her mind. First: Should she tell him the keys were right there slightly behind the vase on the table? Second: Bless his heart he was still a tight ass, which made her keep quiet.

"Here they are."

She watched him pop the collar on the suit that fit him perfectly. Slim, but broad shouldered—he was always a well-dressed man, she thought. However, a man can hide in his clothes just as a woman can under make-up.

"She spends too much time on Facebook. That's probably where she gets those crazy ideas." He mumbled.

"You think that's the problem?" Violet was sure it wasn't.

Taylor stopped fussing with his suit and looked at her. "This is a good thing right?"

"I hope so," Violet said, and right away realized she should have sounded more confident. "We'll be fine, Taylor."

He took a deep breath, "Okay, Silla will do all the cooking and cleaning. She has a couple of prepared meals in the fridge to get you two started, so all you have to do is concentrate on Dahlia. I've made a few additions to the house since you been here. . . . Get reacquainted." He looked at his watch and headed for the door, lingering at the threshold. "If this doesn't work out, you'll call for me?"

Violet nodded her head. She waited until he reached the door of his Audi and yelled, "I'll call alright. I'm gonna call a realtor for you so you can put this museum on the market."

"Uh, Violet—"

"I'm just kidding. Go on now." She'd forgotten how Taylor never could tell when she was joking. Violet shut the door, leaning against it to get a view of the place. It made her think about the boy her daughter, Rose had chosen.

Taylor had made such an effort to appear refined: going on about ski trips, the Hamptons, and the stock market most of his visit. Violet guessed he assumed she and Rueben didn't know a damn thing about any of it. He was right, they didn't. She remembered thinking who does he think he is, coming in her home and talking over her. But Taylor made her Rose smile, and he stood up whenever she left or entered the room. He talked about big plans, and how he was going to make those plans a reality. His clothes were neat and clean back then too, but it was his shoes, polished to a glistening shine, but worn thin at the soles that showed his hand. This house was like the clothing he had worn that day, all shiny and rich, and he the shoes—polished on the outside but worn and tattered underneath. Violet felt sorry for him trying so hard like he did. She'd decided to like him back then, and now.

"Silla, I hope my son-in-law is paying you a whole lot of money," she said out loud and walked slowly through the living room, observing the crystal, and the paintings that she should know but didn't. The furniture didn't look like the kind one would curl up on with a book, but the kind that needed dusting off. She decided it all seemed to work well together though, in a stuffy, *Architectural Digest* sort of way. Violet never purchased the magazine, but she'd skimmed through the pages from time to time while in Kroger's grocery line, so she was aware of what was considered good taste. She came upon another room that was less formal and slightly familiar to her. She pushed a couple of the buttons on the wall. The ceiling fan came on, and then the wall separated to reveal a movie screen. She thought she'd better stop before she pushed a button and the floor dropped her into hell or something. She sat down on Taylor's rigid couch and looked around her. That is when she determined that this house was meant for more than just two. It needed a teenager ready to go off to college, a thirteen year old with braces and music playing too loud. Maybe twins would fit this house. Yes, twins on all fours still, so that the mother would be exhausted from chasing them by the end of the day. It needed soft furniture that molded to any behind. And laughter, lots of laughter that shook the walls and seeped into the foundation.

This house needed life.

She peeped into the kitchen, where the changes to the house appeared most. Stainless steel and concrete replaced the warm woody kitchen she remembered. She saw a teapot on the stove that looked out of place and assumed it was put out for her benefit. Her arthritic hands flared as she looked in six cabinets without handles before finding a teacup. Violet was trying to cut down on swearing, so she refrained from saying something foul. She put two cups on a tray, and filled the teapot with water.

"I don't drink tea. Daddy does," said a voice from behind and only slightly familiar to Violet. Violet's heart pounded and it seemed like an eternity to complete the pivot to face her granddaughter.

"Humor me," was all Violet could think of to say. She'd received pictures in the mail, probably when Taylor was feeling especially sorry for himself: one picture of Dahlia at seven, another at ten, the last on her thirteenth birthday. It was eerie looking at the girl so very much like her Rose. Dahlia was tall like her, same creamed coffee complexion, and long coal-black hair that cascaded down her back. The only difference between the two of them was Dahlia's eyes. Her eyes were of someone Violet faintly remembered, but couldn't clearly forget, eyes that reminded her of why she left.

"Have any honey or lemon?"

"I don't know. I don't do the grocery shopping around here," Dahlia said as if she were talking to someone beneath her. Then she opened a jar and pulled out two packets of Splenda. "Some people just use sugar."

"That's what's wrong with people—always justin'." Violet said. "That ain't sugar anyway." Dahlia rolled her eyes and set the Splenda on the tray. "You haven't seen me in almost ten years and you don't have anything for me but rolling eyes and a pack of fake sugar?" Violet opened her arms to Dahlia, unsure if they would be filled. Dahlia pressed her lips and ambled over to her. Her lackluster hug was one you would give an Uncle Harold, whose hands wandered and breath smelled of cigars.

Dahlia moved away quickly. "I don't know why Dad sent for you."

"He didn't send for me. We talked and I decided to come."

"That must have been some conversation."

"It was."

"It's not your business."

Violet ignored her and picked up the tea tray. "Let's go in the living room and talk for a bit."

"I don't feel like it," said Dahlia, flatly.

Violet suddenly stopped in her tracks, which caused Dahlia to almost run into her. "Now did I ask you what you felt like doing?"

Dahlia stood strangely silent. Her eyes piercing through Violet like an alien observing a human specimen—she was sizing her up. Violet tried to stand her ground even though Dahlia oddly seemed more confident than her.

"Why did you even come here?" Dahlia finally spoke.

"Because I wanted to see you."

"You saw me. Now what?"

"Now we . . . get to know one another again."

"You've been doing fine for ten years without that knowledge, you'll survive."

"But you won't."

Dahlia put her hands up. "If you want to pretend for a while, then fine. Where did you want to go? In the living-room?" Dahlia went in and sat down on the sofa.

"Dahlia—"

"No one calls me that." Her face tightened.

"Alright. . . . Well, they should. It's a beautiful name." This wasn't how Violet wanted their reunion to begin. "Look, let's sit together in this room your Daddy thinks is going to make him stand out and just try." Violet put the tray on an ottoman between the two chairs by the fireplace. "Would you come over here and sit with me?"

Dahlia breathed hard then plunked down on the chair across from Violet. She flipped the switch that ignited the gas fireplace and crossed her arms and legs impatiently.

Violet sighed. "Everything is so convenient these days." She dared to look at the fire only for a second until her heartbeat began to accelerate. It was all coming back to her: she hated the flames, the smell—its power.

"I don't like this room either." Dahlia looked around. "It's archaic."

"What do you like?"

"Nothing," Dahlia said somberly.

"I looked out back where we used to have a flower garden."

"I don't plant flowers anymore. They die."

"Sometimes. Sometimes they're just sleeping and need a little caring for."

"Well, Dad put grass over that spot a couple of years ago."

"Wouldn't take much to clear it again."

Dahlia fidgeted. "I'm sure you didn't come all this way to talk about a garden."

"No." Violet thought a moment. "But I did come all this way to talk about flowers. You said no one calls you Dahlia. What do they call you?"

"It's not important."

"Tell me?"

Dahlia chuckled. "Don't pretend that you care, alright?"

"I've always cared. But I'm human, honey. I'm full of flaws. But you gotta give me some points for trying. Your father called me because he doesn't know how to get to you."

"And you think that after all these years, you do?"

"Maybe."

Dahlia rolled her eyes again and stood up. "I don't want anything from you."

"But you need something from me, and I'm finally here to give it to you." Violet stood up too. "But right now it's getting late. . . . and I need you to set my hair."

Dahlia laughed. "I don't know how to set hair!"

"It's time you learn."

"That's some outfit," Dahlia said.

"You don't like red?" Violet did a quick turn to model the caftan she used for a nightgown.

"I do. It's just that . . . there's so much of it."

She caught a glimpse of herself in the mirror. "I guess I do look like a big red hot air balloon. You'll find as you get older that these are very comfortable."

"I don't think anyone needs that much comfort," Dahlia smirked.

Violet hiked the caftan up at her hip and sat down at the vanity. "I got this on a trip to the Bahamas. That's where Rueben learned that the sun ain't always black folk's friend. He fell asleep on the beach and his skin baked to crisp sienna." Violet giggled and shook her head. "That man argued with me about every little thing after that because his body ached so. He finally realized he was ruining the whole trip and took his aching, red-brown behind down to the marketplace and brought me this caftan. He said he bought it so that every time I wore it, it would remind me of the island and his heart." Violet closed her eyes and drifted back to the Bahamas for a moment, surprised to remember how the warm sand felt under her toes. When she opened her eyes, Dahlia was looking at the setting lotion, rollers and tissue paper as if Violet had put eggs, flour, and butter in front of her and told her to bake a cake.

Violet demonstrated. "Take the lotion, spray a section of hair, wrap it with the tissue and then roll it." She put a pin in to secure it.

"You can't just tell someone to do your hair," Dahlia protested lightly.

"I'm not telling someone, I'm asking you."

Violet flexed her arthritic hand back and forth. She winced purely for sympathy.

"Okay, but your hair is going to be jacked up tomorrow." She gently separated her grandmother's hair, barely touching the scalp.

"Child, you're not performing brain surgery—part my hair."

After a couple of mishaps: hair sticking out of one roller, a section of hair too fat to clip, Dahlia seemed to get the hang of it.

"You know there is such a thing as a flat iron," Dahlia said.

"Honey, I'm still working my way up to a curling iron. Your granddaddy bought me one of those things about fifteen years ago thinking he's going to make my life easier. I plugged it in, and I guess I turned the knob up too high. I still remember the smell of my burnt out hair wrapped up in that thing."

"All you had to do was turn the heat down."

"All I have to do is keep my hair with these rollers, thank you."

Violet stole a glimpse of Dahlia through the bathroom mirror. She reminded her of Rose, who'd stand in the kitchen behind her, talking about the latest boy she liked or what went on in school that day. Rose was quick with setting her hair. It was mindless work for her. Something her hands did while she chattered endlessly or swayed to *Earth Wind and Fire* on the radio. Dahlia was different. She seemed to have to concentrate. She took great care in working the hair around each roller, making sure it was snapped, and patted it with her hand to make it stay put.

"Long hair, is that still important?"

"Huh. Uh, yeah I guess," Dahlia said.

"All these weaves and things you young ones wear don't make no sense to me."

"It's an accessory like everything else," Dahlia said.

"You all are ruining the little bit of hair you got, well—not you. Yours is down your back, but these other girls ain't never gonna have any putting all them glues and clips and things up in it all the time."

"Some of my friends' weaves look really nice."

"And some of them look a hot mess and you know it. . . . And what's with the white girls wearing them now?"

"They call them extensions."

"I call it stupid." Violet said. "By the time you all are my age ain't none of you, black or white, gonna have a bit of hair." Dahlia shrugged her shoulders. A few moments later Violet asked, "What grade are you in now?"

"I graduated early."

"You're only sixteen, right?"

Dahlia nodded.

"A smart one, huh?" Violet smiled up at her.

"That's what everyone tells me."

"What? You don't believe them?"

Dahlia didn't answer. After a couple of flailing attempts to make more conversations about trivial topics, Violet let the room have its quiet. The void between them had ten years to swell. Deflating it would take more than a couple of hours.

"Give me my pills out of that purse over there . . . and don't you go gettin' any ideas. These won't do anything but give you a stomachache."

Dahlia grimaced.

"Hey, we can pussyfoot around what you did, but I figure that's not going to help you. You're scaring the hell out of your father. He's not one of us so I can see why."

"Us?"

"Yes, us. You think you're the only woman in this family holding pain?"

"I wouldn't know that now, would I?" Dahlia said, snide.

Violet shook her head. "Knowing isn't always best."

"Oh, this is much better."

"Fair enough. Fair enough. I guess this is why I came. To give you a past so that you can have a future." Violet sat down on the guest room bed and mulled over where she should start. "I know what it's like to feel alone in a room full of people."

"You don't know a thing about me."

"I know that I left you. And now I have to undo my part in all of this."

"Why bother now? Because I took some pills and you feel sorry for me? Well don't. I'm like that island you went to—Duty Free."

Violet had been with Dahlia only a couple of hours, but she could already see the depth of hurt she'd caused. There was this flat-lined haze of emptiness that sat confidently poised upon Dahlia's face.

"I don't know what you want me to say. I'm sure your father has said it all. So if that's your plan, then there's no way I can stop you. But all I ask is that you give me this time with you. Just for a while."

Dahlia shook her head. "Why should I?"

"Because I'm an old woman. Because I'm here. Because you and me are the last of the women in this family. Come sit down on the bed with me."

"I'm fine right here."

Violet guessed she felt safe across the room. In the scheme of things, it was a small fight that she didn't have the right to battle. Giving her a reason to live was the war at hand. "I don't know why your father didn't tell me how serious this was. Maybe he just didn't want it to happen on his watch. . . . He was always weak."

"Don't talk about him," Dahlia said.

"I don't mean in the way that it matters in this world. He did all the right things." She looked around the lavish guest room. "Provided for you in ways most fathers wish they could. I mean there's a primal weakness in him. Like when catastrophe strikes and instead of—what do you kids call it—manin'up—you just shut down. I'm only saying this because he doesn't have half of the strength that your mother did."

Dahlia's stare turned black. "Don't bring her into it either."

"I have to. She's a part of this puzzle that's missing the glue to keep it together. But I'm not going to start with her. Nawh. We gotta go back further than her." Violet took a deep breath. "I don't know all the details, just the parts that were told to me."

Bedtime Stories

An hour had passed before Lilly's story was over and done with. Unfolding another woman's life was difficult, especially when it wasn't a firsthand account. Sugar coating what Violet knew about Lilly would be a mistake—part of the curse that infected her family.

After Dahlia had some time to soak it in, she asked, "Whatever happened to her?"

"Stewart went before her, but her two boys still took care of her until she died. They buried her right next to Stewart in the Fillmore's family plot."

"It's so sad."

Violet stood up to stretch her legs. "What's sad is Lilly's baby was still alive. Tula never killed her. Instead she sold her to a woman she knew who wanted a child."

"How do you know all this?"

Violet put the remaining rollers back in her bag. "Tula told the woman the baby's name was Violet.

"Violet?" Dahlia leaned forward. "You're telling me Lilly was your mother?"

Violet struggled to keep hold of her emotions. "She gave birth to me . . . but she was never my mother."

A long while passed before either one of them spoke. They were sitting on opposite sides of the room, Lilly's story filling the space between them.

"I'm going to bed now," Dahlia said.

It was a lot of information for one night. Violet knew she needed to give her a little time to digest it. Dahlia stopped at the door. "You have two brothers out there."

"Things were different then. I was colored—they wasn't. That's all there was to it."

"But . . . that would mean that I have more family . . . cousins maybe."

"They were kind enough to tell me about Lilly the one and only time I saw them. But it wasn't like no family reunion was about to take place."

Dahlia sighed. "I'm going downstairs for something to drink. Want some?"

Violet smiled. "Water is fine." Dahlia came back with two glasses of water. "Thank you, baby. My mouth feels like I've been gargling with sand."

A tiny smile escaped Dahlia's lips, but there was still a thick uncomfortable silence between them. Violet didn't want her to leave. She was about to talk about her train trip, and the lady with the lopsided wig—anything, when Dahlia saved her.

"So, you were raised by this woman that. . . ."

"That bought me? Go ahead and say it."

"Yeah."

"I'll tell you all about it if you sleep in here with me tonight."

"I don't think that's a good idea." Dahlia squirmed. "I'm kind of a wild sleeper."

"Come on, then I won't have to stay in this mausoleum you all call a guest room by myself. Besides, I sleep wild too, so we'll cancel each other out."

Dahlia didn't say yes, but since she didn't say no, Violet pulled the sheets down on both sides and got in on one. She patted the bed space beside her. "Want to hear about what happened to me?" The ultimatum worked because Dahlia sat down next to her. Violet grinned. "Well, I can only remember back so far. By the time I was six or seven years old, Millie put me to work. I had to clean the floors, wash the dishes, and wash the clothes out back. Talk about modern day slaves—that was me. She expected me to do all that and go to school too, because Millie wasn't raising no black child to be no fool, she would say. She moved real slow, sneaky like a cat—probably why I can't stand those creepy things now. Only time she moved quicker was when she was about to whoop you with one of those switches she got off the bushes out back. Ooooh she was a nasty kind of mean. Used to have me scratch the dandruff out of her nappy hair when she was finished beating me."

Violet's Heat

"Be glad I took you in because your momma sure didn't want you," said Millie.

"Yes, ma'am," Violet said, quickly wiping off the table.

"If you don't like it here, you got a choice. Leave if you want. Just don't come back."

Violet was only a child, but she knew what lay outside Miss Millie's door on Detroit's city streets. They both knew there was nowhere for her to go. The only glimmer of light in Violet's life was school. Every morning she'd walk past the drunks and the pimps and other street people that congregated on the corner, just two blocks from her school. By the time she was thirteen, Violet was comfortable with them all. They looked out for her because she was "getting some learnin'".

She'd try to guess what dress Beth Ann, the hooker, would have on each morning. Her green dress meant she was going to make some big money. It was low cut and Violet thought it was made out of a material that seemed too shiny for daytime. Her blue dress meant she was going to keep some of the money that she was supposed to give to Big Ray. A pocket cleverly sewn inside the dress was where she kept an extra ten percent of her earnings. Yellow meant she was feeling real bad that day and needed to be in something bright and pretty to cheer her up.

She'd wonder if the gambler only known as Tennessee was going to have on the sharp, white sport coat that he wore even in the winter because he "hit the number," or rags because he had to sell his clothes to get back in the game. Was Skeeter going to be high and singing one of his silly tunes, or pacing back and forth down the sidewalk trying to kick his habit.

In Violet's adolescent mind, they were all her friends. Beth Ann was really a princess waiting for her prince to come and take her off the streets. Tennessee was in fact a magician. He could do anything with a card and always had some new trick to show her. Skeeter was not of this world. He was an angel sent down to make sure she made it to school each day. It was her corner, where all was familiar and safe to her.

Until he came.

"How you doing, Miss Violet?" Red said, running across the street to walk with her to school.

"Fine, Red," Violet answered. Red was a light-skinned freckled face boy, too short for his age. He always called her Miss Violet, which made her feel special somehow. "Did you finish reading *Huckleberry Finn* yet?"

"Oh, I finished that last week," Red said, proud.

"I'm almost done. Miss Millie had me up washing floors last night so I—"

"I understand," he said before she could finish.

Violet figured Red knew all about what went on in Miss Millie's house. She could tell by the way he looked at her—how he pretended not to notice the welt on her arm sliding in and out of her short-sleeved shirt.

"The book report isn't due until Friday, right?" Violet asked.

"Right."

They walked in silence for a moment. Red's crush on Violet could be felt a block away. There were not a lot of black boys interested in getting a good education like Red. Many in the neighborhood had already dropped out. He was smart and forever in a good mood. She didn't see any harm in having him occasionally walk with her to school.

"You want to go get some soda after school today, Violet?"

"I don't know. I guess," Violet answered, wondering how quickly she could drink the soda down before Miss Millie started looking for her.

After school, Violet saw Skeeter, Big Ray, and Tennessee hanging on the corner. All men with nothing better to do, as Miss Millie would put it. They huddled around another man Violet hadn't seen before. Skeeter and the group had their backs turned toward Violet so only the man leaning against the wall was in view. As she and Red walked past, Violet couldn't help but look at him. He noticed her too, looking at her like she was a cold glass of ice water on a cement-hot Detroit day. Violet was only sixteen. No one had ever looked at her that way. Sure, there was Red, but he was a boy.

This was a man.

She felt her stomach do a row of summersaults before she turned away from the stranger's gaze. An uncontrollable sweat saturated her underarms. She waited a couple of seconds, until they passed the corner and then stole another quick glance. He hadn't stopped watching her! Violet turned back around to Red, but not before drinking in the last drops of his hypnotic stare. Millie had taught her about being street smart—about not giving a man a reason. She should have been frightened but she wasn't. Just then, she realized Red was talking.

"They think Jackie Robinson was something, wait till I get there. Yep, I'm gonna steal so many bases they're gonna lose count. But I'm gonna graduate from college first. So I'll know how to manage my money."

Violet smiled. How long had Red been talking? Violet hadn't the slightest idea. All she could think about was the man at her corner. It was the first time she felt like a woman instead of a girl.

In the weeks to come, Violet's games with Tennessee and the rest were put away like old toys. Her ideas for entertainment had matured and had all to do with the mystery man at the corner, who had continuous engagements with a hooker, Skeeter, the police, and a series of comings and goings of which he was the center. Yet each day that Violet walked by, he'd take time to stop to watch her—make sure she knew he was looking.

Even Red noticed.

"I hear he's from Missouri and mean and dirty as they come," Red said, before he broke into a coughing fit.

"Are you okay?" Violet asked.

"Uhmm,' he answered, but coughed deep and grating once more. "My dad said he runs hookers and drugs. Even got Sally Perkins strung out on something."

"Can't get nobody strung out that don't want to be. Sally's been on something long before he came anyway, so you can't blame it on him."

Red frowned. "I'm just telling you what my dad said . . . got the whole neighborhood stirred up."

"Violet! Get in here and get to these nasty clothes!" Miss Millie yelled from the front stoop.

"Yes, ma'am!" Violet called back and said quickly, "I'll see you tomorrow, Red."

"Wait a minute," Red fidgeted and looked down at the cracked cement. "I—I was wondering if you got time on Friday to go to the movies with me."

"Miss Millie don't really let me go anywhere."

Red coughed a couple more times. "She seems to think I'm all right. She knows my dad and she lets me walk with you to school doesn't she?"

"Violet!" Miss Millie yelled again, this time with a tone Violet knew wasn't safe.

"I'll see." Violet ran up the walk.

Red snapped his finger and smiled all the way down the block to the bus. He hadn't seen Miss Millie shove Violet into the house that day, and unfortunately, he never got to go to the movies with her either. His bad cough turned into a serious case of pneumonia, leaving Violet to walk to school alone.

Pencil Skirts

"Come in here, Violet!" Violet was in the kitchen finishing dinner and her schoolwork at the same time. She turned down the neck bones to simmer and found Millie in her bedroom. Millie's bedroom door was slightly closed. Violet knocked. "I said come in didn't I?"

"Yes, ma'am. Violet entered the beautifully feminine room that was usually off limits. The rest of the house looked like a cave, but this room was decorated in florals and draperies to match. It always smelled of heavy perfume that sometimes filtered out into the hallway. It was a room for a lady, not a monster.

Millie held a big brown paper bag in her hand. "You finish dinner yet?"

"Almost. Just waiting on the rice to cook."

"Mrs. Brooks gave me these clothes." She emptied the assortment on top of the well-dressed bed. Violet did all of the chores, except for Millie's bedroom. Millie paid a hundred dollars for the four poster bed. It was hers, and she was going to make it. "These skirts and things ought to fit you nicely."

She sat down on the edge of the bed and lit a cigarette. "Try them on in here, so I can see what you look like in em'."

"Yes, ma'am." Violet undressed and slipped on the grey skirt with a pink button down cardigan.

"Yeah, you fillin out. Don't be letting any of them boys feel all on you."

"Yes, ma'am." Violet said.

Millie looked her up and down. "Sixteen and don't know what to do with yourself," she mumbled.

Humbling herself in front of Millie was commonplace in Violet's life. She didn't dare stare admiringly at the image reflecting back in the mirror. Millie was in her forties, but attractive. The last thing Violet wanted floating through her head was competition. No full-length mirror hung in Violet's room, but she memorized the way she looked. Her consensus: well rounded hips, breasts smaller than she'd like, but she had time. She was sure just a few more months of pressing her palms together in sets of eight would make them blossom, backside—sufficient, legs—very very nice. Back in her room, she undressed and put her new clothing neatly in her drawer. She was growing older. Soon she could get out of there.

The following day Violet flew out of the house. It was library day—her favorite day of the month.

"Look at you, Miss Lady," whistled Beth Ann, who was already out bright and early working her hustle.

"Miss Millie got me some new clothes." Violet said, embarrassed by the attention.

"Well, you be careful with all that busting out of that skirt, girl. It's a whole bunch of men around that corner. Ain't none of 'em got no money, though."

They both laughed and Violet took off across the street. Her skirt's straight cut made her run like a penguin, but if she was late, she wouldn't get to check out a Nancy Drew mystery. She'd already read the three the school's library owned, and on her request, they had ordered two more. She had exactly ten minutes before the first bell rang. She picked up speed, clinging tightly to her books, winding the corner.

Wham!

It was a direct hit with someone coming around the corner just as she did.

She heard a voice smooth and deep, "Are you okay, sugar?"

Violet looked up into the eyes of the man she'd fantasized about every day since he landed on her corner.

"Yes, sir." She didn't know why she'd said *sir*. He didn't appear as old up close as she'd suspected from a distance. She tried to kneel to collect her things, but the pencil skirt wouldn't let her.

He looked her up but mostly down and said, "That outfit is for admiring, not for heavy lifting."

Violet couldn't stop blushing as he handed her the books one by one. His hand slightly brushed hers only once, and it sent a warm tingle racing through her body.

"What are you reading?" he said, withholding one book from her.

"*Huckleberry Finn*," Violet said and reached for the book. He held a tight grip on it, toying with her for a moment before letting go.

"Thank you," Violet said nervously.

"Uhhhhmm," He let it roll slowly in his throat like molasses. Violet was at the curb without realizing how she got there. Her mind and body were working separately. Her mind was in a trance, but her feet must have tried to pull her out of it. She wasn't sure if he'd followed her or if he just happened to be headed in the same direction. She held her books on guard tightly against her chest.

"Is it good?"

Violet's heart pounded so hard it gave her a headache. "What?"

"Huck Finn."

"Oh, the book, uhh, it's alright."

"I wish I had someone to teach me how to read," he said and then his eyes rolled up and down her body again. She couldn't help but notice the hair that crept out of his shirt. She thought that he might be nineteen, twenty-one at the most. He was still looking at her, but at her face now. No, not her face, her lips! It was overwhelming.

"I—I have to go now," Violet could hardly get the words out and hurried across the street.

That night she barely felt the sting of the burn from Millie, who'd thrown a cup of hot coffee on her arm for not finishing the dishes quick enough. She fell asleep with the smell of butter soothing her arm, and the memory of the man with the full lips and velvety voice.

The next morning Violet was up a half an hour earlier than usual. The extra time was so she could dress in peace, before Millie awoke. She wished she had a mini skirt like some of the older girls at school. She'd have to settle for—be thankful for—the purple pencil skirt that showed off her hips. The thought of seeing him took her mind off the burn, which she'd wrapped in a makeshift bandage. It was better today—only a surface burn. She'd finished her morning chores ahead of schedule and had already eaten by the time Millie sat down.

"You're awfully chippy this morning." Millie said.

Violet wanted to tell her the correct word was chipper. But that would be suicide. She set the plate of scrambled eggs and toast in front of Millie. "I have to go in early this morning."

"Why?"

"I—I have to help my teacher grade the math tests."

Violet rinsed her cup and plate and set it upside down on the counter to dry. It was best to look busy. Usually Millie was half-asleep in the morning—more like the walking dead. She definitely couldn't tell her the real reason—that she wanted to take her time at the corner.

"Them teachers getting free work out of you now, huh? Don't you stay after, hear me?" Millie said with her mouth full of food.

"Yes, ma'am," Violet grabbed her sweater and flew out the door. She saw Tennessee a half a block down.

"Hey, buttercup!" he shouted and pulled out his cards. He licked one and slapped it against his forehead. "Guess what card's up there."

"I can't today, Tennessee." Violet hurried past him and toward the end of the street. She'd guess several cards on the way home from school to make up for it. All she could think about was getting to the corner. Once she was a distance away from Tennessee, she put more of a sway in her hips—at least what she thought was a sway. Her stomach twirled with anticipation as she turned the corner.

Empty.

There wasn't a soul around. A stray dog limped toward her and then suddenly changed course and ran across the street. Violet stood there dumfounded, until a loud truck rumbled past and woke her from her slight coma. She laughed. She was all dressed up and ready for a man she didn't even know. What was she going to do if he was there anyway? She felt like a mystified fool, and Millie's words rung in her head. *"Ain't none of them worth the time of day."*

She dragged her feet forward, for she had at least twenty minutes to kill before school started. The last few pages of her Nancy Drew mystery would have to suffice. Tonight she could finish it, if Millie didn't have a million chores waiting for her.

Two weeks passed, and her hopes of seeing him again faded. She'd worn all of the pretty new clothes, but there was no sign of him anywhere. She didn't dare ask Skeeter or Beth Ann about him. They would end up asking her more than she wanted to answer. When he was around there was lots of commotion and people at the corner. When he left, it seemed that he took everybody with him. She figured he'd moved on to another corner, given life to another girl with only a look. The comfort she'd felt along the streets with Tennessee and the rest were now boring and immaterial. Red, who was still recovering from pneumonia, crossed her mind often. She missed his company, even though all he talked about was baseball. Her pace quickened. If she hurried home from school, did all of her chores, maybe Millie would let her stop by and see him today.

She started to think about the Declaration of Independence test she'd taken in school and was looking through her notes. Yes! It was King George III the United States had grievances with, not the II. Violet's nose was in her notes going over the other two questions on the exam she wasn't sure about when she turned the block. She hadn't noticed him part the two men he was with and walk up to her.

"You gon' teach me to read so I can get off this corner?" He'd posed it like a question, but it was more like a demand.

Violet was beside herself.

Her heart beat hard against her chest. This time she was sure he could hear it. She blushed, "I can't. I have to go home." He stepped in front of her to stop her from walking any farther. He was far too close for a stranger. Close enough to feel his breath on her face. She looked around for her safeguards: Beth Ann, Tennessee. She didn't see them. "Let me by," Violet said with no meaning at all.

"You could teach me for a while after school, or in the mornings before you go," he said.

"I don't even know you."

"Billy Hughes," he said with a fulsome smile and reached for her hand to kiss it. Instinct told her to pull away, but she didn't listen. His hands looked like he'd never known hard work—no cuts, no calluses. His breath smelled like bubble gum. She was going to faint. "If you're as smart as you are pretty than you could probably teach me in no time. I'll bet you're the sharpest one in your class aren't you?" Violet was ahead of most of her class. She took pride in it. Being smart made her feel like she was someone—no matter what Millie said. "You don't have to admit it. I can tell that you are." His wide smile was infectious. He had the prettiest teeth she had ever seen on a man. He licked his lips.

"I don't know you . . . Billy," she said his name only to hear herself say it aloud. The "I don't know you" part was repeated simply because she couldn't think with him standing so close to her. It was one thing to have a schoolgirl fantasy about a man, but this was real.

Billy crossed his arms, making his biceps protrude even more. He remained in front of her, quiet, waiting for her to look at him. When she did, he stopped smiling and looked at her dead on. "I know you the way a man knows a woman. Don't even know your name. And you know me too, don't you?" he said with such conviction that she had to step back a bit to keep her balance.

"Violet."

Billy looked puzzled.

"My name is Violet," she said quietly.

"V-i-o-let," he said, letting her name roll slowly off his lips. Then he looked up toward the sky and back down at her, eyes dancing around her as if he'd already had her and was now reminiscing. "Violet and Billy." he smiled.

She was sixteen going on seventeen. All she had was school and Nancy Drew. She needed more.

More

Billy's place was on the top of Uncle Vic's Barber Shop, who in truth wasn't anyone's uncle at all. There was a long set of steps on the side of the building that led to the second floor, with another door leading into a small screened-in breezeway. Violet could see him standing inside it, waiting for her to reach the top. The door to his room was already open. It was small and unadorned, furnished with only a bed and a wooden chair at the window. Violet stood in the middle of the room clutching the Dick and Jane book, *See Spot Run*, tightly at her breasts.

"You can sit here," Billy said and pointed to the bed. He grabbed the chair and sat down across from it. "I'll sit here."

Violet hesitated.

"We don't have a lot of time, Violet. I want to make sure you get to school on time." It was seven a.m. She had to run all the way to his place to save time to teach him before the eight o'clock school bell rang. He motioned with his hand for her to sit down. Violet sat down slowly. She couldn't tell if the sheets were dirty or just worn out. "It's probably not what you're used to, this is only temporary. Once you teach me to read, shit—shoot I mean. I'm out of here."

Violet smiled dimly. She opened the book and pulled out a sheet of paper with the alphabet written on it.

He grinned slyly. "I already know my letters, Violet."

"Oh," Violet felt a rush of embarrassment.

"I'll tell you what." Billy took the book out of her hand and leaned in close to her. "I'll read what I can, and if I get stuck, you can help me."

Violet nodded her head. She could smell his bubble gum breath again.

If Billy hadn't already known the alphabet, if he hadn't been such a fast learner, things wouldn't have progressed so quickly. He went through the Dick and Jane series with ease. *Horton Hears a Who* and *Curious George* gave him a little trouble, so the two of them began to sit together on the bed. That way, Violet could look on with little effort if he needed help with sounding out any words. Soon he could read two syllables, and then three. All the while, Billy was a perfect gentleman. The beginning of reading *Huckleberry Finn* was when Billy started to sit much closer—his leg touching hers. By the middle, he had his arms around her while he read. Toward the end of the book, Billy began to kiss her after each page.

Violet forgot all of Miss Millie's teachings on respectability when he kissed her. His lips were soft and his tongue wet and warm. She kept her hands at his chest and pushed at him every so often—he just pulled her closer. The cat and mouse game went on for thirteen days. On the fourteenth, she told him she would turn seventeen the following week. And on that birthday morning, Billy told her that he had a surprise for her.

"Give it to me!" Violet was comfortable with him now.

"Well, the first part is. . . ." He sat down next to her on the bed and took her hand. "I'm twenty-five."

Violet squirmed. She knew he was older, but twenty-five was too old. She gently removed her hand from his, but Billy took it back. "Hey, it's me, baby." He rubbed her cheek, "You know you're special to me." Then he kissed her lips until she had to catch her breath.

"What . . . about the other part of my surprise?" Violet stood up, still adjusting to his age.

"You're not going to get it that easy. You got to come back after school to get this," he grinned. "I'll see you at three-forty-five. Just come on up."

Violet thought about the surprise all day. Three-fifteen couldn't come quick enough for her. She was at the side of the barbershop by three-thirty. Beth Ann gave her a disapproving look as she ran up the stairs and through the narrow breezeway to Billy's door. The door was slightly open, but she knocked anyway.

"Billy?" She walked in slowly, not wanting to spoil anything.

"Come here," was all Billy said.

Her first time with Billy was loving and gentle. His kisses tender, touching her like she was his most precious, valuable thing. She didn't know where to put her hands, or where to kiss him back. All she knew was Billy was pressing against her and it felt good. He kissed her breasts and bit at them gently, kissed down where Millie told her she needed to keep clean. Her delight left no room for guilt. She was all in—happy, nervous, thrilled with a pleasure she hadn't known existed. The love she felt for him was beyond anything she could measure. Love that transcended the budding phase from the moment she laid eyes on him, to full bloomed adoration. Then he entered her. Fire and ice simultaneously invaded her senses. He had hurt her then, but it wasn't like Miss Millie's blows; it was the kind of pain she'd dream about when she scratched the dandruff from Millie's head.

It happened on a Friday afternoon. Violet had all weekend to reminisce. On Monday morning, Violet rushed to get dressed and down to the barbershop. Skeeter looked at her funny. No doubt, Beth Ann had been talking.

"Hey, Skeeter." Violet's smile uneasy.

"You keepin out of trouble?"

Violet didn't answer. She knew what he was getting at. She breezed by him and down the block, telling herself, she didn't care what Skeeter thought. He was just an old junkie anyway.

Billy picked her up and into his arms once she arrived. "I been missing you all weekend baby." He carried her over to the bed.

"Wait. . . . I'm still a little sore from Friday."

"Auwwh."

"Billy." He unbuttoned her blouse. "I can't." Violet pushed his hands away gently.

"Baby, I need you. You gone be a little girl or a woman?"

"I'm sore." Violet whispered.

"I'll make it alright," he said and pulled her blouse open to kiss her breasts—her belly. By the time he unzipped her skirt, Violet had already forgotten about the pain. His fingers were inside her panties, inside her. Violet thought she was going to pass out. He kissed and caressed her until she thought there was nothing else but him.

"Only you bring that out in me," Billy said when his technique changed after a few weeks passed, and he began to take her with more force. At seventeen, Violet confused it with passion. He pacified her with trinkets that she'd hide under her mattress. She didn't care about school anymore. She didn't care about anything but him. She told her teachers that Miss Millie was sick with the pneumonia that had spread to many in the community, and that she would need to miss school to care for her a week or two. It had been a month and a half. But Violet couldn't stop seeing Billy. He was like a nutrient her body needed to consume to live, and she believed him when he told her he would come for her soon.

"When the time is right," he said.

Boiled Water

"Where have you been going girl?" Millie demanded as she loomed over Violet. It was the middle of the night and Violet was in bed, half-asleep. It took her a moment to wake fully and focus on the belt she twirled in her hand. She'd let Violet go to sleep as if nothing was wrong. She'd even complimented her on how well she had done the ironing. It was a crucial part of Millie's reign. Violet never knew when Miss Millie was going to attack. When she did it was always treacherous, so Violet grew up being cautious of Miss Millie's compliments, her movements, and her manner in general. But Violet was so enthralled with Billy that she had let her guard down these last few months.

"You haven't been going to school 'cause I was there today!"

"I wasn't feeling well today, so—so I didn't go!" Violet cried.

"Oh, where did you go then?" Millie pulled the belt through her hand.

"I-I went to the library." Millie cocked the belt high in the air. I needed a book for school!" Violet yelled as the belt met her skin.

"You gon tell me where you been all this time," Millie threatened with a sharp blow to Violet's thigh. Crack! Violet's skin split open as she tried to crawl into a corner. Crack! Crack! Millie tore at her flesh, her gown, the glass of water by her mattress, anything between the belt and Violet. "I'ma get the truth out of you—one way or another!" Millie taunted and whipped until her own arms hurt. "I can see I'm gon have to boil me some water," she said, grinning and wiping the sweat off her brow. "After I baptize you, we'll see if you can stop lyin."

Violet didn't know where she was going when she ran. She just knew Miss Millie was original evil, and anywhere was better than there. She ended up at Billy's. It hurt to knock on his door because she had tried to use her hands to block the blows from Millie's belt. After three strong knocks and two weak ones, Violet was so tired and sore that she sat down on the breezeway floor and fell asleep.

She opened her eyes slowly, focusing on the familiar voice coming up the stairs. "Baby, save some of that for when we get behind closed doors," she heard Billy say. A woman giggled and moaned, which lead Violet to believe they'd already started what was planned for inside his room. Her first thought was that she must look frightful compared to the glossy woman and Billy. They were dressed as if they were on the cover of *Jet* magazine, which made her feel foolish and ashamed. She tried to cover her whipped legs and straighten her hair.

Billy stood there gawking at her.

The woman tucked her arm in between Billy's and giggled. "Looks like you got a stray puss at your door, Billy." She nudged him. "Get rid of her."

Billy shoved the woman away as if she were a ragdoll and bent down to Violet to caress her bruised face.

"I had to leave," Violet whimpered. "She was going to kill the baby."

Violet took the T-bone out of the icebox and set it in water to thaw. She could cook a meal from the littlest scraps of food from living with Millie. She had to learn how to cook all over again with full cuts of meat and whole chickens. Billy kept the icebox stocked, and after a few mishaps, Violet made sure he ate like a king. She was nine months pregnant when they moved to the most expensive apartment building in the community, a two-bedroom in a building with ten floors. She felt like a queen every time she stepped into the elevator to go to the seventh. Violet would have been content with having a warm bed with sheets, hot water for a bath, and a rug to warm her feet. But Billy had a different life in mind for them. In less than a year, he'd become the Black Prince of underworld Detroit. He never talked about his business with Violet, but he didn't hide it from her either. Violet wasn't naïve anymore. She knew where the money came from. He had cops in his pocket and so many hookers that he had to keep a log inside a lockbox in the back of the closet.

"Rose," Violet said. "That's what we'll name her."

"Hello, Baby Rose," Billy cooed. He sat down on the hospital bed next to Violet and his new baby girl. He gave the gentlest kiss to Rose's forehead. "You and your momma gon have the best of everything," he said, and he kissed Violet softly on the lips.

"Do you know how much money these hoes bring in?" Billy asked Violet.

"I'm just saying you could do something else. With the money we have—"

"How you know how much money we have?" he snapped. Violet looked at him, a bit surprised. He softened and went to her. "I'm goin' legit soon, baby. But first I got to make us some real cash. I've been checkin into somethin more lucrative than hoes anyway." He pulled the small bag of powder out of his pocket.

"This is what's gon get us everything we want."

Violet frowned. "Billy, I'm not proud. . . . I know what you do. As long as you keep your business away from me and Baby Rose, I can live with it. Prostitutes and reefer is one thing, this stuff is a whole 'nother matter."

He held both of Violet's shoulders firmly. "Heroin is big business now, baby. If these fools want this shit, I'm gon sell it to 'em." He slipped his hands around Violet's waist. "It's just for the time bein', sugar. We do this for a little while, and you'll see. We'll have so much money you won't know what to do with it all."

"I don't know, Billy."

He put a silky smile on his face, "Come on now, won't you like your man ownin a nice little blues club or somethin? I'm thinkin 'bout a place where you could go after a hard day's work at the factory, after you cleaned yourself up a bit." He pinched her on the cheek. "Take your lady out."

Violet couldn't hold her smile, yet she still couldn't endorse the idea. The thought of Billy dealing serious drugs frightened her. She squirmed in his arms in protest, but he held her tight and promised, "One day you and me gon live like the white folks do, with a big ol house on a tree lined street, with Baby Rose playin in the front yard not the back."

It became Violet's dream too. She held onto that promise when she bailed Billy out of jail, or when she had to turn her head when he smacked one of his hookers for taking the drug. She overlooked the time Billy beat a German Shepherd to death for barking loudly and scaring Baby Rose while walking down Woodward Avenue. She even told herself it wasn't Billy's doing when Miss Millie was found in an alley whipped and beaten, her face looking as if she'd been boiled alive.

Summer of 1965 was hotter than Violet could ever remember. The kids in the neighborhood constantly opened the hydrants to play in the spraying water, causing an ongoing feud between them and the fire department. Violet sucked on ice cubes to keep cool.

Although they lived in one of the nicest high rises in the community, they were on an upper floor and it was like an oven most of the time. Violet could cope with the heat, although fans in every room blaring on high, overwhelming any other sound coming from the radio or television was a bit annoying. It actually served a purpose in putting Baby Rose down for her nap. The steady buzz seemed to pacify her for a solid hour or two on a blanket strategically placed in front of one. Billy couldn't find relief inside or out.

"I can't stand this place," Billy said.

"It'll cool off soon." Violet had been with Billy long enough to know that if he was in one of his disagreeable moods (which could occur even on the most comfortable of days), then seven days of excessive heat was seven days of pampering she was going to have to give to Rose and Billy as well. "I heard that at the end of the week it's supposed to cool down some." She rubbed a cool cloth on the back of his neck.

"These windows ain't big enough. The water takes forever to warm." He looked at Baby Rose sleeping on the blanket. "You can't even take the baby outside to play."

"It's not so bad, Billy. We're just fine. Rose is too young to play outside anyway."

"She'll be old enough pretty soon," Billy snapped back. He tucked his head under the water faucet over the kitchen sink and drank from it.

"We've got time." Violet curled her arms around his waist from behind and kissed the back of his neck.

"You better slow down before you end up in that back room," Billy said. He didn't need to say it twice. Violet knew what sex was like when he was in this kind of mood, so she quickly unleashed him.

"I'm making you a chocolate cake," she said, tying her apron on fast. "I got to finish before Baby Rose wakes."

Pipe Dreams

In Billy's line of work, it wasn't as if he came home at a scheduled time, but he would call during the day just to touch base with Violet or to hear Rose's baby talk over the phone. It was nine-thirty and this was the third time this week that Violet hadn't heard from him all day. She was beginning to wonder if there was another woman, bearing in mind that she hadn't met him in church, but on the corner. Just the thought of it made her stomach hurt. She'd felt that he had chosen her above all women, devoted to her and Baby Rose. He was still irresistible. She wanted—no *needed* him to still be unbelievably hers.

Violet was sitting at the kitchen table with the baby when he finally burst in. He was lit up like the Fourth of July, and when he grabbed Baby Rose and raised her over his head, Violet knew he was drunk.

"I've been trying to get her to go to sleep all night, Billy! Why are you getting her all excited?" Violet said, irritated. "It's twelve-thirty!"

"So what! She wants to see her Daddy." He leaned over to kiss Violet.

"You smell like whiskey."

"And you smell good," he grinned.

"What has got you all crazy tonight?" She was still suspicious.

"We're getting out of here, that's what, baby!" Billy gloated.

"Getting out of here?"

"That's where I've been the last couple of days. Out looking for a house!"

"What?" Violet took Rose from him and put her in her playpen.

"I told you my baby's gon have a back yard to play in." He pulled Violet over to the couch. "It's beautiful, Violet. It's got three bedrooms and a big kitchen for you to bake all that good food, and a big yard out back with a cherry tree—"

"Wait a minute!" Violet interrupted. He was talking too fast. "Can we afford a house like that? Where is it?" She jumped up and paced the floor, too excited to sit still.

"That's the best part. . . . Dearborn."

"Dearborn?" Violet thought he was kidding. "We can't live out there, Billy. Ain't none of us there."

"Sure there is, and if there ain't . . . well, there is now," he said and smacked his hands together.

"Billy, I don't know about this. We don't want to get caught up in the middle of something."

Billy cupped her face in his hands. "Look, don't I always take care of you?"

"Yes, but . . ." she sighed.

"You gon love it, baby." He picked her up in his arms and kissed her with the passion Violet left school for. "We gon give them people next door a couple more weeks to listen to you holler before we say good-bye to this place."

The home was a brick ranch in style, with a big old oak tree out front. The lawn was immaculate, and flowers lined each side of the porch. The kitchen was big and bright. The window over the sink faced the backyard and Violet could see herself and the baby sitting under the cherry tree. She caressed the Formica cabinets and counters, the refrigerator and the four burner electric stove. The L-shaped dining/living room combination would fit their furniture nicely. Two of the three bedrooms were spacious and lined with carpet. The small bedroom would be perfect for Rose. It was already painted pink.

"It's beautiful."

"I told you."

"Are you sure we can afford all this?"

"You sure you can decorate all this?" Billy was proud of himself.

Violet smiled at him. If she hadn't looked out the living room window, if she hadn't noticed the neighbor across the street's curtain slightly open as if someone was sneaking a look, if Billy hadn't insisted that the only reason they were waiting until dark to move in was because he "didn't want an audience", she could have ignored her stirring gut. Violet watched Billy unload the truck that night. She paced back and forth across the living room bouncing Baby Rose in her arms (the only way these days to coax her to sleep), while Billy moved the boxes in quickly, quietly, as if he were a burglar in reverse.

Aretha Franklin was emerging as the "Queen of Soul," while combat units were deployed to Vietnam. Malcolm X had been shot in New York and Bob Dylan's, *The Times They Are A-Changin'* resonated through the ears of the American public. Times were changing.

Just not fast enough for Violet and Billy.

Welcome Wagon

The neighborhood didn't find out right away about Billy and Violet. Their house sat back from the street and there were lots of trees to shield their identity from the community. Violet busied herself with Baby Rose and decorating: red and white check curtains for the kitchen, cream for the living room. The appliances were old, but Billy promised her a new stove and fridge by the end of the month. It had been three weeks since they moved in and Violet still hadn't attempted to go to the grocer in her new neighborhood. It was just easier to tell Billy a rosy story about how nice the butcher was to her, rather than say she still went back to the old neighborhood to get her groceries.

With Billy gone until nightfall most of the time, Violet tried to remain unnoticed. She ignored the stares from the women who convened a few houses down to watch her as she drove in and out of her driveway. Once a police car followed her all of the way home and parked at the end of her lot. He didn't put his lights on, nor get out of the car. After a few moments of sitting in her own vehicle, Violet scurried inside with the baby and closed the curtains. Throughout the day, she peeped between them, hoping and then praying that the police car would be gone. She knew what he was there for—to frighten her, to make her feel unsettled.

It worked.

Violet was afraid all of the time. But Billy was so proud to have the place, and the scent of the life he told her he would get for her. They were the pioneers—if she could just endure for a while, other Negroes would eventually move in.

One day on a Saturday afternoon, the doorbell rang. Billy was home and answered.

"William Hughes?"

"Yes," Billy said to the man standing on his front porch.

"I'm Brian Nolan, the head of the block association."

"Who?"

"I'm sorry. It's my Irish accent throwing you for a loop. Brian Nolan," he said more clearly.

"How you doin, Mr. Nolan? I'm Billy Hughes," he said with a big smile and shook his hand.
"Please, come in. Violet!" Billy yelled behind him.

"No—no, that's not necessary. I just wanted to talk to you about—"

"Come here, baby." Billy ignored him. "This is my wife Violet."

Violet knew right away this was no invitation to a Tupperware party.

"A mistake was made." The man said in a down-to-business tone, which made Billy stand more erect.

"A mistake?"

"It's probably not the smartest thing, you moving in our—this neighborhood." The man said matter of fact.

Billy gave him a stern look. "What are you talking about?"

"Well," Mr. Nolan fidgeted. "The neighborhood association thought that I should come and talk to you."

"Sir, this is my home. We plan to be good neighbors so tell everybody they don't need to be worryin."

The man looked behind him as if someone was there watching. "You know this is silly don't you? I—I'm trying to be nice to you, trying to help you. I'm trying to keep my property up just like everybody else." The man leaned in a bit. "You know what happens when you people move in. We're just hardworking families who—"

"I work hard too!" Billy raised his voice.

"Let's go back inside, Billy." Violet pulled at his arm, but he pulled away.

"I'm sure you do," The man said, ignoring Violet, too. He put on a forged smile. "Wouldn't it be smarter to go back where you belong? Now my nephew is looking for a house just like this. You sell it back to him before anything bad happens and no harm, no foul."

"Sell it back to him?" Billy was boiling. "It was never his!"

The man at the door leaned back and pressed his lips together. "You're not going to be reasonable about this?"

"I'm not selling my home, sir. Now you can step off my porch and go on about your business."

Billy pushed the door closed, but the man stood there and stared at Billy until it closed all the way. Violet knew that look. She knew Billy did too. It wasn't the best neighborhood, but to Mr. Nolan and others like him, it was all they had.

Two months was how long Violet and Billy stuck it out. The rumors spread quickly and soon the neighborhood banded together against them. Billy tried to handle the daily harassment, the notes, the epithets yelled from cars racing by. There were citations for parties they didn't have, parking tickets, busted windows. Violet stayed in the house most of the time. Billy went to the police, who said, "We'll look into it." He even went back to the old neighborhood, to the white cops he still paid off to see if there was something they could do. Frank and Tony were two of the cops he met with monthly in the back of the grade school.

"You didn't think we was gonna let ya move near us, did ya?" Frank chuckled as he took his pay-off. "Let your little gal play with ours? Just wouldn't be right now, Billy." He poked his head out of the window and motioned with his finger for Billy to come closer. "It's your color, but it's also your line of work. We can't have this sort of thing in our neighborhoods." The police officer opened the envelope full of twenty-dollar bills and ran his thumb across the top. "This is where ya belong, Billy. You're the king of niggerville." He laughed as they sped off.

Violet never got the chance to plant a garden or let Baby Rose play in the yard, for they moved back into their old neighborhood. And Billy began to put the needle to his arm.

Love's Spell

A push, a smack here and there was nothing compared to what Violet endured with Millie. Drugs changed Billy almost overnight, and there wasn't much she could do about it, other than to stay out of his way. He concealed his addiction from Violet at first. He'd get high after listening to the blues, or with his street friends—the ones he'd never bring by the apartment. But after a while, their home was no longer off limits. Billy would shoot up right there in the bathroom. Most of his prostitutes left him, and the ones that stayed looked ragged and unkempt. Billy didn't care that they brought in half the money of the more desirable women he'd once had. It was enough to sustain his habit. Violet just tried to keep some kind of order for Rose's sake. She'd cook, clean, and have the Sunday dinner table dressed, just as she had before Billy started using. But order is difficult when men come by the apartment looking for Billy, who owed more than he sold. An up-and-coming pimp named Stony had taken over Billy's territory without much fuss. Billy would disappear for days and resurface only when he was out of money.

Sunday evening Violet had returned from church, her saving grace the last couple of months. The Reverend and his wife lent a hand when Billy was nowhere to be found. Religion was top priority as a child growing up with Millie. Sundays, usually after getting the crap beat out of her on Saturday, was "the Lord's day," and Millie made sure they got there early to sit up front. Violet often wondered how many others sitting in the congregation shouting, "Yes Lord", and singing, *At the Cross* along with the choir, were monsters like Millie. Since then, the church hadn't been a big part of her life. But with Billy's instability and their financial situation, Violet found comfort within its walls. This Sunday, she'd prayed for herself and Baby Rose, but mainly for Billy. She prayed that he was safe, that he would find strength to kick his habit and that maybe, just maybe he would take a whole new direction with his life.

It had been a particularly good sermon today, about forgiveness and God's mercy. Violet felt her prayers had been answered when she heard Billy in the kitchen. He was home! She took off her coat and set Baby Rose down. In the kitchen she scanned the mess of drawers pulled out onto the kitchen floor. The cabinets were wide open and in disarray. "Can I help you find something, Billy?" Violet said cautious.

He hadn't heard her come in and jerked around. "Where is it, Violet?"

Violet knew what he was looking for—the money he told her not to give him no matter what—the money he told her to hide away for the rent and food for her and Rose. A part of Billy Violet could always reason with, and she would seek out that part when he was like this. He'd put up a fuss or knock something down, or smack her across the face. When it got too bad, she would pacify him with a little money she had somewhere else. It was just enough to get him out the door.

"Look, I ain't playin with you today, Violet. Now where is it?"

"Billy, you just got back. Why don't you let me fix you something to eat and then you can rest." Violet could hardly get the words out before he grabbed her around the neck.

"Where is the money, Violet? And if I have to ask you again, Rose ain't gon have no Momma."

He didn't holler. It was more like a quiet snarl, or a low growl from a wild animal. His usual blows were merciful. He called them "love taps" after he got what he wanted. However, his hands were tight around her neck, and Billy didn't make idle threats.

"It's in my shoe in the bedroom closet," Violet wheezed. Billy loosened his grip. He caressed her neck where his hands had been, looking down and shaking his head in remorse. Then he took off down the hall.

"How are we gonna pay this month's rent, Billy!" Violet cried. She was talking to the back of his head because he was already at the bedroom closet and back at the front door in a flash.

"I'll give it back. I just gotta do somethin first."

"Billy, wait!"

He was down the hall before she could get to the door. He didn't wait for her or the elevator—he took the stairs. Violet was afraid to run after him anyway. He wasn't her Billy anymore. He was somebody else. How was she going to get the money to stay in the apartment? How was she going to feed Rose? Violet looked in the cabinets to do a quick check of how much food was left. She counted three cans of tuna, a can of beans, and a half of a box of Cheerios. That would last about four days if she gave most of it to Baby Rose. In the refrigerator, there was a loaf of bread and two baked drumsticks leftover from the night before. She had planned to go to the store in the morning—Baby Rose needed milk. Eleven months ago, they'd owned a beautiful home in the suburbs. She thought of how happy she and Billy were the first couple of days. "Everything is about to change for the better, Violet," he'd promised that first night. She curled up into a ball on the kitchen floor and cried until Rose woke from her nap.

Billy returned five hours later with blood on his shirt and a brown bag that she guessed contained his drugs. He was already high—stumbling and singing out of tune. Violet tried to quiet the man she thought so intriguing years ago. His pretty smile was yellow from the drugs, and he had lost so much weight that even small time punks messed with him.

He pulled Violet into his arms and tried to dance with her.

"*Mona Lisa . . . Mona Lisa they have—*"

"Billy, please. You're going to wake up the baby."

"I ain't gon wake nobody up." Rose started to cry in the back room.

"Augh. Ohhhh." He put his finger to his mouth and giggled like a child.

"Billy," Violet moaned and headed toward the back room. She picked up Rose and comforted her with a bottle of water. After Violet quieted the baby, she put her back in the crib. When she turned around, Billy was standing at the bedroom door, his eyes dark and cold—the same way he looked when he killed that dog.

"You want me to make you something to eat?"

He didn't answer.

She was about to ask him what the blood on his shirt was from, until she saw the syringe in his hand. Her instincts told her to stand still and quiet.

"I've been thinkin, Violet. Things just ain't workin out the way I planned." His voice cracked and Violet saw Billy cry for the first time. "I tried to give it to you, tried to give you a good life."

"Billy we can have a good life. . . . We can start all over." She went to him and held his face in her hands. "You could get a job at the factory."

Billy pulled her hands away from his face. "You know how I am. I don't know how to work clean."

"You can change, though. The factory is good money, and they're hiring us."

"I'm gon go get a factory job taking shit from them every day while you go find work God knows where? Stuck here forever in this shit hole? Well I say no!" Billy's sudden outburst made her jump back. Rose started to cry again. "I'm tired, Violet. I can't hang on no more." His tone was sad but absolute. "I say let's go to a place where they can't keep us caged."

"We're not caged! I can go back to school—"

He shook his head to silence her, and then he looked past Violet toward Baby Rose, who was getting more wound up.

"Give me my baby," he said.

"Billy, I'll get her. Keep her real quiet so we can talk."

He pushed Violet away from the crib and lifted Rose up and into his arms. "I'm not gon let 'em get you, sugar. We gon go to a place where they can't touch us."

Violet's legs were shaking with terror. She stared at the syringe still in his hand and tried to think of a way to get Rose from him.

"Billy, get some rest okay? You'll feel better in the morning." She attempted to take the baby from him, but he jerked away and almost dropped her.

"It's mornin now," he reconciled. He was rocking the baby back and forth. Rose stopped crying. "It's over, Violet." He kissed Rose on the forehead and pushed up the baby's tiny sleeve. "I got enough for all three of us."

He was suddenly calm and decisive. Violet thought he'd found some kind of peace in this madness! "No Billy, don't!" she screamed. "Do me first—then I can be where you are and know it's right. Do me first, Billy!" She kissed his cracked lips hard until his lips softened against hers. "Let me put her down." He stared at her for a moment, then he handed her the baby. Violet's whole body trembled now—not just her legs. She searched her mind for some kind of scheme to persuade Billy not to do this, but just as she put the baby down, Billy pulled her to him. "Billy, wait a minute—"

He hit her hard across the face before she could get the rest out, and blood spurted out of her nose. "No more talkin," he said. Violet used all of her strength to keep from passing out from the blow. He grabbed her arm and she slid down onto the floor. "This is how they'll find us—all together. *Going to fly high in the sky*," he sang. Rose was whining again in her crib. Billy looked over at her. "Hush, Baby Rose. I'll take care of you in a minute."

Violet closed her eyes tightly, thinking it would be over soon. He tied the rubber tube around her arm and slapped at it to get a vein. She was crying but couldn't hear herself. She couldn't feel the blood dripping from her nose and onto her lap. She felt as if she were looking at a movie—watching this whole scene unfold outside of herself. The needle's tip prodded her skin. She couldn't struggle; her body was frozen with fear. Billy's thumb extended to the back of the needle preparing to fill her veins. He hesitated, looking into her eyes and said, "I love you," for the first time. Violet felt the prick of the needle as he bent down to give her one last kiss.

"Auuggggghhh!" he screamed and buckled over in pain. She didn't know how she managed to kick him in the groin, but she had to save Rose. She got to her feet and tried to run to the door for help. Billy caught her by the hair. "You're going one way or the other!" he growled. She could feel his hot breath on the back of her neck, and then he whispered softly in her ear. "I already knew how to read."

He twisted her around and she stared at him, this man she'd given all of herself for. He was grinning like a Cheshire cat. He slid his hands around her neck to strangle her. Violet could feel her body growing limp, her sight blurring. He was right. It was over.

His spell was broken.

Out of the corner of her eye, she saw the syringe that had fallen out of his hand and onto the couch. Billy had her pinned against it. She groped the plastic covered cushion until she had it firmly in her palm, and in one swift move, plunged the syringe into the side of his neck. Billy looked surprised, as if he wasn't sure what Violet had done to him. His body tensed, and he fell against the wall with the needle still stuck in his neck. Billy never took his eyes off of Violet as he slid slowly down the wall to the floor. Finally, he fell over onto his stomach.

Violet's first instinct was to go to him, pull the syringe from his neck and call someone for help. She acted on her second, grabbed Rose, and ran out the door. She ran with Baby Rose the five blocks to Pastor Monroe's home. His wife Sarah took one look at Violet and pulled her inside.

"You stay with us for as long as you need to," Sarah said.

"I don't have anything. All I got is my baby."

"Don't cry now, honey. You can help me with the Lord's work." Sarah rubbed Baby Rose's head. "You'll earn your keep."

Pastor Monroe

Violet helped Sarah anyway she could. She prepared meals weekly for old widow Delores, who could hardly get around. She swept out the church daily, cleaned clothes, and washed dishes after supper. Each morning and evening, the three of them got down on their knees together, with pastor Monroe leading the prayer.

"Dear Lord, bless my sweet wife with children, Lord. Bless our congregation, and this young woman and child so that they never have to run again."

The women of the congregation thought Pastor Monroe a very good catch, and Violet agreed. He was openly affectionate with Sarah. He complimented her daily on her meals and her work at the church. He was well spoken and ate neatly at the dinner table, used his napkin and chewed with his mouth closed—Billy had eaten like a horse. Violet imagined that she also needed some fine-tuning in manners. She learned a lot about being a lady from Sarah. She was a frail thing—tiny. Violet thought she'd break if she looked at her too hard. She wore her hair in a bun pulled tightly at the nape of her neck, complimenting her high cheekbones.

Sharp pains shot through Sarah's abdomen at times and would make her buckle. She coughed a lot and her eyes popped like an owl when she did.

"I'm fine, Violet," she'd say when the pain subsided. "You just tend to that baby of yours. Me and the pastor will pray on it like we do every night."

"Do you think you should go and get something for it? Let a doctor look at you?" Violet pressed.

"The pastor says if the devil can make you sick then you best believe God can make you well."

Sarah's pain became more severe as the weeks progressed, though, and eventually she had no choice but to go to the hospital. Violet took over all the chores for Sarah so that she wouldn't have to lift a finger when she returned. She prepared the meals, cleaned the house and even took over Sarah's Sunday school class.

"I can't practice my sermon for Sunday with your baby crying like that all the time," Pastor Monroe said one evening.

"I'll get her in just a minute, as soon as I get this chicken in the oven for you." Violet said.

The pastor hadn't said it with anger. It was an eerie, somewhat calm disgruntlement, as if he had just given her a compliment instead of a complaint. The next couple of days were similar.

"When you fold my shirts, I prefer them folded like this." The pastor folded the long sleeves into the center of the back and then flipped the shirt's bottom up to the center.

"Alright," Violet said. Even though she could have swore she'd folded the shirt the same way as he had.

That same night, he'd said, "The catfish was a little on the salty side."

Violet considered the comments just his way of dealing with missing his wife. Violet missed her too. Millie never gave her time to develop friendships with other girls, and with Billy, the only kind of women she came across were prostitutes. Violet went to bed in the spare room for her and Rose thinking when Sarah returned, she would tell her what their friendship meant to her.

Police sirens made Violet nervous. Two weeks had passed with Sarah still in the hospital—two months since she ran from Billy. The police cars passed the house—she could breathe easy. She hadn't seen or heard from Billy so she imagined the worst. There was no news in the papers about him; then again, a drug-dealing pimp found dead wouldn't exactly make the front page. Nonetheless, whenever she heard a police car, she was sure they were coming for her. It was the middle of the night and she needed to get some sleep. Sarah would be coming home and she wanted to get up early to make her a cake. Another police car sped past her window. Violet watched Baby Rose who lay next to her on the bed sucking her fingers in and out fast as the cars passed by. Her eyes pressed tight, then relaxed as the siren became more distant. She was a good baby. Finishing high school was going to be her top priority when Sarah came home. She was smart—she could do it. She even thought about college. Then she could give Rose a better life. Violet kissed Rose on her forehead and turned over falling into a deep sleep.

"Violet. . . . Violet."

She heard her name the first time it was called, but she thought she was dreaming and ignored it. The second time she recognized the pastor's voice. He stood just inside the door. Violet glanced over at Rose figuring that she had dozed off and didn't hear the baby cry, and pastor Monroe wanted to complain about the noise. But Rose was sleeping soundly. He sat down on the bed.

"Do you like it here?"

"Very much. I don't know what I'd have done if it weren't for you and Sarah."

He smiled and nodded his head. She'd thought of him as sort of a father figure: moody, but good. She had on one of his wife's old gowns and she pulled the covers up over herself respectfully.

"You know we can't help you much longer. The Lord's calling me in another direction. There are lots of people that need our guidance."

"I know, Pastor. I'm saving a bit from the chores I do around the church and all. I'm going to try to find some real work that I can do after studying for my diploma. Sarah said she would watch the baby for me till I get on my feet."

He ran his hand along her feet. "Now how is she going to do that and cook and clean and be the pastor's wife?"

She eased her foot away, stunned. Baby Rose was still asleep. "I could still help her with the chores, too."

He crossed his legs like a gentlemen. "I'm sure there's something we can work out," he said and he put his hand on her leg, rubbing it up and down, each stroke a little higher up. His hand was almost at mid-thigh when she stopped him.

"Pastor Monroe!" she moved his hand away. "I know you're probably missing your wife, but I didn't ask you for no massage."

"You're in my house. I don't have to wait for you to ask for nothing."

"The hell you don't!" Violet was on her feet.

He stood up, offended. "You're going to have to leave here."

Violet already knew that. "I'll leave in the morning," she sighed.

"No, you'll leave now!" he demanded. It was the first time Violet heard him raise his voice.

"Can I have a little bit of privacy to get me and the baby's things together?" She couldn't believe this was happening.

He was quiet for a moment, looking her up and down. "As I said, this is my house. Besides, I can't have you trying to take none of my wife's things." Then he leaned against the wall and stared at her. Violet had been through too much with Billy to deal with the pastor's antics. She didn't know where she would go, but Violet knew she had better leave before it got any worse. She stomped over to the corner to get dressed. Baby Rose was awake but still.

"Hey, little pretty girl," he cooed. Your momma is causing all this ruckus over nothing."

Violet turned her back to him and tried to put her clothes on as quickly as possible. He slid up close behind her. "You know things don't have to be this way," he said, running his hand along her hip. "I know who you ran from. I'll pay you."

"If you touch me again I swear I'll kill you!" Violet snapped.

Pastor Monroe didn't know exactly what she'd done to Billy, but he had heard the rumors. "Get out before I call the police on you!" Violet grabbed Rose and the few things she had. The Pastor followed her to the door. "I don't know how I'm going to tell Sarah how you came on to me, girl!" Pastor

Monroe yelled from the door. "There is nothing worse to her than a woman trying to cleave to another woman's man."

Violet had little money, nowhere to go and no one to call. She walked with Rose in her arms until she found a church she could sit in until the morning.

In the beginning, she could easily blend in with the other shoppers, asking questions about the vase in the window, if the sofa could be delivered earlier than two weeks, if it came in other colors. How she would go home and discuss it with her husband, and let them know if she would take it. To keep Baby Rose out of the cold, she'd say anything. But the money she'd saved from church duties disappeared quickly, with buying food and a place to lay her head. And as the days passed, Violet began to look more worn. She no longer had enough to rent a room. She wasn't clean, though she washed whenever she could, but there was only so much that can be done in a public bathroom. Before long, clerks scrutinized her movement through their stores.

A former prostitute of Billy's recognized Violet and bought her lunch. Violet gobbled down the burger and fries and ordered Rose some applesauce and scrambled eggs. "My brother did heroin so I knew where Billy was headed," The woman said. "I went on with Stony. He don't give you what you worth like Billy did before he started using, but he's what's out here now." She shrugged her shoulders. "You gotta be in somebody's stable or you get your ass kicked. Where is Billy anyway?"

"I don't know. He left us," Violet said. She convinced herself she wasn't telling a lie. He did leave them—when he started doing drugs.

"It's a shame that you out here all alone with that baby. Take this." She handed Violet a twenty-dollar bill.

Violet's eyes filled. "Thank you."

"You're welcome, sugar. I got to go now before Stony sees me in here takin a break. Take care of yourself. Keep that baby warm."

The twenty dollars paid for a good meal and a room for two nights before Violet was back on the street. She smelled like fish and yogurt and sweat and smelly socks all rolled up into one. The stolen loaf of Wonder Bread was what she shared with Rose. Violet ate two pieces in the morning, one in the afternoon, and three at night. She thanked God Rose was on solid food and that she was too young to know what was happening to them. Violet was weak from exhaustion and lack of sleep when she ran into Stony.

"Phyllis told me you were out here in the cold with this little thing," he said and caressed Rose's chin. "You look awful, darlin." He had two girls no more than sixteen or seventeen with him, one on each arm. "Why don't you come with me and get out of this weather? Take a hot bath and clean your pretty self up." Violet snuggled Rose closer to her. "Awwwh, don't be like that. . . . Violet is it?" She looked back toward him. He was taller than Billy, with golden brown skin and eyes to match. He was too pretty for Violet's tastes, and there was something artificial about him. He was muscular, but not naturally like Billy. Stony looked like he had to work at being tough.

Billy just was.

"Don't I treat you right, girls?" he asked the two without taking his eyes off Violet. "Come on home with me tonight, Violet. We'll put the baby to bed and talk about your future." He pulled out a thick bundle of cash. "A warm coat, juicy steak . . . we'll move on from there." And then he plucked two fifty dollar bills from his stash and held them out to Violet. Violet's stomach twisted from hunger. No doubt, Rose was starving too. Where was she going to sleep tonight? A hot bath, a good meal, a bed for her and Rose to sleep in—

he wasn't bad looking. "I'll put you up in a nice room." Stony said. "Your customers won't mind the baby, as long as she's not a light sleeper."

"I don't want your money!" Violet pushed by him and across the street, kicking herself for being weak enough to even consider it.

"You'll be looking for me in a couple of days," he called. "I'm usually outside the liquor store around the corner."

His Wing Tipped Shoes

It was getting dark and Violet's feet were freezing. "Lord, don't let it be too cold tonight," she prayed aloud. "A few coins for my baby?" she asked a woman coming toward her. The woman looked past her and straight ahead ignoring Violet's plea. Another woman with a toddler headed toward her, she caught a glimpse of Violet and tightly grabbed her toddler's hand and crossed the street. "A little change for my baby to get something to eat," she begged an older gentleman who frowned at her, but reached in his pocket and gave her fifty cents. "Thank you, sir. God bless you." Violet looked at the big clock at the corner. She had begged for thirty-five minutes and had only collected a dollar and seventy-five cents. She was too cold to feel the humiliation of resorting to begging on the street. There were matters more important— Rose was getting fussy. She needed at least five dollars to sit at the diner all night where it was warm and she could feed her. She could strategically time her orders: coffee first, then applesauce, then toast, then scrambled eggs. She could stretch the orders out until morning. Violet held Rose close to her chest, blowing hot air onto her little face. Violet's warm breath comforted Rose long enough for her to collect another dollar and fifteen cents. But Rose grew tired and what began as fussiness, morphed into a full-fledged wail.

Some of the people on the street knew she used to be with Billy and shook their heads in disgust as they walked by. Some showed compassion and gave a little. Another ten minutes passed and Rose finally cried herself to sleep. During that time, Violet collected two dollars more. The wind nipped at her face and her own tears bit at her cheeks. Her hands and feet were freezing, and if she didn't find somewhere warm soon, Rose would wake to a cold or something much worse.

She didn't look at anyone, just their hands to see if they would dig into their pockets or handbags. She figured she was invisible to most of them. Perhaps this was penance for being with Billy. The community was never ideal, but the Billys and the Stonys of the neighborhood were major contributors to its downward swirl.

"Sir, could you spare a little for my baby?" She begged again. She noticed his shoes first, they had an interesting pattern at the tip—a wing of some sort. Nothing like Billy had worn. He reached into his pocket and counted out five whole dollars. "Thank you, sir! Thank you so very much." Violet smiled at him and stuffed the money into her pocket. She could already taste the grill cheese sandwich and glass of milk in her mouth.

"You're welcome," he said. "…Violet?" She was already halfway across the street, headed toward the diner. "Violet?" She heard again. Violet turned around and watched the well-dressed man come toward her. She coiled for her own protection and stepped back to keep her distance from him. "My God, it is you! . . . Violet, I'm Red!" He held her shoulders gently. "I'm Red!"

Violet stared at this distinguished man, nothing like the short little boy that chased after her when they were in school. He wasn't handsome like Billy, but tall and lean—elegant. She tried to smooth her hair, but realized how foolish that gesture was. Seeing her like this, musty and unkempt was bad enough, but she could smell Baby Rose's dirty diaper and was sure he could too. Looking away from him was her only defense and tears began to pool in her eyes.

"Miss Violet." He said softly.

It had been a long time since she'd had anyone call her that—too long. Shame couldn't keep her from falling into his arms. She could barely stand from the cold. Red took off one of his gloves and wiped her face. "My Violet," he whispered as if it were true. "Whatever has happened to you is over now."

The world around her shut down while he held her and Baby Rose against his chest. Violet closed her eyes, just for the moment, absorbing the heat from his body.

"Come on," he said, coaxing her forward toward his car. He opened the door for her. He put the heat on high.

"I live not far from here."

On the way to his home Violet thought about Billy and the reverend. Again she was helpless. Again her fate left in the hands of yet another man.

"I should of never left school."

Red was quiet.

"I had to get away from Millie."

Red was still quiet.

"Billy was trying to hurt us."

He looked at the baby. "What's her name?"

She stared at him. He didn't want to know about Billy or any of it—at least not now. "Rose." she said.

"Does she like apple butter?"

His home was small, not nearly the size of the home she and Billy had for a quick moment in time. The walls were bare except for the picture of Dr. Martin Luther King—floors could use a rug or two. Yet it was enough for a young man starting out in the world.

"It's nothing special, but—"

"I like it." Violet reassured. "Is there somewhere I can put the baby down?"

"Uh, yes. You can put her down in here." He led her to a back room decorated with olive green carpet and a single bed.

Violet put Baby Rose down and looked at Red standing at the door. She wanted to get things straight. "I would want to stay in here . . . with her."

"I know, Violet. I'll make us something to eat."

She sat next to Rose watching her sleep. He'd been generous enough to stop and get some diapers so that she could change Rose in the car. She'd feed her and give her a bath later, after she got some rest. Before long, the air scented with the flavor of chicken frying. She was starving, so she checked Rose to make sure she was deeply asleep and then headed toward the kitchen, following her nose. Violet stopped at a room right before the kitchen. Red's wing-tipped shoes were on the floor at the end of the bed, so she assumed the room was his. The double bed had one pillow. The top of the dresser across from it was bare except for the case that held his watch and keys. Violet tried to imagine him sleeping in this lonely room.

"I found something for you to change into."

Violet jumped, embarrassed that she'd been snooping around. Red was holding a brown robe in his hand along with a towel set.

"Thank you."

"There's a bathroom right down the hall if you want to take a shower," he said in a somewhat formal, yet encouraging manner. "I'll finish up dinner and listen for Rose."

"She'll probably be asleep for a while," Violet said.

"I'll check in on her anyway."

Violet couldn't wait to get the stench of the streets off of her. She glanced at the tub and dreamed of a long hot soak, but a shower would do for now. She worked the soap into a foamy lather cleansing with her hands several times before she used his washcloth. Then she sudsed the cloth and got down to real scrubbing.

Afterward, she slipped on his robe, rolling up the sleeves to her elbows and crept out of the bathroom to check on Rose.

She wasn't there!

Violet tried not to go to pieces while she raced down the hall.

"Shush," Red whispered when she reached the kitchen. He was setting the table with Rose draped over his shoulder, limp and relaxed, eyes closed, lulled by the heat of the kitchen, away from the noise and cold outside.

It hadn't mattered to Violet that Rose rested comfortably, as if she'd been in Red's custody many times before. She practically snatched Baby Rose from him.

"She woke up, so I thought I'd bring her in here with me."

Violet moved away from him, holding sleeping Rose close.

"I wouldn't hurt her."

Violet didn't say anything.

Red stood there for a moment. Then he quietly resumed setting the plates on the table as if nothing happened. "I have some macaroni from last night to go with the chicken." He went to the fridge and took it out. "I made too much. . . . You want to set Rose on the couch while we eat?"

Violet nodded.

Neither one of them said a word while they ate the meal he'd prepared. Not until Violet relaxed a bit.

"Thank you Red, it was really good." Violet felt she at least owed him that.

"I'm glad you liked it."

"So you decided not to be a baseball star?"

Red smiled. "You remember. Well, I realized I liked books more than baseball. I'm an English teacher around the corner. There's a small library in the closet if you want to read anything."

"I want to read everything you've got."

"Hopefully that will take some time."

She smiled back at him, surprised at her discovery that she'd rushed to judge his appearance. He *was* handsome, in the most pleasingly understated way.

Red loved her still, and seeing her as a woman and how she was with Rose only made his love more genuine. He never pressured her to satisfy him physically, expected nothing but a meal and the respect that a man deserves when he takes care of a woman. He only hoped that she would stay, but Violet found his love to be more comforting and secure than anything she had ever felt with Billy. Watching Red with Rose was one of Violet's greatest joys, and in time, his love for her was reciprocated.

They married in the church near his school and he raised Rose as his own. Now pictures, rugs, and toys garnished each space, and on the double bed lay her pillow very close to his. When Red came home from work, Violet had a back rub and pleasant conversation waiting for him. And when they made love it was tender and heartfelt. She resolved to call him Rueben, his real name, to give him the dignity he deserved.

Violet sat upright on the bed next to Dahlia. "If I had gone with Stony that day, I'd have had a steak and a hot bath, put your momma to bed, and then lay down with Stony, and I don't even know if it would have been in that order. I was in a hole that night, and I would have stayed there if I hadn't believed there was something better for me." Violet thought a moment about her life before Rueben. "You don't know what life has in store for you up ahead. Don't get bogged down by how you feel in the here and now."

Dahlia sat on the bed in silence. Violet didn't rush her, it wasn't an uncomfortable quiet anymore.

"Did the police ever find Billy?" Dahlia asked after some time.

"Wasn't a need to. You know that fool lived and kicked the habit. I hear he moved back to Missouri. So you see, I probably saved your sorry grandfather's life that night."

Dahlia smiled and shook her head. Violet took off her glasses and placed them on the bedside table.

"Are you having sex yet?"

"What?"

"You heard me," Violet said, propping a pillow comfortably under her head.

"No."

Violet gave her the eye. "Fooling with girls?"

Dahlia rolled her eyes. "Nooo!"

"You know you kids now a days don't think it's nothing to experiment with each other."

"Where did you get that information? Oprah?"

"The View." Violet answered matter-of-fact.

They both laughed.

"And what if I did 'fool with girls'?"

"If you're gay you're gay. Just don't be experimenting if you don't know what you're doing." Violet pulled the covers up over her chest. "I would think that another woman would know how to please a woman more so than some of these men out here—you got the same equipment. You switch back to a man, your just setting yourself up for a big letdown. So unless you're feeling something deep down in your soul … leave the girls alone."

"That's life according to Violet?" Dahlia chuckled.

Violet paused. "No, that's life according to your grandmother."

Dahlia put her head down. "Goodnight."

"Goodnight, baby."

Dahlia turned the light off and the two of them lay still for only a few moments before Violet tapped her on the shoulder, "Dahlia?"

"Hmmm?" She didn't turn around.

"Life's full of choices. I made a bad choice with Billy that almost cost me and your mother's life. Sometimes you're gonna make the wrong ones. It doesn't mean you can't reset your course."

Violet closed her eyes, believing she'd taken a small step back into Dahlia's life today. The dark left shadows of words that had not yet formed into conversations between them, but she was lying next to her granddaughter. That was enough for tonight.

Then Dahlia said out of the blue, "I don't like girls."

Violet smiled and went to sleep.

Quiche

"Dahlia!" A woman's voice called from downstairs. "Estas aqui, Dahlia?"

"Who is that?" Violet pulled the covers over her chest. She looked at the clock beside the bed. It was eight o'clock in the morning.

"I'm in here, Silla," Dahlia called back and yawned.

Before Violet could grab for her robe the door swung open. Standing in the threshold was a full figured woman with sun-kissed skin and dark eyebrows. The large mole on the side of her face gave her a seductive quality that didn't quite fit her occupation.

"Oh," said Silla. "Good morning. I didn't see you in your room, Dee. I thought that maybe you were out already." She glanced at Violet in the bed she needed to make. She wanted to finish early, and get back across town to her own home, which needed tidying up before her children came home from school. "Did you want this room cleaned?"

Violet could tell from her tone that the woman wanted to get a move on. Dahlia was already out of bed and headed toward the bathroom.

"You mean to tell me Taylor has somebody making the bed for you?"

"That's what money is for." Dahlia mumbled groggily.

"I didn't know you had a job."

"I don't have to. Daddy does." Dahlia tossed back to her.

"Lord have mercy. What's your name, honey? Sita?" Violet flipped the covers back taking a minute to raise herself off the bed. Silla was already opening the blinds.

"Siilllia," The woman corrected her.

"Now look here, Siilllia." Violet said, just as sarcastic. She took hold of the woman's arm gently and led her to the door. "I know there must be a hundred things you got better to do today then to clean up after a spoiled child and her grandmother."

"Tengo que limpiar la casa," Silla disputed.

"She has to clean the house," Dahlia translated.

"Casa will be just fine today without you. We have two able bodies here to cook and clean."

"I'm not doing it!" Dahlia protested.

"Hush child," Violet said, and led the woman to the door again.

"Señor Taylor told me you would be here and I was to take care of the house."

"I understand that, but you don't have to today."

"I have to do my job, ma'am. I'll be out of here in no time." The woman said and headed back to the bed and started to pull the covers neatly into place.

Violet sighed big. "You're not needed today." She went over to the woman and put her arm around her, escorting her back to the door, all the while the woman protested in Spanish. Violet thought the woman was putting up too much of a struggle for there not to be something behind it. "I'm gonna make sure he still pays you!" Violet finally said. With that, the woman stopped struggling and looked at Dahlia.

"Dilea tu padre que estuve aqui."

"Okay, Silla, I'll tell him you were here," Dahlia repeated in English.

"That's a smart lady, did you see how fast she left when I said your daddy was gonna pay? She must have some black in her."

Dahlia laughed. "I don't know about that, but she is real smart. She's in law school."

"What?"

"I think she graduates next year." Dahlia propped her hands on her hips. "So, now what are we going to eat for breakfast?"

"Quiche."

Violet went downstairs to the kitchen and looked for the ingredients for her quiche. She found some shrimp in the freezer and pulled out mushrooms, spinach, cheese, and eggs from the fridge. She figured Taylor must have remembered the Sunday afternoons when he and Rose came over for brunch and told Silla what to stock the fridge with. A half an hour passed before Dahlia came strolling down the stairs with her arms full of bottles of dark nail polish, remover, and cotton balls.

"I told you I didn't know how to roll it!"

Violet patted her Medusa hairstyle. "It's not that bad. You just need some practice."

"I can always get my flat-iron upstairs. Is the food ready yet?" Dahlia plopped her supplies down on the kitchen table much too close to Violet's ingredients, which Violet countered calmly by pulling the garbage can close to the table and pitching the whole mess of polish and cotton balls into the can.

"Hey!"

Violet slammed the chef's knife down on the cutting board in front of Dahlia. "Save the prima donna show for your daddy and start cutting these mushrooms."

"Is this what you and Dad planned for me? Yesterday I rolled your hair."

"Poor baby,"

"And now you think I'm going to cook all day?"

"Not all day," Violet joked.

"I don't even like to cook," Dahlia said, chopping the mushrooms wildly.

"You're going to hurt somebody, child." She leaned over Dahlia and guided her with the knife so that she cut the mushrooms into uniform slivers. Dahlia was no sous chef, cutting the mushrooms still a little too thick, but they looked much better than before.

"The key is putting in the right amount of cream and about two tablespoons of water," Violet said after she noticed Dahlia watching her whip the cream and eggs together. "I can't stand to eat nobody's quiche dense as a hamburger. . . I know a lady back home that puts raisins in her quiche."

Dahlia winced.

"Ever meet somebody that's always trying to make a good thing better? That's her. She's sweet as can be, just don't eat none of her food." She arranged the shrimp, mushrooms and spinach in the pie dish. "Some things just aren't meant to be messed with."

Some things just aren't meant to be messed with. Violet played the words back in her head. Staying away from Dahlia all these years was not only for Dahlia's sake, but for hers also—up until now. She thought if she could keep the truth buried, leave the hurt behind and start fresh, it would make it easier. But the past does affect the present, and she was going to have to make things right with Dahlia before it was too late.

At first it was the little things. She couldn't find the carton of milk, then she'd find it the next day in the pantry—the bath water overflowing because she didn't remember turning on the water. Once while in heavy traffic, Violet couldn't remember how to put on her turn signal in the Toyota Camry she'd driven for six years. She thought these were normal things that everyone did occasionally. All of us disconnected with the world sometimes, right? But ending up at the grocery store without a clue as to what she was there to buy or how she got there was different. She felt as if she were trapped under murky water when she'd forget. Each time something pulled her deeper—each time she had to fight harder to reach the surface. Her biggest fear was that she wouldn't remember why she needed to reach the surface at all. There were no memories in the shadowy depths—just peace.

Later, after they had eaten the egg pie, Violet looked at Dahlia's empty plate. "Food tastes better when you make it yourself. Now that you know how, you should surprise Silla one day and make her one."

"Maybe I will." Dahlia eyed her polish in the garbage. "Do you mind if I take my things out of the there?"

Violet watched her pull the polish out, putting the tips of her fingers in and plucking out each one as if she were putting her hand in the toilet. "I can't imagine what it's like to be a teenager these days. When I was your age, I was working like a dog for Miss Millie. I was sitting here thinking about how different we are, but actually, you and I are a lot alike." Violet's mood took on a sudden downturn. "I never got to sit at the table and watch my mother cook—never had her sing me a lullaby. Don't even know what her voice sounded like. Ain't natural."

"How did you find out about your mother?"

"There was a woman who lived next door to Millie. Millie told her all about how she paid Tula for me. How I was some white–looking rich woman's baby from Grosse Pointe, Michigan. Rueben helped me track down my brothers. They told me the rest."

"Dad freaks out anytime I bring up my mother," Dahlia said. She sat quietly for a moment. Then she said, "I think you were right about him being weak."

Taylor Crane

"Are you finished with this, sir?"

Taylor Crane nodded his head, barely looking up at the young man at the coffee shop. He was stuck in his own head this evening.

Rose was on his mind.

He'd just landed another big client, his second this month. Instead of celebrating with his fellow partners at Crane, Gordon, and Baxter, Taylor chose to skip the bar and clear his head. Downtown Chicago was only about a thirty-five minute drive away from his home in Olympia Fields, but he was back in town for only one night, and then it was off to Germany in the morning. While he did want to check up on Dahlia, making nice with Violet wasn't his idea of a restful evening.

The quick walk outside of the hotel had turned into an hour stroll. It was getting dark and the sudden nose-dive in the weather had caught him by surprise. The coffee shop was a welcoming place to grab a cappuccino and biscotti and warm his hands before heading back. Despite the evening chill, Taylor decided to take his time, stopping in front of the gallery where her paintings had shown in the window—Rose was the first black artist to get the coveted spot. He could almost feel her tugging him away from the window as he announced to everyone passing by that the painting was hers. The memory lingered for another block until he found himself outside of Garret's Popcorn. At the end of the line, that was well outside the petite shop, was a couple snuggled together to keep warm. Their kisses broke all the rules of PDA and Taylor couldn't help but feel a twinge of jealousy. It had been a long time since he'd shared his favorite caramel and cheese corn mix with someone who mattered. Of course there were fill-ins: Sarah, the artist in Phoenix; Washington attorney, Regina worked out fairly well when he was in town, then there was Carol, who could have made him forget all the others if she had just let things be.

She and Taylor met on a business trip in Montreal two years after Rose's death. It was time to get on with it—at least that's what everyone advised. The pharmaceutical sales rep was a Dartmouth graduate with a butter soft complexion and a smile that made him smile too. Her small frame—five foot three at the most, was not what he usually went for. He preferred the Victoria's Secret type, whose appearance bordered on the impossible. But Carol was built for the comfort of a man on top. Just enough cushion where it mattered most. It surprised Taylor that a total package like Carol was still on the market at all.

They could talk about anything that mattered and everything that didn't: President Clinton and Hillary, the World Wide Web, Seinfeld. And when they were intimate, Taylor let her believe that it was indeed intimate. She never asked for much from him, other than a call after work and a weekend date—usually a Friday night. She understood that after dinner, a movie and a little bedtime bliss, Taylor would take a shower and dress. Dahlia was motherless—there could be no overnight, lazy Saturday mornings. Carol even understood that it would complicate things if she met his daughter just yet. "Let's take it slow." He'd told her. Taylor needed that time which she had said she was willing to give.

Eight months passed before she told him she deserved more. He remembered the last time he and Carol were together.

"I love you, Taylor, and I am trying to give you time to love me back," she'd told him. "I'm a damn good woman, a damn good one."

He'd tried to let her down easy, expressed all the usual things a man says to a woman he knows would be good for him, but thinks he needs something else. What he really felt was fear. He liked Carol and probably could have loved her. But Taylor couldn't trust himself completely with any woman.

Look what he'd done to Rose.

It was after six by the time Taylor stepped back inside the hotel lobby. He caught a glimpse of an old colleague sitting at the bar. Taylor remembered the guy drank Vodka like water, and from the looks of things, he was just getting started. If the man spotted him, he'd insist that they have a least one drink, and then that would turn into three or four before he could get away. So Taylor slipped into the elevator just as it was closing.

His hotel room, tastefully decorated in earth tones of muted orange, olive-brown, and red inspired instant comfort. Someone had tried very hard to make it look effortlessly elegant. He went straight for the bathroom, shed his clothes and stepped into the hot shower. The water felt good streaming down his spine to his backside, the backs of his legs, his cold feet: the objective being warmth—cleansing was an afterthought. He let the bathroom fill with steam, the heavy fog surrounding him like an embrace.

Room service was room service, a standard of meals that rolled from one country to the next. Taylor planned to eat quickly and then try to catch up on his sleep, but it was autumn and the city lights cast a splendid glow on the fall foliage from the window. Slow down was something he had to tell himself every once in awhile. He took pleasure in eating the bacon and blue cheese burger cooked to a perfect medium. Not medium well, not medium rare, but medium—just the way he liked it. He continued to gaze out of the window well after he finished his meal, until the darkness closed in on him and he could no longer see the colors of the trees. The thought of the sienna leaves succumbing to the arctic winter ahead saddened him.

He usually shut his mind down at night by finding a woman to keep his body occupied or by drinking enough Scotch to dull any memories that had the potential for danger. His usual safeguards for self-preservation wouldn't work tonight. He had to be at O'Hare by five-thirty in the morning, and neither shooing a woman out the door by four, nor nursing a hangover seemed appealing. Instead of fighting it, Taylor slid under the covers and let the thoughts flow in about the women of his life.

The first woman wasn't his.

Charlie's Angel
1976

"Hey, little Dude," said Taylor's cousin, Simon.

They smacked hands and Simon patted him on the back. Taylor was all smiles when Simon visited. His father only came around every once in a while, which had more to do with seeing his mother for the night than it had to do with Taylor. Simon, at twenty-five-years old had become father, brother, and mentor to fourteen-year-old Taylor. He stood six-foot four inches tall and sported a mammoth afro, which he picked out incessantly.

Taylor clung to his every word.

"Aunt Vivian!" Simon kissed Taylor's mother on the cheek. He had an exaggerated smile on his face. "This is Shannon."

It took a moment before Vivian spoke. Her dagger eyes did all of the talking. She said a tepid, "Hello."

"Hi," Shannon grabbed Vivian's hands before they were offered and squeezed them tight. Her glossy lips parted, showing all of her pearly whites. "You two are all Simon talked about on the way over here. I feel like I know you already." She looked at Taylor, "Hi there."

"Hi, Shannon," Taylor smiled big. His mother cut her eyes at him too.

They all sat in the living room, Vivian's favorite space in the brick bungalow identical to most on the block. Taylor hated this room. The sofa and loveseat's plastic covers stuck to his legs in the summer and needed at least five minutes to warm up in the winter. It didn't bother him today though, not even the piece of torn plastic that stabbed at his bare thigh. He was in a dreamy state that trumped all other senses. He could only hear his mother and Simon in muted tones, but Shannon came in loud and clear. The breeze from the window behind the couch caught her hair ever so often, making it dance at the top of her shoulders. It was golden, similar to one of the Barbie dolls his little sister played with. She had blue eye shadow on her lids and cheeks that blushed rosy all the way to her ears. Looking at her, Taylor determined that some girls wear too much make-up and look horrible, and some wear too much very well.

"How did you two meet?" Vivian asked, obviously uncomfortable.

"She was at my friend Frankie's party. You remember him don't you, Taylor? The cat that thinks he's Bruce Lee."

"Yeah, I know who you're talking about," Taylor laughed.

Vivian didn't. She sat across from them like a stone, eyeing her favorite nephew stroke the girl's arm.

"Is that my favorite pie I smell, Auntie?" Simon turned to Shannon, "She makes the best pies in Chicago."

Vivian looked at Shannon, ignoring Simon's efforts to butter her up, and with all of the courtesy she could muster asked, "Would you like some pie?"

"Sure, that'd be great," Shannon said.

Taylor was glad his mother went to the kitchen—she was embarrassing. At least now he was free to admire Shannon without her watchful eye. The south side of Chicago didn't present much opportunity to socialize with whites, other than the few teachers at school. Shannon sure didn't look like Mrs. Kackmeyer, his homeroom teacher, whom he and his buddies called Mrs. Quackmeyer behind her back because she looked like a duck. (Quackmeyer became Cockmeyer if they were heard and sent to the principal's office.) He wanted to call those same friends and tell them he was sitting across from this chick who looked like Farrah Fawcett in the flesh!

"Taylor!" his mother called from the kitchen. "Come help me with the plates, please."

"Okay," he said. Damn it! He thought. Taylor took his time getting to the kitchen, hesitating at the door. He hadn't stepped two feet in before she turned to him and said, "Don't you come in here with no white girl, hear?"

Taylor knew all too well the back-story on how his mother felt about black men choosing white women. More and more of the athletes and professional men were passing up "quality black women" as his mother would say, for white girls. Simon was her dead sister's son. She'd practically raised him, so Taylor guessed it must have been a personal blow to her ego. She pulled the pie knife out of the drawer and pushed it shut with her hip—her classic "I'm pissed" move— a signal that he should keep quiet until she was finished blowing off steam. After she had started with, she didn't know what was wrong with our men, to knowing what was wrong with them—"They just want what they been told for two-hundred years that they can't have," then eventually getting around to how she was raised to treat everyone as a proper guest in her home, the lecture was over.

"Get the plates and forks and come on," she said.

They returned to the living room with her sweet potato pie, only to find Simon and Shannon nestled tightly together. Taylor thought that for sure they'd been kissing.

Shannon didn't like the pie, although her attempt at masking it was noteworthy. She scooted it around her plate—cut it into little pieces, but took very few bites.

"I've got to get ready for work," Vivian had had it. She nudged Taylor hard to break his fixed gaze on Shannon. "Make sure you lock up when they leave."

"Uh huh,—Yes, ma'am," Taylor said, barely taking his eyes off the girl.

"It was nice meeting you," Shannon said, perky.

"Uhmmm." Was all Vivian could force in return.

Once Vivian left the room, Simon grinned. "Man, ain't she fine?"

Taylor didn't answer, but it was obvious he agreed. His cousin leaned in and kissed her glossy lips. Taylor was just a boy, so the kiss was enough to do him in. Simon winked at Taylor and pulled her mouth open with his thumb—sliding his tongue in and out of her mouth until she giggled and pulled away.

"Stop it," Shannon said halfhearted and wiped the excess lip-gloss from around the outer corners of her mouth.

"You don't want me to stop," Simon cooed and then he grinned back at Taylor, "White girls are what's happening now, man. They treat you right."

Shannon blushed and Taylor watched his cousin pull her to him again. The adolescent bulge in his pants remained most of their visit. After they left, Taylor went into the bathroom, locked the door and made himself feel better.

From then on, neither Denise, the girl he'd had a crush on since the fourth grade, nor any other black girl would turn his head. Taylor didn't even go to his own prom. However, he did make sure his grades were good enough to get a full scholarship to Michigan State University.

Halloween

Ronald Reagan was well into his Presidency and Taylor was well on his way to receiving his B.A. from Michigan State. East Lansing allowed Taylor the freedom to pursue what he wanted. And he didn't have much trouble finding white girls who were oh-too-happy to try out what their father's feared.

He had settled on Penny, a steel blue eyed bleached blond from Florida. She was smart, a journalism major with a minor in theatre. Taylor had dated better looking girls than Penny, but she had the kind of girl-next-door charm that gave her an advantage. People liked her. She was well known on campus as the girl that headed lofty campus organizations, as well as the girl that could out drink a guy, and still walk out of the party in full control. They met at a young democrats rally and had been together ever since.

"You could just stay with me you know," Taylor suggested to Penny.

"It's better that I stay on campus."

"You're going to have to tell your parents about us when we're married," he half-joked. It was a frequent topic between the two of them.

"I know, and I will. Soon." She wrapped her arms around his waist from behind. "Just let me get through this last year, and we'll tell them . . . together."

Taylor wondered how they were going to have any privacy with Penny moving back into the dorms. After a year and a half of dating, she had decided to give up her apartment and become a resident advisor. They were seniors and had passed the neophyte stages of loud music and drinking throughout the night, so Taylor wasn't crazy about the idea. But Penny moving back to the dorm wasn't as bad as he'd anticipated. The floor was relatively quiet when he stopped by. In fact, Taylor studied there quite often.

"So where is this mysterious next door neighbor of yours?" Taylor asked, peering through the bathroom door that connected Penny to her suitemate.

"I don't know. She studies a lot."

"A freshman studying—I'd have to see that to believe it. She's probably curled up with some frat boy being fresh meat right now."

Penny grabbed a handful of the Mickey D's fries that she and Taylor shared. "She's not a freshman. She's a transfer student from some black school in the south."

"Any new girl, transfer student or otherwise still classifies as fresh meat," Taylor said.

She wedged a fry into his mouth. "Not for you, Mister."

November First, Taylor woke to an immobilizing headache. Halloween was a big thing to Penny, and the two of them had dressed up as Apollonia and Prince. Taylor hadn't partied like that in a long time—mixing beer and cheap wine. He ended up crashing at Penny's, which was somewhat tricky considering she was the resident advisor and was supposed to be setting an example.

Penny had made a quick run for coffee, apparently unaffected by the alcohol—Taylor didn't know how she did it. He found the purple pants to his costume on the floor next to him and crept slowly out of bed. Foreseeing how ridiculous he was going to look leaving her dorm later on made him chuckle.

"Prince, my brother, a white ruffled shirt on a straight black man is a hard feat to pull off."

If he left now, he could bypass the redundant commentary he was sure he'd hear all the way back to his apartment. However, that would take energy he just didn't have this morning. Aside from the room still making a slight orbit, his head felt like a truck had rolled over it. He decided to stick around and wait for last night's spirits to wear off. Luckily, his notes on foreign policy were still there from a couple of days ago. After a sobering cup of coffee, he'd hunker down and get to work on his paper.

First, he heard the water run in the bathroom, then a quiet knock on Penny's bathroom door.

"Penny, would you give me eight quarters for two dollars?" The voice called from the other side.

Taylor went to the door and yelled back, "Penny went out for a minute. She'll be right back."

"Oh, —I'll come back later," the girl stammered quickly, as if hearing a man's voice so early in the morning had startled her.

"No, it's no problem. She'll be back in about ten minutes. If you want I can check to see if Penny has any change and—" Taylor heard the girl's door shut and lock before he could finish. "Okay, suit yourself." He shrugged his shoulders and went back to his notes.

By the time Penny returned, he was well into typing his paper. "Man, it's cold out there," Penny said. She put the coffee down and rubbed her hands together. "It was warm last night."

"California's calling us, babe," Taylor said.

"I can't wait." She pressed her cold lips to his and handed him a cup of Dunkin' Donuts coffee.

"Thanks for making the coffee run. You know you didn't have to."

"I know, but it felt kind of good to get out and get some fresh air." She nudged him. "It might have done you some good, too."

"Me no like the cold," he joked, "Especially when I'm hung over." He pulled the plastic lid back on his coffee and sipped. "I'm making a mental note to myself though, from now on, I only drink the best or nothing at all."

"Awwh, you're no fun."

"Just because you have an iron stomach. . . . Oh, your suitemate asked if you had any quarters. I tried to tell her you'd be right back, but she took off."

"Is she still home?" Penny passed through the bathroom before he could answer and yelled, "Rose, I'm back if you want some quarters!" A moment later Rose walked in. "I think I have it. Just hold on." Penny pulled a tin box out of the closet and rummaged through it. "I did laundry last Friday, but I thought I'd put some more change in here. . . ."

"If you don't that's okay, I'll go over to Spartan Grocer or something and get change. I should've stopped off yesterday and got it."

"Wait a minute. I've got some in my coat pocket." Penny dug deep inside the pockets of her bomber, pulling out a handful of coins. "Here's five quarters . . . Taylor?"

He deliberately hadn't even looked up at the girl. She had her chance earlier. He probably did have a few quarters in his pocket, but he wasn't about to go out of his way to look unless he was asked.

"Honey, this is Rose."

"Hi."

"Hi," Taylor said looking up at her coolly. His double take took him by surprise. There was a small chance that she hadn't noticed—more importantly, that Penny hadn't.

"Do you have any quarters?" Penny was holding out a dollar bill.

"Hm?" He'd heard her, but he was attempting to make time stand still.

"Change?"

"Oh." Taylor reached in his pocket. A sudden awareness of his attire caused a slight panic. He hoped Rose knew it was a costume and thanked God he didn't have on the purple jacket. "I think you took the last of it to get the coffee."

"Sorry. I thought I had a lot more in here." Penny went back to rummaging through the nickels and dimes in the tin box.

Taylor forced himself to look back at his work, pretending to read his notes while Penny looked in another coat pocket, and then the bottom of her purse. Her overly helpful nature bugged him at times. This wasn't one of them. Holding the notes up to hide his face worked as a good decoy, careful not to block his view of the mirror reflecting the two girls—his eyes fixed on the one. Rose. Her name twinkled in his head.

If looks could kill, then he was dead and happy for it. Taylor could appreciate a good-looking black woman. What man couldn't? He would argue that he had great admiration for his grandmother, his two sisters, his mother. He just had another preference. But Rose was Helen of Troy, Cleopatra, Isis, Nefertiti, Aphrodite, Robin Givens and Vanity and Lisa Bonet all rolled into one—Caramel fine! A brandy he'd love to take a few sips of sweat from—who was he kidding, a girl this beautiful didn't sweat and didn't shit. He was sure of it. Her eyes big and clear, like Bambi's. Bambi was actually what came to his mind. No human had eyes like that! Looking at her lips, all he could think of was Mrs. Quackmeyer to defuse the bulge in his purple suede pants. The paintings in art appreciation had nothing on her. Rose's beauty was infinite—absolute. He was lost in it.

"This is enough quarters to get started, Penny." Rose said, pocketing the change. "Nice meeting you."

"You, too," Taylor said back to her. He was going for detached but courteous, and except for his uncontrollable leg jiggle under Penny's desk, he was putting up a good front. Had she seen him fidget in his chair? Had she spotted him staring at her? Had she noticed his lips quiver when he said "You, too"? He stole one last glance at her before she passed back through the door. *Her ass—oh-my-God!* He sensed a hurricane coming. Rose. He said one more time in his head.

He was sick.

In the weeks that followed, Taylor hoped his crush on Rose would fade. Penny went home to Florida for Christmas, and he went back to Chicago. He busied himself with interviews and plans to graduate in the new year. His future was with Penny, he convinced himself. They were getting married and moving to L.A. He needed to keep his eye on the prize. But every time he visited Penny, hopes of seeing Rose remained. She was under his skin now, burrowing deep.

What disturbed him most was that Rose seemed completely disinterested. She never gave any extra conversation or attention other than what was appropriate for the task. She smiled politely when he cracked a joke or helped her carry a heavy box up the stairs. She answered his many questions about the differences between Spelman College and Michigan State, how her dad got tenure, why she transferred.

Taylor couldn't figure out if the lukewarm conversations between them were intentional on her part, or if it was just her nature in general. He thought himself to be outgoing and articulate. He was well liked around campus. He kept his slim frame in shape; fifty push-ups a day required to be considered slim but built, rather than just tall and skinny. His ebony skin had a pleasing glow that emphasized his firm features. He had white teeth and clear bright eyes. He wasn't vain, just convinced that he was on the better side of passable. If only Rose would notice. He hadn't thought it through enough to know what he would do if she did.

Had Taylor given into Penny's craving for a bacon burger, they would have gone to Clara's Restaurant for the best charbroiled patty in town. But Clara's was all the way down by the Capital. He wasn't in the mood for a trek down Michigan Avenue, so he convinced Penny that La Rana Verde was the way to go. It was his desire for Mexican, a wet burrito with beans and rice to be specific, that gave the two of them a swift kick down the road to the end of their relationship.

Penny pinched Taylor's butt at the restaurant door. "You're looking pretty good tonight."

He grabbed her hand and opened the door for her. "Are we going to have a little under the table action this evening?" He winked at her.

"Nope, that's it," Penny grinned quickly before the waiter greeted them. They were just about to sit down in a cozy little booth, when they caught sight of Rose at a table across from them.

"Hi, Rose," Penny said.

"Hey."

Rose's date extended his hand to Taylor. "Dallas," he said.

Taylor introduced himself and waved to Rose. The waitress stood next to them with the napkins and silverware in her hands while they greeted one another.

Rose turned to Dallas, "Is it okay if they sit with us?"

"Uh, I guess—yeah. Of course."

Taylor could tell the "of course" was for Rose's ears. He'd seen him around: on the football field, in the paper.

"Want to?" Penny asked.

Taylor flipped his hands up, "Why not?"

He would have preferred to say that the two of them just wanted to have a quiet evening alone, but thank you—anything to dodge the torture he was about to endure. But Penny had posed the question as if it had already been decided.

"We're leaving for Florida next Saturday," Penny explained about their plans to visit her family for the first time.

"Are you two gonna be alright down there?" Dallas asked.

"It's not that bad. We're near Tampa, so people are used to seeing interracial couples because of the army base nearby."

"Yeah, but we're not in the military," Taylor warned.

"You better sign up, my man," Dallas joked.

"My parents and everyone else is going to love you just like I do." Penny smiled and leaned into him. Taylor kissed her hand. It was all he could think of to do, for he was a mess.

She ordered the taco and quesadilla platter. She wiped her mouth after every bite. She didn't take a sip of her coke with lemon until after she'd finished her meal. She ate all of the yellow rice on the side. Penny continued with her take on Florida, but this table was all about Rose. Taylor glanced at her neck and wondered how she smelled up close. He simply couldn't keep his eyes off of her. Dallas must have taken notice, because he suddenly put his arms around her. Rose and Penny were unaware, and it appeared that Dallas wanted to keep it that way. Nonetheless, he let Taylor know what was what with a glance. And just to rub it in, he played with her shoulder length strands of brilliant black curls. Then he leaned in closer and whispered something in her ear that made her blush. Touchdown! Taylor's whole body ached with jealousy. He imagined the many ways he could kill the guy, tortured between wanting the night to end, and never wanting it to.

He was going insane.

Spring

Taylor graduated and was happy to finally have his B.A. Kinko's popped up all over the country and everyone scrambled to learn how to use a Macintosh or PC. Taylor wanted to start a computer consulting firm to tap into this new business environment. Penny, preoccupied with making plans to move to California and sending out tapes for her budding broadcasting career had been in and out of town for the last couple of weeks. They never made it to Florida that Saturday, or any weekend after that. They both knew they were falling apart. They just didn't know how to end it. Then at a mutual friend's graduation party, Penny pulled Taylor into the kitchen.

"Does she know?" Penny asked. She looked at him dead on.

Taylor thought about the many things he could say: How it just happened, and that he didn't want to hurt her, that he would always care about her. "No, not yet," was all that he could come up with. He wanted to crawl under a rock.

Penny nodded her head as if to confirm what she already knew. She stared at him, her arms crossed. Taylor started to move toward her. "Don't." Penny put up her hand and started to cry, but chuckle at the same time. "If I hadn't asked, would you have gone to California with me? Married me?"

Taylor moved in closer. "Penny—"

"I said don't!" Just then, a fellow graduate walked in, took one look at them and exited quickly. After what should have been emotional attacks, and tactical plots of how they could work things out instead of dead silence, Penny finally said, "I'm going to California." Her eyes filled again. "Looks like you're headed somewhere else."

Loving Rose was clear and easy for Taylor. For Rose, love didn't come as quickly. She and her parents were in front of her dorm packing her things into the back seat of the car. Taylor wasn't going to let Rose slip away without letting her know how he felt.

"I Love you, Rose. . . . I love you." Taylor said again, as if saying it twice would somehow give the words more weight.

Rose stopped packing and stared at him. So did her parents.

"We're going inside and grab the last of the boxes, Rose." Rueben said. He put his arm around Violet to signal that they needed some privacy. Violet went along, but took a long look back at the two of them.

"You're crazy," Rose said once they were alone.

"Marry me."

"What! You *are* crazy. Don't you think you ought to talk this over with Penny first?"

"I already did. You and I need to talk now. I know you know how I feel about you. You had to have felt it."

"Yeah, it was kind of obvious." She looked at him for a moment and then shook her head. "I can't deal with this right now." She tried to move away from him but he cornered her.

"Then when? When can we talk, Rose? Give me your home number so I can explain."

"Taylor."

"Please, Rose." Her parents headed toward the car again. "Give me a chance," he whispered.

Rose looked at Rueben. He shrugged his shoulders—it was up to her.

She tore off a piece of a paper bag and wrote down her number. "Here," she said and slid into the back seat. Rueben started up the car and drove off.

"I love you, Rose!" Taylor yelled.

Rose didn't look back.

There were already three messages from Taylor on the answering machine when they arrived home. Rose didn't call back the first or the second night.

"You're going to have to pick up this phone," Reuben said on the third day of endless calls.

"He was going with my suitemate, Dad."

"He's obviously not going with her now is he?"

The phone began to ring again. Reuben stared at her, "Girl, if you don't pick up this phone!"

"He likes white girls!"

Reuben's eyes widened along with his mouth.

"You know I didn't mean that. I don't care if Penny's blue with pink polka dots."

"I'm glad you cleared that up," said Reuben. "We raised you better than that."

The phone stopped ringing.

"It's just awkward, Dad. She was my suitemate."

"*Was* your suitemate. Relationships take all kinds of turns, baby. Ask your mother about that. Now we are tired of taking all of these long messages he wants to leave." The phone started up again. "I'm a professor, not your personal secretary." Rose gave him a face as he picked up the ringing phone. "Hello. . . hold on. She's right here." He covered his hand over the receiver. "I guarantee that this man wants you. Don't be afraid to see if you want him." He handed Rose the phone.

They were on the line for two hours that night, and four the next. Taylor had waited three weeks for a kiss—Rose wanted to be sure.

It was worth the wait.

He met Rose's family more formally two weeks after that kiss, and revolved the rest of the summer around getting his consulting company off the ground, and weekend trips to East Lansing to see Rose. Every time he saw her, his determination to have her belong to him deepened. He talked about Chicago, and the art scene and how his business was taking off there. He spoke often about how much he wanted her to come and visit, but Rose resisted. They hadn't been intimate yet, a form of torment Taylor was sure was the cause of his migraines. If he could just get her to come to Chicago—his loft—his environment, then he could show her how much he wanted her in his life—in his bed.

Thanksgiving

"Ms. Crane, everything was wonderful."

It was Thanksgiving and Vivian having heard that Rose was "one of ours" wasn't going to miss her chance to pull out all the stops. Taylor was shocked to see so many relatives— some he hadn't seen in years. Vivian buzzed around the room introducing Rose to his two sisters, Katrina and Jackie, Great Aunt Barbara and her third husband Randall, Grandma Lil, old lady Kelly from next door, and his cousin Simon.

Simon pulled Taylor aside and gave him a big hug. He'd replaced his massive afro with a jerry curl that dripped onto his red leather jacket.

"You're gonna get jerry curl juice on me!" Taylor joked. "*Beat it . . . Beat it.*" He did the classic Michael Jackson move.

Simon crossed his arms, "You know this jacket is fly, man." He turned his attention to Rose across the room. "Ummmmmum," he moaned. "You did real good."

"Don't look at my lady like that."

"Respect Cuz, respect, but she fine as hell!"

Taylor grinned, proud.

"You able to handle all that?"

Taylor gave him a look. "Come on, it's time to eat."

Taylor stuffed himself on turkey, ham, macaroni and cheese, greens, dressing, butter beans, cranberry sauce, spaghetti and bread. Breadcrumb remains scattered across his plate. Rose did a pretty good job of keeping up with him.

"You out-did yourself, Mom."

"I haven't seen you eat like that in a long time. She looked at Rose. "Must be the company you're keeping, got your appetite all worked up."

Taylor grinned at Rose, "Must be."

Vivian was beside herself. She asked Taylor's two sisters with a smile spread wide across her face, "Have you ever seen him this happy, girls?"

"No, Momma. I have never seen Taylor this happy," the eldest sister, Jackie teased in a perfect drone-like voice.

"Silly girl." Vivian still called them girls even though they were eighteen and twenty-one years old. "Come help me get the pies."

Taylor swore he saw his mother skip to the kitchen.

"She's just glad she didn't have to serve pumpkin pie," joked Katrina, the youngest.

Silence resonated around the table for a few seconds, and then they all broke out in laughter, including Taylor. It was visibly clear that there was a sense of relief that Rose had given the family. She even ate all of her sweet potato pie and asked for seconds! Taylor had never seen his mother perform so. He couldn't help but feel good about it.

"You come back anytime, okay?" Vivian said. Her arms laced around Rose like she was already part of the family. "I don't know why you all are staying downtown. We got plenty of room right here."

"I want to show her around Chicago. It's the holiday season, Mom."

Taylor didn't dare tell Vivian what he had in store for Rose. He'd planned everything carefully. They roomed at the Westin Hotel in the heart of Chicago, where he had flowers and candy waiting, along with a view of the Chicago River. Candlelight and fondue at Geja's Café for dinner. Later, he took her on the no-fail romantic horse and buggy ride around downtown. Taylor wasn't about to take a chance at being original—he was betting on the sure thing.

"You like the city, Rose?"

"I love it! Look at all the lights."

"Yeah, they're really something." He had his eyes on her not the lights. "Want to get off and get some popcorn?"

"Sounds good."

"Let me pay the guy and we'll get off at the next corner." He reached into his pocket and pulled out the small robin's egg blue box. "I've loved you for a long time, Rose. I'm at my best when I'm with you. Marry me." He slid the full carat marquise diamond onto her finger. "Loving me is all I'll ever ask of you. You're perfect, you're beautiful, you're smart, and you make me happy, Rose. You make—"

Rose put her finger up to his mouth. "I'll marry you."

He kissed her long enough to make a couple of onlooker's cheer. Then they walked along Michigan Avenue, eating popcorn until they reached the hotel.

The following morning, Taylor watched Rose sleep. Despite the cold outside, the room itself was warm, and Rose had pushed the blankets down leaving her bare to the waist. He lifted the sheet and smiled, realizing that at some point in the night she'd put her panties back on. It was a night of firsts—her first time, and his first time with a black woman. He looked at the ring on her finger he had saved for since that first two hour call. Her hair fell across her mouth. He pushed away her soft curls and gently kissed the breast of the woman he loved before lying back with his hands behind his head. It was going to be a good life.

Happiness?

Rose moved to Chicago and landed her first job as an assistant to an art dealer. With Taylor's business taking off so quickly, they were able to purchase the five bedroom, three and a half bath home in Olympia Fields that Rose had stumbled upon while delivering a piece of art. The diverse, upscale neighborhood was immaculate—the perfect place to raise a family. The house needed some updating on the inside, but by the time Rose finished putting her artistic spin on the décor, it looked like something out of a magazine. Taylor worked hard on his consulting business and soon partnered with a couple of buddies from college.

"Rose, this house is gorgeous," Beverly said. She and Taylor's other partner's wife, Laura, couldn't say enough about the new home.

"Thanks, I've been working hard on it." Rose refilled their wine glasses.

"You're lucky you have a wife that can do all of this," Charles said. He winked at his wife Beverly. "Decorators are death to the checkbook."

"My mother always said, 'Keep a man's pockets light and there'll be no room for trouble,'" Beverly explained.

"This one thinks a penny earned is a penny spent." Taylor's other partner Brian joked.

"Pennies! What's that?" Laura said and the three women clicked their wine glasses together in laughter.

Taylor listened to his business partners joke about their wives' spending habits and cooking skills, while at the same time praising Rose in comparison. He was annoyed with them and everyone else Rose met. He had heard too many times how lucky he was to have her, and now it was like a mosquito buzzing at his ear. Yes, dinner was always there when he came home. Laundry never piled up. No fuzz balls in the corner when he closed the bathroom door. How Rose was able to work a full time job as an art dealer (she was no longer just an assistant), and managed to finish the last of her credits at DePaul to graduate was unbelievable to him. He glanced at Rose in the huddle with the other two women; his partners stood listening nearby, as captured by Rose as their wives.

She did know how to work a room.

When Rose was on, she was on. It didn't matter that within their circles, most of the time she was the only black woman in the room. Rose had a knack for making everyone feel instantly comfortable with her. A calm confidence resonated in conversations from politics to gardening. They'd forget about color when she was around, or at least think about it differently. She and Taylor were the perfect "black friends" and Rose did it without even trying. But Taylor was always aware that the invites to North Shore parties, to the Hamptons, to golf outings were mainly for Rose's sake. If it weren't for her, he probably wouldn't even be standing in his own living room with Brian and Charles and their wives, despite them being partners.

He wasn't jealous of Rose. He just wanted a little of that star power shined his way instead of being treated like an afterthought, someone she would get to when there was no one else around. It was as if she had told a joke and let everyone in on the punch line but him. Rose loved him—he knew it. He loved her; he knew that, too. At thirty-three, he had the perfect life, and the perfect wife—a real 'super-woman'. There were no big arguments between them like some of the other married couples he knew. He just couldn't figure out why he wasn't happy. He watched Rose throw her head back in laughter, charming the hell out of the four of them. It came to him that he was standing away from the group, alone and on the outside.

"Did you need something, honey?" Rose asked.

"Uh, no. I just . . . need to make a quick phone call," Taylor said and headed toward the kitchen.

"You'd better hurry back or I'm taking Rose home with me," Brian joked.

"Not that kind of party, Brian." Taylor shot back. They all laughed while Taylor went to the kitchen and pulled out a bottle of cognac. He poured himself a full glass and drank it alone.

When Rose lost their first child, the doctor told them that it happened sometimes with the first pregnancy. Taylor remembered her saying that she would be extra careful the next time, as if it were her fault. When she lost the second child five months in, things changed rapidly between them. The second was a boy, and Taylor had visions of watching him play little league and throwing a football with him in the front yard. He would be nothing like his father—he was going to be there to raise him to be a man. He was as heartbroken as Rose, but Taylor knew her sorrow was more important. She was the one who needed nurturing.

He tried not to think about the "what ifs". What if it was always going to be just the two of them? What if there wasn't going to be a big family around the dinner table on the holidays. What if there would be no packing the car full with groceries—no juice boxes, no Fruit Roll-Ups. He tried to convince himself that Rose would be enough. But he'd done all of this: a successful business, a fabulous home, a wife whom he was sure would make a good mother, and for what? He wanted kids—a family.

By the summer of 1990, Rose and Taylor had been married for five years. Sex was all about taking temperatures, charting ovulation, and trying to make another child whom Rose could carry to term. She practically tackled Taylor as soon as he walked in the door, for which he was a willing victim the first two months. It brought the spark back for a while. But after six months of trying, they were right back where they'd started—childless. Eventually, sex with Rose became a chore.

Arguments over nothing erupted frequently. Taylor felt like he was on pins and needles around her most of the time. There was no one thing you could point to that could explain the growing distance between them. It just was. Resentment and doubt grew until Taylor could no longer lie to himself. Rose's flaw was worse than any aesthetic deficiency in other women. At least they could accomplish the one thing that made them women. For all of her perfection, Rose couldn't give him a child. He knew it was irrational.

It didn't matter.

Taylor's Delight

The flight home from Texas had Taylor waiting an additional forty-five minutes while it taxied in line at O'Hare. He needed to stretch his legs and grab a quick bite to eat before driving home to Olympia Fields. The idea of French fries and a burger sitting on his stomach all the way home kept him away from fast food, so when he saw the small bar just a few blocks off the expressway, he thought he'd take a chance. The place was practically empty, dark but not uninviting, and smelled of hot wings and corned beef. He took a seat at the bar.

"What'll you have?" The waitress had a look that said she was ready to go home.

"Do you have a menu?"

She rolled her eyes. "No. We have hot, barbecue, and teriyaki wings, or a beef sandwich. Take your pick."

Taylor wondered what smelled like corned beef. "I'll just have the sandwich."

"To drink?"

"Bud Lite."

"Harry, a Bud Lite!" the waitress called to the bartender.

He wanted a Lowenbrau, but he didn't want to look like a total yuppie, although his Rolex and lamb leather jacket were dead giveaways. A couple of losers were probably checking out his BMW right now. The Bud was surprisingly refreshing. He'd kept his college promise to himself to drink only the best. At home, his bar was stocked with Grey Goose, and Gentleman Jack. His wine cellar housed bottles from Sonoma Valley, to France, to Australia. The beer reminded him of days when his future was still unknown but promising.

A few barstools away sat two women with empty shot glasses in front of them. Taylor nodded his head to them and looked up at the TV in the corner. The bar was still quite bare, early evening, around six, so the news was on with coverage of Ross Perot announcing that he would run as an independent.

One of the women said, "Idiot! He's going to fuck up the Democrats."

Taylor couldn't help but smile, surprised that the beautiful one of the two had a mouth on her. He hadn't realized he was staring until she caught him looking at her. She whispered something to the other woman and laughed in an unsettling way that was both demeaning and enticing at the same time. The pretty one glanced at him again, and the process started all over.

Looking.

Whispering.

Laughing.

This went on for a couple of minutes.

"What's so funny?" Asked Taylor, but instantly thought that he should have just paid for his sandwich and left.

"You don't know?"

"No, I don't."

"You really don't know why we're laughing?" The pretty one was doing all of the talking.

"No, but you'll have to cut me some slack. I've been traveling all day; I'm a little slow right now." He rested his head on his hand and leaned toward her. "So why don't you tell *me*. . . . I could use a good laugh."

"That's all you could use?" The attractive woman winked.

It had been a long time since Taylor blushed. He told himself this was harmless. The waitress returned with his sandwich, catching him off guard. A guilty rush soared through his body, even though he hadn't done anything. He cleared his throat and turned his barstool forward, away from the two women.

"Where is your restroom?" The other woman asked the bartender, leaving Taylor at the bar alone with the brunette beauty.

He took three bites of his sandwich before he looked her way again. She smiled back at him. He thought of *Lost in Space* where the robot says, "Warning! Warning!" Deciding to ignore the alarms going off in his head, he asked, "I don't know where I'm going with this, but are you going to tell me what was so funny?"

"Are you sure you want to know?"

Taylor peeped at her long legs crossed at the thigh, which forced her already short skirt even higher "I'm sure," he lied. Her short dark hair swept across one eye. He wanted to move it back out of her face.

"My friend and I were guessing that you must be getting quite a bit at home because you haven't noticed me."

"Oh, I noticed you," Taylor grinned, the beer giving him nerve. "A man would have to be blind not to notice you. Where are you from?"

"Croatia."

"You have a beautiful accent, Miss Croatia," he said, leaning forward, "What's your name beauty?"

"Mira, and you still haven't noticed me."

"You have my full attention, Mira." *It's just a little flirting.*

"Do I?" The woman swiveled back and forth in her seat.

Taylor was enjoying himself too much to leave. He couldn't put his finger on why he was so attracted to her, maybe because she reminded him of a foreign spy in one of those old movies. Maybe because she had lips that looked like they could do all kinds of tricks. He'd never done this before—at least not as a married man. Still, leaving was out of the question.

Mira stopped swiveling and parked her chair directly in front of him uncrossing her legs slightly wider than was proper. Taylor gaped. "You seem to have forgotten something."

"Didn't see any need to wear any."

"I don't either," Taylor said and swiveled his barstool back toward her so that he sat directly in front of her. He hadn't come across a woman this bold since college. And it had been years since he'd had this much excitement. "Get her another one of whatever she's drinking," he said to the bartender.

"Nope, I'm finished drinking for the night." The woman grabbed her coat.

Taylor couldn't help but to feel a little relieved that she'd just been toying with him. She'd stopped this from going any further; before any real damage was done. He'd already chalked it up to the beer and the ambiance as she headed toward the door.

Mira looked back at him as if she'd thought he was behind her the whole time. "You coming?"

Taylor was acting on the anticipation of the hard, intentioned muscle between his legs. They drove their own cars to the hotel nearby, and went up to the room separately. He had a plan in his head on how things would progress, but that plan dissolved not two minutes after they entered the room. Mira put her purse down on the table and leaned against the dresser facing Taylor—waiting. Taylor slinked up to her and tried to kiss her, but she gave him a hard shove against his chest. It startled him. No woman had ever done that to him. He grinned and moved back in. Smack! She hit him hard across the face.

"You crazy. . . " Before he finished he'd already roughly pulled her hands behind her back and wrestled her to the bed. Once he had her hands pinned over her head, his kiss was harsh—brutal, yet a warm sensation surged through his entire body. It was quick, fast, and to the point. No romance, no niceties. Mira was far less inhibited than Rose and pushed the limits of sexual pleasure, which enchanted Taylor to an unbelievable level of desire that he didn't know existed within him. He had never experienced that kind of passion. She coached and coaxed him into a raw, primal heat that was refreshingly unrefined. He'd been uptight and synthetic most of his adult life. It was a night of release. On the way home, he resolved that he would see her again.

Did he feel remorse—guilt? Yes, but only after—always after, for when he was with Mira, he was with her all the way. Mira's imagination fueled their encounters. She had skillfully drawn him in, opening a Pandora's Box that he saw no need to close. She liked it when he restrained her—arms pulled back and the knots tied tight at her wrists. Taylor was surprised at how easy it was for him to indulge her. He told himself that he was doing it for her because she liked it, but in the innermost part of him, he knew that what they did together was for him too. She made him feel like a man, like he was in control. With Mira, he forgot about Rose and the children he didn't have, and *driving while black*, and the looks on his client's faces when they met him for the first time—after they'd realized the person on the other end of the line wasn't white. He would clear his mind of all of the uncontrollable details of the outside world. With Mira, he had the power. He was leading two lives. This one with an anticipated fervor he could hardly contain.

Mira was no low budget tramp. She was a member of Mensa and employed with a leading marketing firm in Chicago. Why she was in the bar that night, why she had chosen him, Taylor didn't know and didn't ask. She was captivating, and he had never met anyone like her. He convinced himself that she was what he needed.

The irony of Taylor's infidelity was that Mira eased some of the pressure between him and Rose. Rose was his safe haven after dipping into the most provocative sexual fantasies with Mira. He cleansed himself in his wife's arms and after five months, Rose was pregnant again.

This time she took her doctor's advice and had complete bed rest the remaining three months. Taylor was elated that it looked like she would make it to term and catered to her every whim. Rose slept most of the time and Taylor made sure she was comfortable—tucking her in and watching her go to sleep. She was used to Taylor working late, never questioning him about leaving her once or twice a week to go back to the office. He was meticulous about his whereabouts, the time he would return, and followed those plans to the letter, carefully executing each rendezvous so that there would be no marks and no clues.

It was absolute euphoria with Mira. However, Taylor made it crystal clear to her that Rose meant the world to him and that he would never leave her. If Rose so much as received a funny look from across the street from her, he threatened to not only end the relationship, but also to make her life a living hell.

"Yes, Daddy," Mira had whispered in his ear then bit it hard, but careful, ever mindful of the no traces rule.

Doe Eyes

The weather report forecasted only two to three inches of snow the night Rose went into labor. However, there was already five inches on the ground, and it was still coming down by the time they arrived at the hospital. At six-forty-seven a.m., after ten hours and fourteen minutes, Dahlia Marie Crane was born: five pounds, two ounces. She was frail, with a head full of curly black hair that framed her round little face. She had big, doe-like eyes, espresso brown like her mother's, and lips that formed the perfect little pout.

Something happened to Taylor that night. An overwhelming feeling of remorse, responsibility and hope combined. Seeing Rose with the baby—his beautiful little girl, made him feel sheepish for being so proud.

"You want to hold her?" Rose raised the baby to Taylor.

He choked up. "No you . . . you're doing fine."

Rose looked at him for a long moment. Taylor started to cry freely.

"Will you lay here with me?" Rose asked. Her eyes filled too.

He couldn't speak so he nodded.

She snuggled Dahlia next to her, leaving enough room for Taylor. He lay with Rose all night like that. Rose didn't sleep as many mothers did after giving birth. She talked about their marriage and the two of them as a couple, and what she wanted for their future.

He listened.

Two months had passed and Taylor was still seeing Mira, though she was beginning to want him to do things that even he began to question. Like the time she brought in another woman. Mira's head was buried at his groin when he felt a mouth on his chest.

"Who is that!" he jumped, wiggling madly until he could peep out of the bottom of the blindfold.

"My friend," Mira said and buried her head again.

"Don't you remember me?" She kissed his mouth hard.

Taylor pulled away, straining at the ties around his wrists. "No!" He knew he shouldn't have agreed to let Mira tie him up.

"She was with me at the bar, Taylor," Mira said as if they had met in church and he should have remembered. Mira slinked up to her friend and kissed her. "She just wants a taste of you, too."

The other woman ran her hand down the length of Taylor's stomach, quickly maneuvered a condom onto him and climbed on top. Before he could think, he was inside her. The tie on his left arm was loosening as the woman moved up and down. He knew he could wiggle free, untie the other arm and push her off.

But he didn't.

Later that night in bed with Rose, Taylor felt as if he were having an anxiety attack. He looked over at his wife sleeping soundly. He tried not to think about the "what ifs" again, but his mind was already ahead of him. *What if that other woman had herpes—or worse? What if she'd poked a hole in the condom and she was pregnant and wanted money! What if this was what the two of them planned all along? I don't even know the other woman's name. And what the hell am I really doing with Mira anyway?*

He lay awake thinking about the answers to all of the possibilities that could conclude from that night. He looked down at Rose again. Her hair had grown out from the pre-baby bob and fell over her face. It reminded him of their first morning together, when things were simple. He moved her hair away from her face to look at her. Then he kissed her lips softly. She smiled but didn't wake.

Happiness

"Taylor, can you get Dahlia for me?" Rose called. She was in the kitchen making a quiche as Violet had taught her.

"No problem," Taylor said. He didn't mind. It was Saturday, and he loved this time with Rose and the baby. Rose had gone back to being perfect. Not only was she preparing breakfast, but she was also reading the page of a new artist's bio on the other counter. She'd even returned to her pre-baby size six.

"There's my baby!" Rose cooed to Dahlia, pressing her lips to Dahlia's cheek and making quirky farty sounds with her mouth, which made the baby laugh. "I just have to finish this up and then I'll take her."

"No rush, I got her," Taylor rocked Dahlia back and forth so that Rose could finish her work. He was enjoying the moment with the three of them together, enjoying watching Rose.

"What?" Rose narrowed her eyes.

"Nothing. I just like looking at my wife." Rose smiled and poured the egg mixture on top of the cheese to finish off the quiche. "Mommy sure is pretty isn't she, Dahlia?" He watched Rose pop a piece of cheese into her mouth and then wipe her hands with the dishtowel tucked into her jeans. They were delicate, faultless hands that ran his home. He'd never really noticed in the six years of their marriage how beautiful she had made it. He loved the living room, decorated with finds from their honeymoon in Thailand, antiques from their travels to Europe, and the last minute Mexico trip. He thought about the family room; a warm and elegant place where family and friends gathered frequently. He looked around the inviting kitchen with the stone fireplace and sofa across from it. Rose had opened her own art gallery and had bought several pieces for their home. She had an eye for quality, whether it was from local or well-known artists. She even had a few of her own scattered in between; with every piece juxtaposed, visually complimenting another.

Taylor often heard Rose singing to Dahlia. He teased her about reading *Pride and Prejudice* and *Roots* to Dahlia so early, to which Rose countered, "It's never too early to develop a love for the classics."

She was a good mother, a good wife. She had done all of this with him barely noticing.

They were a family.

Breaking Mira

Taylor had it all planned.

He decided to spend one more afternoon with Mira at their usual spot, a hotel fifty miles out of Chicago in a sleepy little town not yet fully developed. He would explain to her that he was a family man now, and that she should get on with her life too. When he opened the door, she was sitting on the bed. Mira had a way of bringing him into the moment right away. Her leather bra with the cutouts around her nipples was cause for some concern, but the chain attached from the bottom of the bra that extended down between her crotchless leather panties blew him away. She lifted one leg up on the bed, running her hand down its length.

"Do you want some?"

Mira was too much for Taylor to resist. He had her— then again, trying to get every last drop of her. This was the very, very last time.

"Who do you think you are?" Mira screamed.

"I don't think I'm anybody. I'm just a man who won't ever leave his wife."

"I didn't ask you to leave your wife! I don't give a shit about her!"

"Well I do." He was trying to stay calm.

"Look, baby." She coiled her arms around his neck. "This is a good thing, who do you think is going to satisfy you the way I do?" She snuggled her lips against his neck. "Certainly not that boring thing you have at home."

"Things are better now." He pulled away from her and started to button his shirt.

"Why didn't you tell me this two hours ago, huh? Before you—"

"I don't know! I don't know." He rubbed his forehead. "I'm sorry."

"The sorriest!" Mira was out for blood.

With that, Taylor quickly dressed, half expecting a kick in the back as in the movie *Fatal Attraction*. Mira was still half dressed and barefoot as she followed him screaming obscenities all the way to the elevator—Glenn Close had nothing on her.

"Mira, stop it!" He kept trying to calm her.

"Go to hell!"

He was about to take the stairs when he heard the ding of the elevator and the doors opened. He hurried inside, hoping she wouldn't get on with him—there was no telling how far Mira would go. She stopped at the threshold when she saw the well-dressed elderly couple standing inside.

"What are *you* looking at?" She pulled the half-buttoned blouse over her shoulder and spit at the couple as the door closed.

Taylor had never been so humiliated, apologizing profusely to the couple as the man handed his lady a tissue.

When the couple stepped out of the elevator at the lobby, the man looked back at Taylor and said, "Learn to handle your trash."

In the car, Taylor thought about that man's words. Mira was well respected in her field. She was up for partner. She wasn't some trailer park tramp. And what did the man think of him? Did he think he was some drug dealer arguing with his whore? He would never put himself in that position again, and from now on, he was going to be the husband Rose deserved.

Fifty Miles

The fifty miles home seemed more like five hundred, shedding the memories of Mira and the hotel, and the last year with each purifying mile. It would take focus. He would have to let Rose in. Let her know when things weren't right between them. He had to stop behaving like a jealous little boy and start acting like the man Rose married. He had a good woman at home: beautiful, smart. She might not do summersaults in bed but that too could be worked on if he opened up. He had to admit it to himself—he had fucked things up. Now he had to muster up the courage to make it right again. He felt high with hope. He was coming home to Rose for the rest of his life.

The flashing lights stunned him when he turned into his neighborhood. His first thoughts were of the old woman with the weak heart who lived across from them. An ambulance had been there twice this year. But there was smoke in the distance and the overpowering smell of it became more pungent as he drove toward his street. He flew around the corner. Shrouds of smoke blended into the night sky, trucks and men with hoses surrounded his home ablaze.

His heart pushed against his chest as he jumped out of his car and ran. People clamored toward him, talking at him—all of them talking. He pulled away from Bill, his neighbor who had helped him with some investments earlier that year. Trish and her husband—he couldn't think of his name at that moment, were yelling something about Rose.

"Rose!" he called out.

A fireman tried to push him back, but Taylor pulled away and ran closer to the house. He prayed that the commotion was what was keeping Rose from coming to him—the haze from the smoke was too thick to recognize anyone. Then he saw the old woman with the heart condition holding Dahlia in her arms. Two firefighters held him back from his efforts to get to the house—to Rose—his thrashing so insistent that they all fell to the ground. They were saying something but he couldn't hear them. All Taylor could hear was his own voice screaming for Rose.

He could never love another woman. This was his punishment for being with Mira while Rose burned.

BOOK 4

Dahlia

Five days.

That's how long it had been since Dahlia and Violet talked about the past. The spark of a possible relationship with her grandmother had dimmed and she was alone again. She felt like an idiot for believing that someone cared enough about her to tell her about the family she knew nothing about. For the last five days, Violet had practically ignored her. Dahlia wanted to grab her by the shoulders and yell that you just don't do that to people. It had been a betrayal of her trust yet again. Violet was either off in the backyard or in the kitchen cooking something, reading—anything and everything that had nothing to do with her. It was the same feeling Dahlia had with her father, sharing the same space, but alone. Violet was at one end of the house and she was at the other—unless Violet had a sudden burst of energy and wanted her to help cook some laborious meal that included at least seventeen ingredients.

Dahlia looked out the kitchen window. Her grandmother was in the backyard with bags of dirt and shovels surrounding her.

"What are you doing?" Dahlia yelled.

"Why don't you come outside and find out?"

Ugghh, I hate it when people answer a question with another. She slipped on her Uggs and went out back. Dahlia caught the look her grandmother gave her.

"Yes, I'm wearing shorts with boots," Dahlia confirmed.

"Flip flops and boots, that's all I ever see you young ones in. Hand me that bag of bulbs over there."

Dahlia set the bag of bulbs down next to her grandmother and dusted off her hands. "Dad's going to kill you."

"Your daddy is the one who told me to use one of the signed checks he left to pay for all of this." Violet dug a hole with the shovel and dropped a couple of bulbs in.

"You did all of this by yourself?"

"If you'd stop acting like a stranger and come out of your room sometime, you'd have seen Silla's friend come by yesterday and clear it for me."

Dahlia pressed her lips, "I've been out of my room, and you're the one that's been acting strange."

Violet put the shovel down. "Strange how?"

"I don't know, just wandering around. Ignoring folks."

"Anything else?"

Dahlia looked at her. "Why?"

"Just answer me!"

"This is what I'm talking about. Strange." *Crazy old lady.* Dahlia looked at the fresh patches of dirt where Violet had already planted. "Why are you planting stuff in our back yard anyway? You won't be here to see it."

Violet dug another hole. "Slide me that other bag of dirt . . . trying to put some life back into this place."

"Well, you keep working on that. I'm going back in."

Violet took off her gardening gloves. "Daisies are over there. They don't need much but watering. They'll come up in late June or July. These bulbs are Casablanca Lilies—their scent is gonna knock you out midsummer. The ground cover is Violet—your state flower. Along the back, you can help plant the Dahlias. They'll grow like tall soldiers protecting the rest. And right here . . ." Pointing to the three small bushes already planted, ". . . are Rose bushes. You don't need to do much but bury some banana peels every once in a while and cut the spent petals."

Understanding what Violet had done, it hit Dahlia like a ton of bricks. "I'll kill them," she said, suddenly very uncomfortable.

"No you won't."

Standing in this refreshed space, fragments of a garden's past filled Dahlia's head: memories of playing with worms and making dirt mounds, feeling the earth sift through her fingers, and her grandmother's hands guiding her along, letting her carry the watering can to dowse each flower.

"Why'd you do this?"

"Because you needed something to hold on to. Something that you could touch and feel, smell. I did it for you."

Dahlia could feel herself warming toward her. She didn't want to give Violet a chance to hurt her again. "Seems like a lot of work."

"It's nothing. Here."

Dahlia took the bulb and stood over the hole Violet had already dug. She dropped the bulb in and scooted the dirt over it with her boots.

Violet handed her another. "A garden is like a person. It needs attention to thrive, to want to live. . . . At least until it can manage on its own. Then I guess you still have to tend to it every once in awhile. Prune its stems, or transplant it to a more adaptable location."

Dahlia didn't respond, but she guessed Violet was leading up to something by the troubled look on her face.

"Sometimes I feel like I'm in a forest, deep into its thickness. It's kind of peaceful, quiet-like, you know? The kind of place you dread packing for, but are glad to have finally arrived. . . . When the doctor told me that I'd begin forgetting things, I wanted to scream. Instead, I just laughed." Violet said as if they were already deep into the conversation.

Dahlia hadn't a clue. "Forgetting things?"

"Just listen. The doctor asked me if I'm alright." Violet closed her eyes. "I wanted to smack him. No, I'm not alright, I said. But I told him I got my mind today." Violet chuckled. "Even after I left his office, the giggles kept cropping up. All this time I've spent trying to not think about Miss Millie, your real grandfather Billy, what happened to your mother—with the onset of Alzheimer's disease I'm gonna lose it for good."

"Alzheimer's?"

Violet nodded.

Dahlia went silent, mulling it over. Then she said rather than asked, "You won't remember anyone."

"Don't know. Everybody's different. I'll just have to see when I get there. . . . That's why I planted this garden for you. I'm naming it Dahlia's Bouquet. Love it . . . take care of it . . . nurture it."

Dahlia's eyes watered, though she didn't know why. She barely knew this woman whom she was supposed to call her grandmother. She had learned not to care too deeply—her father taught her that. He gave her everything she asked for, but she felt that he was just buying time when he was home. It was hush money until he could leave again. She was sure she made him nervous, so she'd hide her feelings just so she wouldn't scare him off. But Violet was making her overemotional—making her dwell on things she didn't want to. Before she could think, before she could turn it off, the words spilled out of her mouth, "Tell me about my mother," she said. Violet sighed. "Tell me! All Dad's ever said about her was she was a good mother and that she loved me. I mean, I know she died in a fire, but that's it. That's all he's willing to tell me."

"Willing?" Violet said, astonished. "That man was gone. Gone I tell you." She sat down on the weathered bench under the maple tree. Dahlia sat down next to her and waited for more. "Me and Rueben took over for your father after your mother died. He just couldn't do it. He ended up in Brazil, left his company and all." Violet looked at the sky as if she needed something up there for support. "At first your instincts kick in and you do what you're supposed to. I took care of you without even thinking about it. I was on autopilot I guess—trying to raise you while Taylor was God knows where."

"Then you left," Dahlia said. "You made Dad come back to be with me because you didn't want me."

"Feelings creep up on you sometimes." Tears swelled in Violet's eyes. "I just couldn't do it anymore. . . . I just needed some time, too."

Dahlia stood up, crying. "You got plenty of that didn't you?" She ran into the house.

Violet wanted to go after her, she just didn't know how.

She was leaving tomorrow. That would be the end of it. Dahlia lay in the claw foot-soaking tub her father bought special to go with her bathroom's Victorian remodel. She thought about her grandmother's words. *I just couldn't do it anymore.*

She was glad she hadn't stuck around to listen to her excuses. She remembered that phone call as if it happened just yesterday. Dahlia was only six at the time and had come downstairs. She was playing with her new dollhouse and wanted to fill the tiny doll cups with water. She hadn't quite made it to the kitchen when she overheard her grandmother.

"I shouldn't have to do this by myself, she's your responsibility."

She remembered how it frightened her because Violet sounded like she was going to cry. "I can't take care of Dahlia anymore. . . . She reminds me too much of Rose."

Dahlia remembered wanting to cry, too. Her grandmother didn't want her anymore. She remembered the fear, and hiding, waiting to hear what would come next.

"You're going to have to take her."

Dahlia guessed that whoever was on the other line didn't want her either because her grandmother was trying too hard to convince them. Then she heard Violet say, "What do you mean you can't! You're her father!"

It frightened Dahlia to death because Violet had said that her father had a business out of the country, and that he could only come to see her ever so often. She'd told Dahlia that he loved her very much. Lies, all lies. Hiding outside of the kitchen, she'd heard what no child should hear, that neither her grandmother nor her father wanted her. That was the only reason Dahlia wanted to know more about her mother—because maybe she had.

The last of the water filtered through the drain before Dahlia stepped out of the tub. Once in her bedroom, she picked up the French talcum powder and spread it over her naked skin. The smooth consistency felt cool against her shoulders. She leaned back on her bed and closed her eyes—taking deep breaths. Self-pity was the last thing she wanted to feel. She wanted anger to envelop her. That's when she was at her best. She told herself aloud, "I won't cry!" She wanted to hold the anger close to her, keep it nuzzled next to her heart. She was angry that she wasn't like other teenagers, angry for not giving a shit about the world, angry at her mother for dying. She was tired of feeling empty.

"What are you doing!" shouted Violet.

Dahlia leaped to cover up with her robe. "Don't just burst in my room like that!"

Violet swiped her hand across the bed table, pulling the spilled talcum powder onto the floor. "I told you about my time with your pitiful grandfather, Billy, and you have the nerve to snort that mess while I'm in this house?" Violet grabbed Dahlia's arm, yanking her off the bed, the jerking motion almost pulled Dahlia's robe off.

"What the hell is your problem!" Dahlia shouted, trying to keep covered.

"I'll kill you myself before I let you snort that up your nose."

Dahlia was completely baffled until she caught a glimpse of herself in the mirror and saw the talcum powder under her nose. "You think that this is cocaine, you ridiculous old woman!" She tied her robe tightly in a double knot as if it were armor. She grabbed the bottle of talcum powder off the dresser. "Talcum powder, see! God! This family would turn you into a drug addict. I can't stand any of you—*even Rose!*"

Violet's hand came across Dahlia's face so hard it left a print. She drew a quick breath, "I didn't mean to hit you!" she shrieked just as fast as she struck her.

"Oh, yes you did," Dahlia scorned. "Only I expected a fist!"

Violet went numb for a moment. Then tears streamed down her face. "Lord, what happened to you child?"

"What happened to me? *You* are what happened to me!" Dahlia was shaking now, all her pain at the front of her mind's eye. "You think I don't know how you want to bash my face in!"

"What are you talking about, girl!"

"You know what I'm talking about. . . . It's not my fault! And Daddy buying me things so he can feel good about staying away." Dahlia wasn't making sense to anyone but herself. "I'm done!" She screamed and ran in the bathroom, locking the door behind her.

"Dahlia! Open the door!" Violet pushed at the door with all the strength her sixty–three years could muster. "Dahlia!" Dahlia didn't answer. Violet stepped back from the door slowly, ringing her hands. "Come out and we can just talk. . . . There's nothing that can't be fixed, baby. You want to be alone. I understand. But just come out so I'll know you're alright."

And then she heard a muffled cry.

"Dahlia!" Violet felt her stomach flip. "What are you doing!" Violet listened—prayed for the words from Dahlia that she was alright. It was silence that spurred her to action. "Where's the key, Dahlia!" She scrambled around the bedroom yanking open dresser drawers, searching wildly though the bras and the tank tops, pulling pajamas and shorts onto the floor.

No key.

She snatched open the top drawer of Dahlia's jewelry box: bangles, earrings, and headbands—still no key. She jerked open the jewelry box's bottom drawer which contained a handful of letters and a small pocket diary. Violet pulled all of it out and there in between the pages fell a picture of Rose. She froze, suddenly only hearing her breath. She felt as if she were in slow motion as she reached down to pick up the picture of her daughter, the feelings churning in her, crumbling her. The pain was there again, deep and low.

"Dahlia!" Violet screamed. She knocked over the lamp by Dahlia's bed, feeling for the key around the table. She cried as she tore the room apart, searching, until she reached over the top of the door frame and touched the small metal key resting on top. Her heart raced as she opened the door.

"Oh baby, No, No, Nooo!" Violet wailed.

Dahlia sat against the claw tub, her wrists dripping. She looked up and said, "Everybody leaves me."

Buds

It was six a.m. Taylor had taken the first flight home from Germany, and he and Violet sat outside Dahlia's hospital room.

"She can get the best care here," Taylor said in a drained, dull tone. "I'll take some time off."

"She's resting now, Taylor. Why don't you go home and do the same?"

"I'm not leaving her!" Then he said more quietly. "I won't."

"Alright, Taylor—alright." Violet tried to settle him. "I know you trusted that I'd take care of her and I didn't but—"

"I don't blame you, Violet." His voice cracked. "She needs help."

Violet put her hand on Taylor's shoulder. "When she wakes up, let me be there for her—just this once."

His eyes brimmed with tears. Violet pressed his head on her shoulder and for a second time they were wedged together in sorrow.

Dahlia awoke confused.

"You're in the hospital—the psychiatric ward," Violet said softly but matter-of-fact. Dahlia looked away. "Your father is outside. He's been here all night. We both have."

"You should have let me finish it," Dahlia said, lifeless.

"You have to finish me too then, and your daddy outside." Violet said angrily. "Hell, let's all do it." Violet stood up from the chair next to Dahlia's bed. "All of us are just a big pile of shit." She looked out the window for a moment, calming down before she turned back to Dahlia. "I came because I knew it was time to let go. . . . Let you finish it? Her eyes filled. "Child, I'm here to give you life. Your father loves you. Know that! When you do this, you do it to him too." Violet sat back down, carefully choosing her words, "He can't tell you about your mother. He just don't have it in him to talk about her. It was my responsibility, and I'm sorry."

"I don't want to know about her anymore," Dahlia said, weak.

"Well, you're gonna know."

"Rose," Dahlia said, her eyes filling. "Even now, it's about her."

"No, for the first time this is about you." Then Violet smiled, shaking her head. "Your mother was my greatest gift," she said. "After I married Rueben, we moved to Atlanta and Rose blossomed like her name. She played the piano like—" Violet closed her eyes to reminisce. "She was smart too. Rose loved to learn. She was the one who got me into gardening. Every summer we'd plant cucumbers, peppers, tomatoes . . . and flowers. Lord would we plant flowers. You could smell them from around the corner. At seven, she would sit and read about the names for them all. It used to tickle me to listen to her at the nursery asking for the plants she wanted by their scientific names. I was so proud of her. We sent her to college—she wasn't going to be like me, Rose graduated with honors. I wanted her to go on to grad school, be an attorney or a doctor or something. She had other plans though . . . that silly art. But she was talented. . . . What wasn't burned I have. Your daddy didn't want to look at her paintings anymore. She wanted to have a baby sooo bad. She tried twice before you, and each one of those babies that died took a little life out of my Rose. But the joy came back to her when she had you."

"Was I a good baby?" Dahlia surprised herself by asking.

"Hell no!" Violet laughed through her tears "Oooh you were terrible—one of those colicky babies. I would have to leave the house because I just couldn't take the screaming—but your mother could. She would walk and talk to you for hours. Telling you how beautiful you were, how sweet you were. She would be kissing and cuddling you, all the while, you're just hollering. Wasn't nothing sweet about you," Violet said with a grin. Dahlia gave a weak smile, which gave Violet the fuel she needed to continue. "She was content with just watching you blink. It was as if all the love I had for her had spilled over into her, so she had both my love and the power of her love to give to you. I stopped hounding her about grad school. Right then, she was doing what she was supposed to do: be your mother."

BOOK 5

Rose

Rose had made a mistake. She'd taken the chicken breasts out of the freezer four hours ago. However, she should have taken the slim chance of catching salmonella poisoning and put the thawed chicken back in the freezer to cook another day, and had Taylor bring home something for dinner. She'd called his office and left a message; twice. It would be easier to just season the chicken and put it in the oven, rather than to keep trying to catch up with him. Harriet, her assistant, needed her to stop by the studio later to okay the final choices for Friday's exhibit. She still had to drop off one of her own pieces to a realtor friend for an open house, and of course, there was Dahlia—she needed a bath. It was crunch time.

"I have got to get a maid." Rose said out loud.

She didn't mean it. She was sure she could do it all and have it all. That was part of her claim to fame.

The fireplace crackled from the roaring fire off the kitchen. Rose glanced over at Dahlia and was relieved that it didn't startle her. Her constant crying had stopped about a month ago, so Rose could finally enjoy her baby the way other mothers did. The baby swing, set up permanently in the breakfast nook, was the perfect place for Dahlia to sway back and forth while Rose prepared dinner. She would nap soon. Her eyes were already opening and closing with the constant sway of the swing. This was the most productive time of the day for Rose. She figured by the time she had dinner in the oven, Dahlia would be asleep and she could select the piece for the open house before Taylor came home.

The doorbell rang three times fast before Rose could set the chicken down into the oven. "Hold on," she mumbled and looked over at Dahlia, whose sluggish eyes popped open and then slowly weighted shut again. Rose wiped the marinade residue from her hands and quickly went to the door.

"My sister and brother are fighting! Can you tell them to stop?" The little girl from next door cried.

Usually the girl's mother came home about twenty minutes after the children returned from school. Rose glanced at her watch—it was almost five-thirty.

"My sister is crying!" the little girl pleaded.

The girl was no older than five, and she didn't have any shoes on. That bothered Rose, since it was the middle of November. Rose knew that the girl's mother and father were going through a divorce because the mother had confided in her that her soon-to-be ex-husband was being difficult. While the court sorted it all out, she needed to take a job.

"Let me grab the baby," Rose told the little girl.

She rushed back to the kitchen to take Dahlia with her, but she had already fallen into a deep sleep. Rose thought about the show on Friday. If she couldn't get the baby back down for her nap, then Dahlia's schedule would be off and there was no telling when she would get her back to sleep. Taylor would have to take care of her while she ran her errands, which would mean he would have a rough time of it, especially if she was cranky.

It'll only take a minute.

She wound the swing's spindle tight so that it would continue to glide back and forth while she was gone, and then ran next door with the little girl.

"Cut it out!" Rose yelled and broke up the fight. "That is your sister, not your enemy." She held them apart.

"She started it!" the boy accused.

"I don't care who started. Aren't you older than her?"

"Yes, but—"

"But nothing! Act like it," Rose scolded. "Now do I have to treat you like my baby next door and sit here with you two like you're infants?"

"No." The boy crossed his arms.

"Then keep your hands to yourself," Rose said in a deep

growl that let the boy know she meant it. "Go to your room until your mother gets home. And you," she turned to the girl. "Stop picking with your brother." Rose stood back and looked at the two of them. "I wished I had sisters and brothers to play with, and here you two are fighting like animals."

BOOOOOOM!

Rose and the children jumped back from the shattered window off the living room. Rose thought it sounded like a cannon in one of those old John Wayne westerns, right before her thoughts shifted to her baby sleeping next door. She shot out of the house, her body moving before her head had time to catch up. Dahlia would be screaming from the noise she told herself. The neighbor's children ran out of the house behind her.

Rose saw the old woman across the street first. The woman rarely came out of her house since her husband died, but the noise had pulled her out of hiding. Rose felt as if her neck rotated in slow motion following the direction of the woman's horrific stare. Her stomach twisted into a labor-like pain and she was back in real-time again. *Her home!* The front part of the house looked like it had swallowed a stick of dynamite, war-torn and open in the front and burning in the back. The remains of the winding staircase severely mangled, but still standing.

Rose tried to scream but nothing came out.

Her fear was one hundred times worse than the terror a mother feels when their child is lost in a store—one thousand times worse than the panicky, sick feeling ten seconds before she finds them.

"Where's your baby!" The old woman ran over to Rose.

"She's in there!" Rose screamed and attempted to climb through the rubble in front of her home. Up close, smoke and flames licked through the remains consuming the hallway toward the kitchen. Its thickness made her run back out into the street to catch her breath.

"I called the fire department!" The old woman assured her. The neighbor's kids stood motionless in the street, except for the five-year-old who was now crying.

"Did you tell them that my baby was in there?"

"Yes, I told them." She tried to hold Rose still.

But Rose knew there was little time. "I—I can't wait!" she said, frantic and out of breath. "I know she's still alive!"

Rose could hear the woman calling for her to come back while she climbed back through the rubble. Fear surrounded her, a force field of protection there to remind her that she was merely human. It stopped her cold. She could hear the fire engines in the background. "They're coming, baby," she wept, cloaking her shirt over her mouth, coughing and crying. She crouched down, helpless. She didn't know how much time had passed—seconds, minutes. It seemed like an eternity since the explosion. The smoke was getting to her, making her feel light-headed.

Then she heard the whimper.

Everything flashed before her. Her real father Billy standing over her crib looking down at her, planting in the garden with Violet, her wedding to Taylor—the two babies she'd lost. What kind of mother can't keep her children alive?

She wasn't going to lose Dahlia. Rose pushed her legs up under her to stand. "Please Lord," she prayed, then she sprinted down the hallway before the heat could turn her around. In spite of her quickness, the flames still took pieces of her. *It's just flesh. If my baby can take it.* . . . The rubber soles of her shoes were melting from the gauntlet of flames in the hallway—Keds weren't meant to get hot. When she reached the kitchen and saw that Dahlia's swing was inside the nook, not yet attacked by the creeping flames, an overwhelming feeling that supernatural powers were assisting swept over her. Her eyes burned from the smoke, but she tried to focus as she pulled Dahlia from the swing. Her baby's eyes were closed and Rose didn't know if she was still alive, or if she held in her arms another child of hers that had died.

The hallway blazed full-force now. They were trapped. The smoke and heat made Rose nauseous and she was losing consciousness. But the sharp, white-hot pain from the flames creeping up her pants kept her from it. Death would have taken her sooner, but her love for Dahlia was stronger. Stronger than her desire to hold her close one last time, strong enough to keep her at a distance, protecting her baby from the flames stoking up her own body. If she was screaming, she wasn't aware of it. Only the pain and Dahlia registered, as there was no time for anything else. The small window in the nook was just big enough. Dahlia was her legacy—her life.

"I saw something fly out of the window and land in the bushes." The elderly woman told the fireman, shaking. "It looked like her baby, so I ran over and pulled her out. What I saw when I looked up . . . she was at the window." The old woman crossed one hand over her heart and the other over her mouth. "She was screaming." She broke down, unable to continue.

"Calm down, ma'am. Take a deep breath," the firefighter said. "Hank, get the medics over here."

The old woman pulled at him. "Did she make it?"

"You saved that baby's life," the firefighter assured her.

"No, I mean the mother."

The firemen cut through the flames to the kitchen—they were just minutes behind Rose, precious minutes that meant the world. They found Rose's burned body under the nook's window.

Requiem

"Your father couldn't take it," Violet said, reliving the pain of that night. "I never saw a man crumble like that. They had to sedate him, leaving me to handle the ugly details." Violet cleared her throat. "I never forgave him for that. My only baby lying there burned beyond recognition. No fingers, no hair. I couldn't grieve, she was still alive."

"Don't tell me anymore," Dahlia said, weeping.

"I have to," Violet gently held Dahlia's hand. "You got to know from what you came. They said only a mother could stand that kind of pain—burning, but still coming to get you. I sat next to her bed at the hospital just like this. She was bandaged all over . . . tubes coming out of everywhere. But my baby was under all of that." Violet started to cry again. "All I could do was talk to her, thinking maybe she can hear me. I told her how much I loved her, how proud I was of her. I told her that she had saved you—that she was the best of me. I kept on talking untill the monitors stopped beeping."

Violet grabbed a tissue off the table and wiped her nose. "They said gas work had been done in the neighborhood a couple a days before, though investigators couldn't conclude that that was the cause of the blast. There was no time to grieve, or fall out like mothers do when their child dies ahead of them—here you were. Taylor was in no condition to care for you. It was as if he had killed her himself. I had to step up. You were the child my Rose gave her life for."

Violet was determined not to let her emotion misguide her, so she changed course. "Me and Grandpa Rueben took you everywhere—zoo's, parks, Disney World."

"I remember," Dahlia said. "I got sick on the teacup ride."

"You remember that?" Violet searched her mind, but couldn't remember the specifics of the trip.

"Why did you leave me?" Dahlia asked directly.

Violet stood up and paced the room. "I fought with the feelings I was having about you, but my Rose was gone. You were her child, but she was mine. I couldn't grieve, couldn't sit around crying. Even at her funeral, you cried so much that I had to take you from Taylor and pacify you downstairs." Violet sat back down next to Dahlia. She wasn't going to be a coward and say the rest from across the room. "I started thinking . . . if she hadn't gone in there and just let the firemen do their job."

Dahlia's eyes swelled again. "I was over and done with as soon as she died. All I am is a constant reminder of what you and Daddy lost."

"Listen baby and you listen good. You didn't let me finish. I used to feel that way. Not anymore." Violet tried to stroke Dahlia's face, but she turned away. "You are all that's left of Rose. I understand why she went into that fire. It's why I fought Billy for her—why my mother went crazy. A mother will do anything for her child. I don't blame you— your father doesn't blame you. He's just sad because for all the clothes and money and things he gives you, he can't give you your mother back." Violet smiled through her tears, placing her hand on Dahlia's cheek. "I had to come back to know that Rose still lives . . . in you."

They sat together and wept for Rose until the room filled with sadness, until the remnants of her death were exalted. Both of them were broken and shattered. Violet was the first to clean up the pieces and rebuild.

"The women in this family have a legacy of pain. But it's gonna stop with you," she said. Dahlia looked away again, still injured, still wronged. Violet turned her face back to her. "I'm not going to let you go," Violet said. "I'm not going to leave you this time, baby. We've got to love each other for Rose . . . for my mother, and her mother before."

Violet's Visions
One year later

People say spring is the beginning. I like fall, when the colors of the earth are strongest. There's a quiet peacefulness in autumn.

Taylor and Dahlia have been going to counseling once a week. Taylor went with her to give Dahlia support at first, but it turns out that there's a lot of stuff he needed to work on himself.

Dahlia has her own support group for teens. She's kept up pretty well with her garden out back, even planted petunias. I don't know why she did that—we don't know anybody named Petunia! It's her garden. I guess she can plant what she wants to. Taylor sold his share of the company to spend more time with Dahlia. She ought to be careful about what she wishes for. He drives her crazy—always underfoot. She is glad he finally got a steady girlfriend, though. A petite, smart lady named Carol he said he's known for a long time. Rueben and I sold the house in Georgia to a nice young couple pregnant with triplets. We were going to get a condo near Taylor and Dahlia, but Taylor insisted that we move in with them. There's certainly plenty of room. We even use the fireplace sometimes.

Rueben likes it here. He likes to go downtown for lunch on Saturdays and afterwards walk up and down the Mag Mile.

As for me, I go in and out of this world. Alzheimer's disease is harder on the rest of the family than it is on me. When I'm with them, it's noisy and happy and I feel like they want to tell me everything that's going on. Like they're trying to get it all in before I leave again. I try to tell them that it's okay where I go. The words aren't there for me to describe it, but it's okay. The forest and I are old friends now. There's a woman deep in that forest. I don't get too close to her. I stay far enough away so that I can come back to Rueben and my family. She looks familiar, soft—beautiful. She calls to me with a melody that my mind somehow recognizes.

About the Author

TAMMARA AGUADO is the author of the novel *Dahlia's Bouquet.* She was a realtor for ten years, but has written most of her life. She lives in Illinois with her amazingly supportive husband. This is her debut novel.

You may connect with the Author here:

www.Tammaraaguado.com
By Email: Goodbooks@Tammaraaguado.com

Cover Photography TAMMY GRALEY PHOTOGRAPHY
Cover Design NOLA SUMMERS

A Conversation with Author Tammara Aguado

How did the concept of *Dahlia's Bouquet* unfold?

Tammara Aguado: This novel unfolded over a couple of years, actually. When I was young, there was a rumor going around in our family about a great aunt who passed for white. *Dahlia's Bouquet* is a work of fiction but I started to think about the life of a woman who would have to live with a constant betrayal of her true self. What kind of relationship would she have with her children, her husband? What effect this secret would have on the generations to come. I had so many questions that I started to write the answers and *Dahlia's Bouquet* unfolded.

Did the actual writing process follow the path you imagined?

TA: LOL. Absolutely not! There are so many twists and turns in this story. I couldn't have imagined it until I sat in the chair and started typing. I knew where I wanted to end, but the meat and bones of the story took me down paths I had to prepare myself to go.

Who do you think will be your reader's favorite character?

TA: Violet. Readers get to see her whole life unfold, and she's been through some pretty rough times, but she still found some humor in it all. Violet's the matriarch, full of wisdom, but wisdom usually comes after making some serious mistakes.

Who is your favorite?

TA: Oh, that's like choosing a favorite child. Of course I love all five of the women that drive the story, but the men that share their lives with them I find to be just as intriguing. Taylor is a complex mess of a man. He doesn't know what he wants and goes from one shiny penny to the next. It was fun getting inside his head and just letting him go. Taylor had a very small part at first, but he just kept shouting in my head. "Pay attention to me!" Billy is the guy that can't catch a break and wouldn't recognize one if he could. Charisma, animal attraction, what is that thing, that something that attracts a woman to the wrong man?

Dahlia's Bouquet deals with love and the lengths we go to protect the ones we love: Do you believe in this?

TA: I think that none of us can know exactly what we'd do in some of the situations or conditions involved in Dahlia's Bouquet, and I still get chills when I think about it. But I will say that I'm a wolf when it comes to my children. Love, especially between mother and daughter is so powerful.

Tell me something you used to worry about that you don't anymore.

TA: I'm the kind of person who likes everything in its place, (no dishes in the sink, beds made, every hair in place…) Writing filled so much of that space that there's no room for my neurotic behavior. There are only so many hours in a day, and I have so many stories I'd love to tell. I don't worry about trying to be perfect anymore.

...and something about you that would surprise your readers if they knew?

TA: Readers would be surprised to know that I also enjoy writing light-hearted stories. And that I'd love to write a great horror story.

If you could sit down with anyone, past, present or future, who would it be, what would you talk about, and what's for dinner?

TA: This might seem odd, but I'd love to sit down with myself 50 years from now and ask how was it and what would you do differently? Life is so short and most of us don't get a chance to appreciate all the great energy and blessings we have. I'm having my older self over for dinner, which would mean I wouldn't have to stress about what's for dinner. It would be all my favorites...sushi, ribs, fries with mayonnaise, a glass of Pinot Noir and a slice of chocolate cake, (I don't know how I'd get through the ribs with no teeth.)

Where is your writing taking you now?

TA: I have a novella coming out called *28 days at Princeton*, a funny story about the hopes and dreams we put onto our kids. And I'm writing the screenplay for *Dahlia's Bouquet*. I've also started on *Dahlia's Bouquet part two*, so I'm pretty busy. I look forward to getting these stories out and connecting with readers on my website. www.Tammaraaguado.com